The Sanctity of Marriage

Amelia Winkle

CHAPTER 1

Rose walked into the courtroom and found an empty seat. Finally. After almost two years, she was there. She looked around, but her husband wasn't there yet. Sometime in the next few hours, he wouldn't be her husband anymore, and she was looking forward to that. She wasn't, however, looking forward to seeing him. He had called her just yesterday, asking her to reconsider. "There's still time," he said. She refused. It was easier to say no to him over the phone, but it was still one of the hardest things she'd ever had to do.

Toby was the kind of man almost any woman found difficult to refuse. He was confident, charming, and had the whole tall, dark, and handsome look that made him irresistible. She had felt so lucky the day he asked her out. It wasn't long after another day in a courtroom similar to this one. That time, however, was different in how she felt. She was hopeful. She still believed she could find someone amazing. She thought for a little while that Toby could be that someone.

They dated for a few months, and then a day came that made her feel even luckier than the day he asked her out. He asked her to marry him. She excitedly screamed her answer without a thought. After that, things started to change, but for a while, she thought it was just the stress of planning a wedding…a wedding she didn't even really want. She'd been married twice before and didn't care much about a big event. She tried to get Toby to have a small ceremony at the courthouse and then a little party afterwards, but he wanted a wedding. So, she planned one. When it was over and they moved into their new home, things changed. Toby's charm slowly turned to demand. He was impossible to please. But she was married and didn't want to give up. Just like her other marriages, her husband wasn't the man she fell in love with. That man didn't exist. The man she loved was simply a character in Toby's one-man show. After a relatively short marriage of two years, she caught him cheating. That's where she drew the line. She packed her things, moved in with her parents, and filed for divorce.

Toby refused to accept the divorce. He came by her parents' house to try to change her mind. He called and texted. He wouldn't sign the papers that gave him pretty much everything except her personal belongings. The visits stopped when she found a house a few weeks later and refused to tell Toby the address. The calls and texts stopped for a while when she changed her phone number. It took him a couple of months to get someone to give her the new one, and then the calls started again. She started dating someone else. Toby threatened him. She dated a couple of other times, but found that she just couldn't trust anyone. Finally, after a year, she gave up.

In the courtroom today, she hadn't been on a date in six months and wasn't planning to change that. The dating apps her friends had talked her into downloading had been deleted for a while. She just wanted this marriage to end. She wanted Toby out of her life, and she wanted to concentrate on her job and friendships.

There was a time that Rose believed in love. Not just some comfortable safety of having someone around, but true love. The kind of love that you feel deep in your heart. That makes you want to be a better person so that you deserve to have that love. The true love that makes you happy just to be in its presence, with no expectations and no judgement, and that makes you believe that anything is possible.

But not anymore. That's not quite right, though. The absence of love isn't exactly what Rose believes in. But she doesn't believe in the things that all the movies try to tell us is real. She had seen real love, but not her own. Her parents were still happily married after almost forty years. They had arguments, but those arguments didn't matter in the big picture. They were together, loved each other, and always would. Other couples truly loved each other. Rose had seen it, so she knew it existed. It just didn't exist for her.

She had married three men who weren't right for her, but she didn't figure it out until after they were married. All of this was because she had hope – hope that they could make it work for one reason for another. She loved them, but it wasn't that kind of true love. And it wasn't enough. Not enough to make a liar stop lying. Not enough to make abusive relationships work. Not enough to make a cheater stop cheating. It was never enough.

So, Rose decided that she wouldn't try again. Not for love. She was 35. Three marriages in 15 years, with several years and several empty relationships between each marriage, made her believe that she would never make anything work. She believed she had tried, but she wasn't sure whether she didn't try hard enough or the men she chose didn't bother trying at all. There wasn't enough trying somewhere, and so it was the end for her.

So she waited in the courtroom for her attorney, Jim Carter. He had perfect timing, walking in and sitting next to her just before Toby appeared standing in the aisle. "Rose…" he began.

"Don't talk to her, son," Jim said firmly. Jim was older – old enough to be Rose's father – and a big man. He was 6'5" and muscular, and when he stood to his full height, he struck an imposing figure. She couldn't imagine anyone refusing an order from him, and that's one of the things that made her adore him as a divorce attorney. His deep voice made Toby stop midsentence and turn away. Toby sat on a bench a couple of rows back. Thirty minutes later, he tried to argue with the judge, to get him to dismiss the divorce. Rose felt relief when the judge, an old, balding man with glasses, raised one eyebrow and told him that the only thing he could try to do is change the terms – not the divorce itself. When Toby couldn't persuade the judge to see his side, it was over. The judge told them he would have the papers signed that afternoon, and they left the courtroom.

Toby tried to follow Rose and talk to her, but Jim walked her to her car and stood there until she was gone. Rose drove to work, finished the day, and then went home. Her friend Leann would be over for dinner that night.

"Rose, honey, you're going to have to stop acting so hopeless. There's a guy for you out there somewhere," Leann sighed. "Your divorce is barely over."

"Oh, please, Leann." Rose looked down at the gray cushion with the word *Love* printed across it in sparkly letters. There was one just like it, except with *Family* on it, at the other end of the red sofa. They were among the few things she'd taken when she left Toby – gifts from Leann that she didn't want to give up. "You know very well that I've had more than my fair share of marriages. I'm done." She picked up the *Love* cushion and threw it across the room. She meant to throw it at the tan wall, but her aim was off. Instead, the cushion hit the entertainment center, knocking over DVDs that were stacked on top of it.

Leann sighed again, standing up and walking across the room to pick up the DVDs.

"Don't worry about them," Rose said. "I'll get them later." She laid down on the sofa with her arms behind her head.

Leann didn't stop. She knelt next to the entertainment center and started picking them up anyway. "It's a good thing you didn't hit those candleholders. I'm not planning on sweeping up shards of glass."

"Funny. Besides, those are just the rom-com DVDs. I was going to give them to you or burn them anyway. Pointless lies."

Leann looked up, her blue eyes glaring at Rose, who was looking at the ceiling. "You mean you took the time to go through all your DVDs and take out anything dealing with love?"

"Yeah. So?"

"So that's a little extreme. What about *The Princess Bride*?"

Rose turned onto her side. "Throw the cushion back, would you? I didn't think about how uncomfortable this damn sofa is on my head."

"No. Get up and get it yourself. And you didn't answer my question."

"It's not in there. I can't give it away. But I won't watch it. Please throw the cushion back."

"Nope," Leann said. "I'm picking up the movies you knocked everywhere. How'd the hearing go, by the way?"

Rose sat up and reached across the sofa for the other cushion. She threw it on the arm of the sofa, then laid back down, adjusting it as she studied the popcorn on the ceiling again. "Just like we expected. He argued, the judge basically told him to shut up, and now it's over."

"I wish I could have been there."

"It's okay. You had to work. Besides, these are kind of normal for me at this point. Good thing I'll never have to go through it again." She reached over to the table for her glass of wine. Instead of getting up, she tried to take a sip while still lying down and spilled a few drops onto the purple top she was wearing. She got up and walked to the kitchen, reaching over the counter for a paper towel and absently wiped at the top. "Good thing this was white wine. Why am I so clumsy?"

Leann was now standing up to set the stack of DVDs back on top of the entertainment center. She rolled her eyes at Rose and turned back towards the overstuffed white chair she was sitting in. "You're clumsy because you just are. And why won't you have to go through it again? I keep telling you that you'll find someone."

Rose threw the paper towel into the trash as she walked back to flop on the sofa. "You said that last time, remember? Except I think you also said something about…" she switched a sing-song voice and plastered a fake smile across her face, "…third time's a charm. Blah, blah, blah."

"Well, it's *supposed* to be a charm, right?" Leann laughed.

"Or three strikes and you're out, which I am."

Leann laughed again. "No, you're not. Keep going, and you'll be married as many times as Elizabeth Taylor."

Rose thought for a few seconds. "How many times was she married, anyway?"

"Oh, I don't know. A few. Easy to find out."

Rose reached for her phone, carefully avoiding the wine glass, and swiped it open. She tapped the Chrome app to open it and typed for a minute. "Eight. She was married eight times. Just seven men, though."

Leann laughed again. "Well, you're almost halfway there. Might as well go ahead. Find your next ex-husband."

Rose laughed. "You think she has the world record?"

"Maybe. I mean, eight is a lot. Hell, your three is a lot." Leann turned and faked a flinch a little after she spoke, jokingly anticipating that Rose would throw her phone at her.

But Rose rolled her eyes and kept reading, ignoring Leann.

"You know, I thought you'd just go through men like crazy now. Be like a man, date without feeling, use them, dump them, and go on."

Rose barely glanced at Leann. "Yeah, right. I've done that before. It's pointless. They're all morons or liars, or they want a relationship when I tell them I don't. I don't even know which of those things is worse. I'll just be a nun."

"Nun? Don't you have to be Catholic?"

"I can convert, silly. There's a convent in the Bahamas or something that looks cool. I found it the other night. Hmmm…the woman with the most marriages had 23, but there's a man who did it 29 times. Why stop at beating Elizabeth Taylor? Why not just go ahead and break the world record?"

Rose set her phone down and reached for the wine glass again, but she sat up to gulp down the quarter of a glass that was left so she wouldn't spill it this time.

Leann reached for her wine and drank the last sip, then got up to go get the bottle from the kitchen. "So you've got options. Convent, or twenty-something marriages? Be real. You know you're not going to join the convent. You'd regret it within a week. Are you going to break the woman's record, or the higher one?"

"You have to ask? If I'm going to do it, I'm going all out. 29. I'll have to be married 30 times, dahlin'." She said "dahlin'" in the sugary-sweet, exaggerated Southern drawl that they both used for the word when they were being sarcastic.

"Yeah, break that record. It would be hilarious."

"Seriously. I've only got 27 left. You think I could find 27 men who'd marry me?"

Leann walked back into the living room and refilled both glasses. She set the bottle on the simple oak coffee table before she answered. "You've already found three. I'm sure 27 more wouldn't be a problem." She looked up at Rose. "Wait. You're not serious? You have that look on your face."

"What look?"

"That mischievous look you get when you're up to something. Please tell me you're not really thinking about this."

Rose was still sitting up. She reached for the wine and took a sip. "Why not? It'd give me a goal. Something to work for."

"It would be hard to date if you were married all the time. How would that conversation go? 'Wanna go out?' 'Just so you know, I'm married. It means nothing, but I've got to be upfront with you.' I'd love to hear how that goes."

"When's the last time I went out with anyone anyway? Five months? Six? It's not happening."

Leann had been trying to get Rose to go out again for a while. She was convinced that it would work out eventually. Rose just had bad luck. "So what's the point of marrying that many men again?"

"Purpose in life. Goals."

"And, you've already got your job and all kinds of things to work for. What on earth would that get you?"

"Yeah, I have my job. Been there almost as long as it took me to get married three times. You know everybody sees me and asks themselves who I'm going to marry next, right? Might as well keep them really guessing. It'd be fun. And it'd be a big 'screw you' to the so-called sanctity of marriage, which, by the way, I've already proven isn't all that great."

"And I still say you're going to find someone great. You just have to be patient. And you won't find Mr. Right just trying to beat the record on the number of marriages. How would that work, anyway? Who's going to marry you knowing you're just going to divorce him anyway?"

"Patience has gotten me nowhere. I should just do this while I'm still young enough to find someone who'd have me. And none of that matters. You know very well plenty of men would get married if they know it's just for a few days. I can get married, divorce the next week, and start again. What do you think it'll take, a month to find a new one?" Rose was thinking carefully. "Who do you think would marry me next? Anyone we know?"

"Are you going to have sex with all of them? And how are you going to afford all the lawyer's fees for these divorces? What about prenups?" Leann's concern about her friend seemed to be waning. She was starting to laugh again instead.

"You know, I really do need to think about all that. I'll see if Jim will cut me a deal, assuming he doesn't go all dad mode and tell me it's stupid. I don't think I need to worry about a prenup. These marriages are going to be short. No judge would give these men the little bit of stuff I have after a week."

"You didn't answer about sex," Leann said, taking a sip of wine.

"Because I don't know. Might depend on the guy."

Leann quickly swallowed her wine and laughed. "I figured something like that. So, who's the first victim?"

"Oh, they're victims now? Is the prospect of being my husband *that* bad?" Rose picked up her phone again and tossed her long blond hair back as she bent her head to type again.

"What are you looking up now?" Leann picked up the remote, found the music app on the tv, and started Rose's playlist on random. The first song was a slow Allman Brothers tune, but she knew there'd be something heavier soon.

11

"Oh, I'm not looking up. I'm seeing if I can get a list of my victims."

"Haha. So you agree they're victims? How are you getting a list?"

Rose didn't stop typing. When she finished, she said, "Check out Facebook."

Leann opened her mouth in surprise. "No. You're not. You know they'll all just laugh."

"Maybe. Maybe not. Maybe I'll find my next 27 husbands quickly."

Leann picked up her phone and opened Facebook. Rose's post was at the top of her newsfeed. *New project: beat world record of marriages. 27 to go. Who's up for helping me out by being my next ex-husband?*

There were already a couple of laugh reactions. By the time Leann reacted to the post, there was a comment from a guy they went to high school with. *I'm in!* Henry had said.

"There you go. Henry Watkins is your next hubby."

Rose had already set her phone back down in favor of the wine. She took a sip and just held the glass, smiling. "Not him. He messaged me a while back saying he had a crush on me in high school."

"Seriously?" Leann asked. "Go out with him. He's nice!"

"Nope. I'm not dating anymore. He's nice. And cute. But no."

"You're not even going to answer his comment?"

"Does it look like it?" Rose leaned back against the sofa and took another sip of wine. "I'll wait until tomorrow. Besides, I've got to think about how this is all going to work. You know, rules and stuff."

Leann sat her phone down and sipped her wine, too. "Oh, so stuff like, no sex unless you're hot?"

Rose's smile was the first real one she'd had that night. "Yeah. And they don't get money, and I won't pretend to love them, and they're not moving in here, and I don't even know what else. Stuff like how long the marriage will last, who pays for the divorce, whether it can be annulled."

"Oh, yeah. Would it count towards the record if it's annulled?" Leann was starting to get into the idea just as the first notes of "I Am the Fire" by Halestorm song played.

Rose thought for a few seconds. "I don't think so. We might have to call and find out what counts for the record. Maybe you should go online and get ordained or whatever so I don't have to pay as much for these marriages."

"And I ask again, how are you going to date for real while you're getting married all those times?" Leann asked.

"Date? Are you serious? I just said I'm not going to date anymore. I don't want to. Love is bullshit."

"Come on," Leann urged. "You know it's not."

"It's bullshit for me. I'm never falling again. There's no point in trying. Like I said, three strikes. I'm out."

They both stopped talking about marriages so they could sing along. Leann figured that Rose would forget the idea by in the morning and laugh at her tipsy Facebook post.

CHAPTER 2

Rose woke up the next morning to get ready for work. Why had she decided to drink on a Wednesday night? She wasn't exactly hung over, but she didn't feel amazing, either. Oh, yeah, that's right. She got divorced again yesterday. That always calls for a few drinks.

Today, though, she had to work. She had hit snooze a couple of times before getting lazily out of the bed, so would have to rush a little to get to work on time. After starting the coffee pot, she took a quick shower and decided drying her hair wasn't worth the time or hassle. It would dry by the time anyone at work saw her, anyway. She threw on a little makeup, found clothes that matched, and walked into the living room. When she passed the entertainment center, she saw that Leann hadn't taken the movies she set out for her. She'd get them to her soon. She also noticed that she hadn't cleaned up the wine glasses and bottle when Leann left.

She walked into the kitchen and filled her travel mug, adding milk and sugar. Then, she looked at the clock. She had a few minutes to at least put last night's glasses in the sink. After taking a couple of sips of her coffee, she set the mug down and went into the living room. She picked up the bottle and found there was nothing left, so threw it away and then set the glasses in the sink.

She picked up her mug to take another sip of coffee. The lid wasn't on very well, and she spilled some onto the white top she was wearing. "Dammit!" she said and then walked into the bedroom to find something else to wear. Standing in her closet, which was barely a walk-in, she went through all her tops on the left side. "Too tight, doesn't look right with these slacks, wrong color to wear with black. Why don't I have any clothes?" She finally just changed into a gray dress that looked decent, almost wishing her office didn't have a business casual dress code. The jeans on the other side of the closet were easier to match. She loved wearing her dress clothes, though. They were just sometimes annoying to match.

There was some traffic on the way to work, so she barely made it on time. She hadn't even thought about the joke she and Leann were talking about the night before until one of the girls on her team, Elsa, said something about her Facebook post. "So, boss lady, how many of those guys are you going to marry?"

Rose was the manager of the web development team at a marketing firm. She and her team designed and built web sites for the firm's clients. They were a pretty close-knit group, and all of them were friends outside of the office, including on Facebook.

She stared blankly at Elsa for a second, but then laughed when she remembered what she'd done. "I don't know. I haven't looked since I posted. Do I have 27 yet?"

Everyone else on the team – two guys and another girl – were looking up expectantly from their computers already. It seemed that Elsa had been chosen to pick on Rose about the post, but Rose knew it was probably just that Elsa had gotten to it first.

Will, the one person who'd been there when Elsa got promoted, spoke up before Elsa could. "You don't have quite that many, but there are a few. So who's first?"

Rose smiled and drank some coffee. "Don't you all have work to do instead of Facebook stalking me? I haven't even gotten to my desk yet."

"Well," Bianca laughed, "some of us got here early and have already done a lot of work for the day. You're on time, but you're late."

Rose laughed along with everyone else. "Yeah, which means I need to catch up." She started walking towards her office.

"Oh, come on!" Bianca said, laughing. "We want to know how *this* got started!"

Rose kept walking, smiling. But, even as she ignored the laughter and pleas to be let in on the joke, even from the guys, she was thinking about it. She was thinking that maybe it wouldn't be that horrible of an idea. Maybe she could pull it off. Marriages and divorces would be a lot easier without feelings to deal with. The only problem would be finding enough men who would marry her without falling in love or living together - enough who could view it as a business arrangement or laugh instead of viewing it as something as serious as marriage is supposed to be.

She started working, leaving the door open as usual. Every once in a while, someone on the team walked by and said something about the world record. One of the guys from the copywriting department stopped at the door, bent to one knee, and asked jokingly for her hand in marriage. She giggled along with them, but turned back to her computer. Today, she was plugging hours into project planning sheets, figuring out her team's workload for the next few weeks.

When it was almost lunchtime, Penelope, one of the accountants, came by and asked if she had plans. They decided to go to an Italian place they both loved.

They sat down in the restaurant, waiting for the server. Rose still hadn't looked at Facebook since the night before. Obviously, though, Penelope had. "You know everybody's laughing about how many marriage proposals you've gotten, right?" Penelope didn't waste any time getting to the point.

"Really?"

Penelope tucked a wisp of her short brown hair behind her ear as she opened her eyes wise in surprise. "You sound like you don't even know!"

"No one's proposed, except for Dan. He came by this morning and made a mockery of a proposal."

"I mean on Facebook, silly!"

"Oh, I haven't even looked." Rose picked up the menu and looked at it, even though she always got the same thing.

"You have to look!" Penelope was a little younger than Rose, and she was lively and energetic. Rose was surprised that everyone in the restaurant hadn't heard her. She looked around to see how many people were staring at them, but they were all immersed in their conversations or meals. "I think you're going to have to break some hearts when you tell them you weren't serious about getting married that many times."

Rose laughed and looked up from the menu. "You're kidding. No one wants to marry me. They're all joking."

Penelope shook her head, still smiling. "Nope. I don't think some of them are. A couple, yeah. You really need to look."

The server arrived then, so they both asked for sweet tea and talked with her for a couple of minutes. It was Linda, one of the servers they got regularly. She said she'd go ahead and bring them salad while they decide what they want to order.

When she left, Penelope said again, "Look on Facebook. Now."

Rose was still holding the menu. "I'm trying to decide what I want to eat."

"You're going to get the chicken parmesan, as usual. You could look at that menu for an hour and still get the same thing. Get your phone out and look."

Rose sighed and dug in her purse for her phone. She unlocked it with a swipe and pulled up Facebook. Not only were there over 40 comments on her post, but she had 10 new messages. She scrolled through the comments. There were two guys she'd dated casually before, one of whom had commented *Wanna try again?* and another who commented *I thought you'd learned your lesson on the whole marriage thing.* Several comments were from her female friends, laughing that they could play matchmaker. There were a few guy friends who were laughing, but besides Henry, whose comment Leann had seen the night before, there were several comments from guy acquaintances with different versions of *I'm in!*

One of the private messages was from Leann, asking what she thought of her popularity with the men. She replied to that one, but left the messages from various guys on read for the moment. There were several who claimed to seriously want to help her with the new project.

Rose still didn't think any of them would really do it. Penelope disagreed, so they spent most of the time until Linda brought their drinks, and then their food, discussing why Penelope thought these guys were really serious. Even though Rose disagreed with almost all of them, Penelope's points were that Rose was pretty, successful, and a much better catch than she would admit.

"But Penelope, they've got to know that me being a good catch isn't even an issue here. If I need to get married 27 times, it's kind of common sense that none of these are going to last long." She took a bite of her chicken.

Penelope rolled her eyes. "You can act so stupid sometimes. Some of them think you might change your mind and stay married to them. And do you seriously think they don't expect to sleep with you as part of the deal?"

Rose laughed so hard that she almost choked on her food. She chewed for what seemed like forever before she could swallow and answer Penelope. "You don't think they're just looking to get laid?"

"Not just. Some, maybe. But I think some of them really wouldn't mind being married to you, even if it's just for a joke or goal or whatever the hell you were thinking. And some of them would just like to be in on the joke. Being one of the husbands who helps you break a world record might be cool." She took a bite of her own food.

"Look, even I'll admit I'm not horrible. And I might actually try to go through with this thing. It would be fun. But a couple of weeks of fake marriage? I'm sure I'd have to give some kind of incentive for this kind of thing. Like money or something."

"Don't make me roll my eyes again. I'm getting a headache from it. Look, you're attractive. That blond hair and blue eyes, not to mention that you actually have a nice body, which I'm jealous of, I might add. You're nice. I'm telling you. You won't have any problems finding 27 husbands. How long are you thinking? A year?"

"It might take longer than that. Maybe two years. I'm thinking it'll take time to find each husband, then get married for a couple of weeks, get a divorce, and start over."

"So you *are* serious?" Penelope didn't act surprised at all. She was, as usual, a little bit excited as she asked.

Rose had to think for a minute. She had really been thinking about it, but she still wasn't completely sure. "I think I am," she finally said.

"Good. I'll help you."

"How?" Rose was genuinely curious. What help would she need with getting married? It's not like she was going to have actual weddings; she figured they'd go to the courthouse or something. There wasn't any reason to have a big ceremony and party if the plan was to divorce the guys quickly anyway.

"You need a manager. I know Leann will want to help, too. We'll help you find guys, set up the weddings and divorces, and we'll also need to interview these guys and make sure you don't end up marrying some psycho who refuses to divorce you. You don't want to go into a 2-week marriage just to have the divorce take two years."

Rose knew she was right. The last divorce had taken almost two years, though that had been a marriage for love instead of for something silly like breaking a world record. "I'm going to have to find out the rules, too. Like, do annulments count? What even qualifies for an annulment in Georgia? How long does each marriage have to last? What if I actually do have to have sex with all of them?"

"I'll be at your house Saturday afternoon. Get Leann to be there, too. We'll figure it all out. And screenshot those messages I saw you looking at. Send them to me. I need to look these guys up on Facebook and check them out."

"Are you serious?" While Rose was getting pretty serious about breaking the record, she wasn't sure why Penelope was.

"Yep. It'll be fun. For all three of us. And PLEASE tell me we can make you wear wedding dresses for all of these. I'll bet we can find some great venues closer to Atlanta. We'll be your bridesmaids." She laughed so loud Rose was absolutely sure the entire restaurant heard her this time.

Rose laughed, too. "I'm not spending a lot of money on weddings, and we're certainly not driving 45 minutes for the weddings. I didn't want to last time, and I'm absolutely not going to do it 27 more times. We'll figure it all out. First step is going to be to make sure we play by the rules."

While they finished lunch, they talked about work. They both had to meet with a client the next week, and this particular client was difficult. All he did was try to lower the budget, which meant they spent almost as much time working with him on what to cut out of his original request than the company would spend on just doing the work. It was a fine line, but they were always the ones who had to deal with him, mostly because no one else wanted to. He was a pain, but they didn't get to decide what clients they kept and what clients they let go to another agency, so Rose and Penelope had the meetings and cut the budget to what he wanted, cutting services along with the money. The other managers just did whatever they said after the meetings so they wouldn't have to go. Kenneth was his name, and they spent the rest of their lunch talking about how they thought the next meeting would go.

When they got back, Rose spent the rest of the day in meetings, so she didn't have to see the few people come by to pick on her about getting married. She did get a text from Leann, though. *Penelope texted me. You're cooking dinner Saturday.* She didn't have to respond. Leann knew she would.

CHAPTER 3

Since Penelope was picky, Rose planned a simple meal for Saturday – baked chicken, salad, and pasta. She knew the girls would be fine with it. She'd been thinking since her lunch with Penelope, and she'd decided that she really did want to try to do this, whether they were serious about helping or not. She had no idea yet how she'd make it happen, but she'd figure it out.

Penelope got to the house first. She bounced in without knocking, setting a bottle of wine on the counter and immediately opening the refrigerator to look for a snack. While she got out some cheese and then rummaged through the cabinet for crackers, she asked Rose what she'd been doing that day.

"I slept late, then had to go to the store to get stuff to cook for you two freeloaders." She opened the oven long enough to check on the chicken, closed it again, and salted the water for the pasta.

Penelope started towards the sofa, then turned back to the refrigerator and took out a can of Diet Coke. "Well, we couldn't be freeloaders if you didn't make it so easy. Besides, I'd cook if Steven would get out of the house occasionally so we could have a girls' night."

Penelope's husband, Steven, was a sweet man. He did actually leave the house more than Penelope claimed. His job as a lawyer meant that he worked a lot of late nights. It was just an excuse for Penelope to get out of the house. Rose liked being at her own house, anyway, and both Penelope and Leann knew it. They didn't mind. They lived close enough that it really didn't matter whose house they hung out at.

Leann showed up a few minutes later. She did knock, but didn't wait for Rose to answer the door. It was more a courtesy to let her know she was about to walk in. She saw Penelope with the cheese and crackers and sat next to her, helping herself to part of Penelope's snack.

"Get your own," Penelope said, pushing the plate between them so Leann could reach the food better.

The three girls had grown up together. Rose and Leann had been friends since they started elementary school, and Penelope wasn't as close to them until she got the job at the same marketing agency where Rose worked. Leann currently worked at a department store. She was the manager, and she had come straight to Rose's house from work.

"I skipped lunch today," she said. "One of the girls got sick, and we were busy. I'm starving."

"I'll have real food in a few minutes," Rose said as she dropped pasta into the now-boiling water and set a timer. "We know the store's busy. People are already starting to shop for school. Besides, I drove by when I went to get groceries."

"And you didn't stop to see me or bring me lunch? I'm hurt," Leann pouted. She couldn't pout long, though, because a smile covered it up within a couple of seconds. She never could fake a pout.

"I would have, but I figured you couldn't talk anyway. Penelope brought Moscato."

"Yay!" Leann said, excited. "Oh, and I have some rum in the car. I forgot to get it. I thought I'd just stay here tonight. It's not like there's anyone at home anyway. The kids are at Brent's."

Leann had a son, Jeremy, who was 10. Her daughter, Bev, was 8. The kids were at their dad's every other weekend. They had the same reddish-blond hair and blue eyes that Leann had. Rose was their godmother.

"When they come back, tell them Aunt Rose will be over soon to play Xbox or something."

"Will do. I think Brent's bringing them back early tomorrow. He said something about having to go out of town for work."

"Awesome. He can just drop them off here if you want. But go out and get that rum. It won't take long for the wine to be gone. And take those DVDs to the car while you're at it," Rose said.

Leann gave her an exaggerated sigh and walked towards the entertainment center. "Do you really want to get rid of them?"

"Yes," Rose replied. "I don't need them. I've got plenty of other stuff to watch. Actually, I'll help." She walked over and picked up half of them, handed them to Leann, and picked up the others. They walked towards the door and looked back at Penelope.

"I'll just sit right here and work on these crackers," Penelope said. "It looks like you two can handle it."

The two girls walked out to the car, dropped the DVDs into the trunk, and got the rum. They set it on the counter when they got back to the kitchen.

Penelope finished her snack and took a long drink of her soda. "So, when are we figuring out how to get Rose hitched a few times?"

Leann looked back and forth between the two of them. "Are we really serious about this?" she asked. She reached for more cheese, but then realized it was gone. Instead, she walked to the kitchen, got a wine glass, and opened the bottle Penelope had brought.

Penelope looked at Rose. "You know, we could make Leann do it. She's single again, too," Rose said.

"Oh, no," Leann laughed. "I have my kids. They can't see their mama getting married that many times."

"But they can see their aunt do it?" Rose feigned shock.

"You've already been married three times. They won't think anything of it."

Rose rolled her eyes. "Right. It's not like they'll meet any of these guys, anyway. Besides, marriage is a joke. I might as well make it even more of one. This way, they'll know you can do anything you want, even if society tells us we should all be like Penelope and her 15 years of bliss."

"I would hardly say bliss. But yeah, Steven's great most of the time. I actually picked okay, didn't I?"

Rose and Leann said, "Jealous!" at the same time.

Then Rose stopped smiling and looked at them, Penelope sitting on the sofa with her feet up on the table, and Leann standing next to the chair with her glass of wine. "If I really want to do this, what do y'all think?"

Penelope was the first to speak up. "I already said you're doing it, and I'm helping."

They both looked at Leann. She took a sip of the wine and said, "It's crazy, like pretty much everything you do. But as usual, I'll do what I can to help."

So it was on. Penelope took a notebook out of Rose's office. They ate dinner, made a list of things they needed to find out and do, and drank the bottle of wine. Penelope would play matchmaker, making sure the men weren't psychos, and Leann was going to research some specifics to make sure they planned all of Rose's marriages to count for the record book. When the wine was gone, they opened the rum. By the time they were finished planning, Penelope had to call Steven to see if he wanted to come get her or let her sleep on the sofa. He drove over to get her, hugging Rose and Leann before he half-carried Penelope to the car.

CHAPTER 4

Rose woke up to loud music Sunday morning. Leann had turned on Red Sun Rising's newest album. She got up and walked into the living room, stretching, where she immediately found the remote and turned down the volume. Leann was dancing in the kitchen, making eggs and bacon with toast.

"You know I don't want any of that," Rose yawned.

"Of course you don't. Breakfast is the least important meal of your day," she answered.

"Nonexistent meal, unless I decide to eat breakfast food for dinner. Eat up. Just remember to add to my grocery list if you eat all of something. And have you started coffee?"

She had. Rose got her favorite cup – favorite because it was the biggest and had a scene from Alice in Wonderland painted on the side – and filled it with the hot coffee. She added milk and sugar, then sat on the sofa. She listened to the music for a minute, and then found the remote again to turn it off. "Are you seriously not feeling anything from drinking last night? My head is killing me."

Leann looked at her slyly, "Oh, I didn't drink all that much. I let the two of you have most of it. I didn't want to wake up feeling like you do right now."

"Bitch," Rose groaned. "You were the one filling the glasses."

"So I was," Leann agreed. "And making sure you two had plenty. There's still a little rum left if you want to add it to your coffee."

"No. I'm good. Besides, I'd use Irish cream if I was going to put anything in the coffee. Where's that notebook, since you were sober?"

Leann was sliding eggs onto a plate that already had bacon and toast. She rinsed the pan and set it in the sink, then picked up the notebook from the counter as she carried her plate to the living room. She already had a cup of coffee sitting on the table. She handed the notebook to Rose when she sat down. She took the remote from Rose and found an old sitcom to watch, but she did turn down the volume a little more. It was really just background noise while they talked.

Rose began scanning the pages they'd written last night. Thankfully, Penelope's handwriting was perfect, even when she was drinking. If Rose had been writing, there's no telling whether they would be able to read it or not. It depended on the day and how fast she tried to write.

"So, you're going to get ordained and perform all these weddings for free?"

Leann answered through a mouthful of eggs. "Yep. I might even make it a side business if anyone wants a real wedding."

"And I'm just supposed to sit around and wait for Penelope to find me a husband. I wonder who she's going to come up with."

Leann swallowed her food before answering this time. "What do you care? Though, I did already find out this morning that you have to consummate every marriage."

Rose's eyes opened wide. "Dammit. Then Penelope better find good ones. I'll have to let her know I have veto power. She'd better not try to make me marry somebody I won't want to *consummate* with." She said *consummate* slowly, making a disgusted face as she said it.

"I'm kidding. I found out just the opposite. Nothing says you have to. In fact, the current record holder had a couple of annulments, and the last marriage was just for publicity."

Rose's sigh of relief was loud. "Good!" she exclaimed.

"But you know, if you want to, no one's going to hold it against you. You'd be married after all. Not a sin if you're married to him, right?" She laughed as she took a big bite of bacon.

"Maybe. Depends on the guy. And whether you look at multiple marriages as a sin anyway. But we'll have Penelope tell them it's not going to happen, just in case."

"Oh, she will. I already talked to her."

"Damn, woman. How long have you been awake?"

Leann looked at the clock. It was 10:30. "A couple of hours. I let you sleep for a while before I turned the music up. I know you'd still be asleep if I wasn't here."

"Yeah, I would. And I'll probably go back to sleep when you leave. It's not like I have anything else to do today."

"Yeah, you do. You have to send those messages to Penelope."

"Didn't I do that last night?" Rose grabbed the *Family* cushion and curled her arm under her head on the arm of the sofa.

"Nope. I checked. Go ahead and do it. Your phone's over there next to you, on the end table."

Rose lay where she was. "Remind me to do it when I wake up better. Since you've already been looking stuff up this morning, how long do I have to be married to these guys?"

"Doesn't really matter, as long as you're married. The world record guy had at least 29 days on all of them. I'd say we need to try for a week or two each. Even though it's basically fake, you do want to at least be married for a little bit. Besides, it'll take some time to get divorce papers through. At least Penelope's going to make sure all of them are going to sign the papers, so it'll be quick divorces."

"Perfect." Rose sat up to get her coffee, and her phone rang. She reached over for it. "It's Penelope." She answered the phone on speaker. "Hey! Leann's here, too."

"And so is Steven! Say hi to the girls, sweetheart!"

Steven didn't sound like he was any more awake than Rose. He liked to sleep late, too. It was one of the few things he and Penelope didn't have in common. "Hey, girls."

"Morning, Steven!" Rose and Leann said at the same time, Rose groggy and Leann through a bite of food.

Penelope took over. "So, I was talking to my sweetie this morning, and he said he'll help us out with Rose's divorces."

Rose looked at the phone. "Why didn't he help me out with my last one, then?" she asked.

Steven must have still been around the phone. "You know very well that's not what I usually do. I'm a corporate lawyer. But for this, if you're really going to do it, I can get you a simple, standard agreement. All you'll have to do for each one is fill in names, sign it, and file it. I'll tell you everything you need to do. It's not like there will be assets to divide or custody of kids to deal with. It'll be easy. But are you really going to do this? It's insane, and…"

Penelope interrupted. "We talked about it. It's happening. Just go with it, Steven."

They could hear Steven groan. "So, girls, he walked off. He thinks we're crazy, but he'll help. Like he said, it'll be easy divorces. We'll just have to pay the filing fee each time. It's something like $100."

Rose calculated quickly in her head. "Okay. That's not too horrible. Try to talk my future husbands into paying half."

"He said you may also want to consider prenups. You don't want them trying to take your stuff. But it's more about dealing with courts than anything. He said it's unlikely that a judge will give anyone anything of yours with such a short marriage."

Leann swallowed food. "Good. Seriously, though. See about getting those guys to pay half that filing fee."

"I will. Oh, I've already got one, by the way," Penelope giggled.

"A set of divorce papers?" Leann asked.

Penelope laughed again. "No, girl. I've got Rose a husband!"

Rose and Leann looked at each other. Neither of them spoke. Leann stopped chewing.

"You girls still there?" they heard Penelope ask.

Leann found her voice first, speaking through the food in her mouth.

"Yeah, we're here. Who? When? Where? Is this guy going to agree to everything we talked about?"

"Yeah, he's good. He doesn't expect anything. He thought it was hilarious when I told him what Rose is doing. Thought it'd be even funnier to be in on it himself."

Rose finally thought she could speak again, "Well, who is it? You still haven't told us that."

"Luke."

"No!" Rose screamed, and Leann laughed so hard a bite of eggs fell out of her mouth. Rose stared at the yellow eggs on the white carpet for a long few seconds while Penelope tried to get their attention.

Leann finally stopped her laughter long enough to tell Penelope they were still there. Then, she used her napkin to pick up the eggs. "My brother Luke? Hahaha! This is going to be amazing. We'll really be able to tell people we're sisters after this!"

Rose snapped out of her shock. "Yeah, but you're the one who, just a few minutes ago, told me to get laid while I'm married to these men."

Penelope practically screamed through the phone, "She gave you permission to sleep with Luke? Oh, that's awesome!"

Leann stopped laughing as suddenly as she'd started. "No. That is absolutely not what I said."

"Oh, but you really did," Rose replied, rolling over onto the sofa holding her stomach.

Luke was Leann's older brother. They were all close. He hung out with them sometimes. Rose and Penelope loved him like part of the family, but neither of them ever stopped reminding Leann that her big brother was hot. He was also still single. He'd been engaged a couple of years ago, but broke it off when he found the girl cheating on him before they even really started planning the wedding. He was as opposed to marriage right now as Rose was. She'd never actually date him – she didn't feel that way about him – but a fake marriage wasn't dating, and she knew him well enough to know he'd be fine with the arrangement. They could get married for a couple of weeks.

Penelope was still on the phone and interrupted Rose's fun. "He said he's calling his parents now."

"Oh, my God!" Rose screamed. "No! Please tell me you're lying. I hadn't even thought about my parents. How am I going to do this without letting them know? You both know they'll try to commit me!"

"Totally lying. He's not telling anyone. But yeah, we need to figure out the whole parents thing. You know they won't like this." There was a voice in the background on Penelope's end, but they couldn't tell what Steven was saying. "Gotta go. Steven wants to go to some new place for lunch. You two figure out what you're going to do about your parents and call Luke. I'll talk to you later."

"Bye!" Leann said, and Rose hung up the phone. She picked up her coffee, took a sip, and then turned to Leann.

"Seriously, we cannot tell my parents about this. Call Luke and tell him."

"He's your fiancé. You call and tell him." Leann shrugged and turned back to her breakfast.

CHAPTER 5

For the next couple of weeks, Rose got frequent calls from Penelope, Leann, and Luke. Luke really did think it was one of the funniest things he'd ever heard, and he was as excited as the girls to play a role in it. He even showed up at Rose's house Monday evening with a plastic ring. She opened the door to find him kneeling on the mat, holding the ring up to her.

"Oh, my darling Rose! Would you make me the luckiest man on earth and be my wife? I promise to love, honor, and obey you for two weeks before providing you with a quickie divorce so you can marry a lot of other men before you die alone with your hundred cats."

Rose took the ring, but it would barely fit on her pinkie finger. She looked at it in fake disgust. "I guess I will, even if all you're giving me is this crappy ring." They both laughed, and then Leann came around the corner.

"We couldn't resist," she said. "I picked out that *crappy* ring, so you'd better like it. It came in a lovely little pack of wedding jewelry in the toy section at the store. There was even a tiara, if you want to wear it on your big day." She handed the rest of the package over to Rose, who started to take it and then stopped.

"Give it to Bev," Rose said. "She might like it. I'm keeping my engagement ring, though."

Leann used her phone to become a minister while she, Luke, and Rose were out eating chips and salsa at their favorite Mexican restaurant. It didn't take long, and all she had left was to wait for the certificate to show up in the mail. When Leann had that, Rose and Luke could go to the courthouse, get the marriage certificate, and they'd get married in a quiet ceremony with just the three of them, Penelope, and Steven.

"So, am I supposed to move in with you, or you move in with me, or how's this going to work?" Luke asked as they were getting their main dishes at the restaurant.

Rose picked up one of her tacos. "We don't actually have to live together. The marriage certificate is all that matters."

"Okay, but we have to put it on Facebook," Luke answered.

Rose stopped for a second, then swallowed without finishing chewing her food. She almost choked but got the food down without too much of a problem. "Why?" she asked.

Steven just looked at her. "Well, there are reasons for both of us," he said. "I want Samantha to see it. And you want people to know you're serious about this. When we change it to divorced after a couple of weeks, these guys who are telling you now that they want to marry you will know that you're really just getting married for the sake of the record. It's…what do you call it, Leann?"

"Setting a precedent," Leann answered as she cut into her enchilada.

"Yeah, that's it. You want to do that, or some of those morons will think you're really getting married."

Rose chewed her bottom lip as she thought. "You're right, except it's really getting married, just temporarily and without all the benefits they might think they'll be getting. But your parents are on your Facebook. How do we keep them from knowing?"

"I'll block that post from them or something. We'll figure it out." Luke went back to his fajitas.

"Fine," Rose said. "Tell your friends, though. I wouldn't mind marrying Kurt for a couple of weeks."

"Gross!" Luke whined, pushing his plate away. "Now I can't eat. You really want Kurt?"

Leann shook her head. "You know, if Kurt's game, I might want to start getting married like this, too."

Kurt went to college with Luke, and both the girls had begged Luke years ago to set them up with him. He was tall with dark hair and dark eyes. He was usually clean-shaven, and he had an amazing jawline. But the last time Kurt was single, they were both married. Now, however, the girls were both joking. Leann was too focused on her kids to date right now, though she may again later, and Luke already knew that Rose didn't plan to ever date again.

Luke pulled his plate back towards him. "He's dating Jen again, anyway. You know she's not going to let him marry either one of you, even a fake marriage."

That was the end of the discussion about Kurt, but they had more plans to make. Luke informed him that, as her first husband for the plan, he wanted a say in her other 26 husbands.

Rose didn't have a problem with it. "Sure. Why not? Tell Penelope to let you in on the interviews or however she's doing it."

Three weeks later, they all took a personal day from work to go to the courthouse. By the end of the day on July 17, the marriage certificate was filed with Leann's signature, and Rose and Luke were officially husband and wife.

The couple of weeks after that didn't feel any different than usual. The only thing different happened the Monday after she and Luke got married.

CHAPTER 6

Rose walked into the office and passed her team, already working at their desks. Bianca threw confetti over her head. "Congratulations!" they all shouted.

The reason for the celebration didn't even register at first. "What?" she asked.

"Ummm...you got married?" Terry responded.

Rose hadn't thought much of the Facebook post. She and Luke had changed their relationship statuses Friday afternoon and pretty much ignored Facebook for the weekend. They knew what would happen during the "first" marriage. "Oh, that," she said.

"We want to throw you a shower tomorrow," Elsa said. "We want to do something for you, even though you didn't even tell us about it!"

They were all excited about her marriage. She almost didn't have the heart to tell them it didn't mean anything, but she also couldn't have them trying to throw bridal showers every few weeks for the next couple of years. "It's not like that. It'll be over in a couple of weeks. No showers, no parties."

"What are you talking about?" Bianca said. "You got married. That's forever, right?"

"You guys really don't remember asking me not all that long ago about my plan to beat the record of number of marriages?"

"You're really doing that?" Will said. "We thought it was a joke!"

"Well, it started as a joke, but I'm really doing it now. Luke's a good friend. We're married, but not for long. We're not moving in together or anything. We'll get a divorce, and then I'll get married again to someone else. Seriously, I'm looking for 26 more after this one."

None of them believed her. They knew that she and Luke were good friends, and so the marriage didn't really surprise them very much. Elsa had even met Luke when she ran into them and the girls at a restaurant one night.

No one else in the office believed that it was a joke, either. Letting people know that they were not going to have a surprise bridal shower for Rose was the most fun Penelope had had in a while. Rose had to tell her team every couple of days that she wasn't getting a wedding ring because there was no point. After a week, Rose finally broke down and bought a cheap ring at Leann's department store so she could shut them up.

She, Penelope, Leann, and Luke hung out every few days as usual. Luke had some of the same problems. People just stared at him in disbelief when he said the marriage wasn't meant to last. After two weeks, they all met for dinner at Rose's. Steven came with Penelope.

After dinner was cleared and they were trying to decide on a board game, Steven pulled out a printed copy of the standard divorce agreement he had promised, along with a pen. He had already filled in Rose and Luke's names. The divorce agreement was only two pages – the shortest one Rose had seen yet. But then, her other divorces had included assets and money owed. This one was simple. Steven let them both read it and then handed Rose the pen.

"Well, Luke, I have to say that you are most definitely the best husband I've ever had. This has been an awesome marriage. I don't hate you at all."

"Coming from you, that's really saying something," Luke said. "And this was absolutely not the marriage I ever thought I'd have. But it was actually a good one. And I don't hate you, either."

Penelope piped in. "Well, maybe you won't hate your next husband when it's over, either."

"Is it lined up?" Luke asked her.

"All ready. Just waiting for her to be legally able," Penelope replied.

"Who?" Rose wanted to know.

Luke shook his head at Penelope, who was already speaking up. "I can't tell you yet. When the divorce is final, we'll talk about it."

Rose and Leann looked at Steven. "Attorney-client privilege," he said, holding up his hands. "Or wife-husband privilege. Whichever. Either way, I've been sworn to secrecy."

They tried to get some kind of hint, but Penelope, Luke, and Steven were all adamant that they wouldn't say a word.

Finally, Rose and Luke both signed the papers. Steven explained to them how to file the paperwork, where to pay the fee, and how long it should take to have a judge sign off on an uncontested divorce. He also told Rose that he'd already emailed a PDF of the papers to her so she can do everything herself, but he would still help out with the next couple of divorces if she'd like.

Since it was so simple, it didn't take long with the court. It probably helped that Steven let the county's judges know what was going on. Within two weeks, the divorce was final. They received their papers on a Tuesday and both changed their relationship status on Facebook back to single.

That Wednesday morning, Rose's team stopped her again before she got to her office. "You were really telling the truth!" Elsa exclaimed.

"Yes," Rose answered. "And it'll happen again."

"Did you at least get some fun out of it?" Bianca asked suggestively.

Rose laughed. "No. It wasn't like that. We agreed not to make it complicated."

Will told her she was crazy through his soft laughter. Bianca asked if she needed some more men to marry, because she knew her cousin wouldn't mind being married for a couple of weeks. They were all in on the fun now that they knew it was for real.

The owner of the agency, Jessica, was in the office that day. She came by Rose's office later that day to try to console her and see if she needed anything. But after Rose explained everything, Jessica just said, "As long as it doesn't interfere with your work, get married a million times. Have fun, though. Marriage is supposed to be fun, right?"

CHAPTER 7

Rose closed the door behind her. It had been a long day. She had meetings with clients all morning, including one with Kenneth, who tried to get them to cut their estimate in half. He didn't succeed this time; Rose and Penelope had been able to convince him that the current plan was best for his profits. That meeting had run over, of course, so she didn't get to take a lunch. When she got back to her office, Elsa told her that a client had changed code on his web site and was now complaining that nothing was working right, so the team spent the entire afternoon trying to find what the client had tried to change, revert to the previous version, and then figure out a way to correctly do what the client had tried to do. They finally finished at 6:00, and Rose spent the next 30 minutes on a call with the client, explaining as nicely as possible how his effort to save money had actually cost him more, because she would have to bill him for the time they spent fixing his mistakes.

When she got home, she leaned against the door for a minute, looking at her kitchen. She thought about starting dinner straight away, but shook her head, set her purse and laptop bag on the table, grabbed a Diet Coke from the refrigerator, and walked to the sofa.

The second she sat down, her phone rang. The phone was across the room on the dining room table.

"Forget it," she muttered. "I'll call them back later."

The phone finally stopped ringing while Rose was looking for something to watch. She picked a movie she'd seen a million times and set the remote on the table. She sipped her soda and thought she may take a short nap before finding something to eat. She wasn't very hungry, even though she hadn't eaten all day, but she was exhausted. In addition to the long day at work, she had been up late talking to Leann the night before.

So she settled back and closed her eyes just as the movie was starting...and then the phone rang again.

She ignored it, but as soon as it stopped, it started again. She started to get up to turn it off so she could rest, but Penelope walked through the door, holding her phone to her ear. "I swear, Rose, you need to start answering when I call."

Penelope hung up her phone, silencing the annoying ringing from Rose's.

"I was trying to take a nap," Rose answered. "And since when is it necessary for you to call if you're coming over anyway?"

"You've been divorced for a week. It's time to get married again."

"And that deserves you interrupting my nap?" Rose asked.

Penelope flopped on the sofa, almost spilling the can of soda she had just taken out of the refrigerator and opened on the walk to the living room. "Yes!" she practically yelled.

Rose cringed and leaned back again. "After I sleep."

Penelope reached over and pushed Rose's arm. "Don't you want to even know who you're marrying so you can dream about him?"

Rose didn't open her eyes, even to push Penelope back. "You know very well that I'm not dreaming about anyone. There's not a man alive who's worth nightmares."

"Oh, you won't have nightmares about this one. Do you remember Neil, from high school?"

Rose's eyes finally opened. She looked at Penelope in surprise. "You're kidding."

"Not at all. Saturday's the day, my dear. He'll go get the marriage license Friday. He did say he wants to be able to take his wife to dinner, though."

"I haven't seen him since the day we graduated. And he barely spoke to us anyway."

Penelope scoffed. "Spoke to you, you mean. He and I talked a lot. He played basketball. I cheered at all his games, remember?"

"Yeah, that's right. Didn't you date him for a bit, too?" Rose asked.

She shrugged. "Kinda. It was like a week. We had one date. Didn't last long." Penelope pulled her phone out of her pocket and started scrolling.

"Why not?"

Penelope shrugged. "I liked Paul better. He asked me out when he found out Neil asked me out, so I picked."

Rose laughed. "And then you dumped Paul for Steven. I remember that."

"Ah, high school. I do kinda miss that a little bit. Now, I'm stuck with Steven forever."

"Nothing's forever, Pen," Rose sighed. "Steven could still screw you over."

"Not likely," Penelope laughed. "I think he's too comfortable with me. Plus, he loves me."

"Don't forget that love is bullshit."

Penelope scowled at Rose, who had leaned back again.

Rose hadn't closed her eyes yet and saw the scowl. "You're right. That's just for me. Other people can be happy with a man. Maybe I should get a few cats, though. Prepare for my future as the crazy cat lady."

Shaking her head and rolling her eyes, Penelope laughed again. "You don't need those cats. The number of ex-husbands you're going to have will be enough for people to call you crazy, even if they don't know you."

She showed Rose her phone, where she had found the messages from Neil. He had agreed to Saturday afternoon, and did actually say he wanted to have dinner afterwards – with just Rose. She was surprised.

"So is he wanting an actual date, or what?" she asked.

"Well, I kind of met him for lunch today. He does want a date," Penelope replied.

"Forget it," Rose said. "I'm not dating. And what did Steven say about you going to lunch with him?"

"Yeah, I know. You'll marry 30 men, but you only dated the first three. But he really wants to!"

"And I don't," Rose said. She got up and started walking to the kitchen.

"I'm getting a real drink. Do you want one? And again, what did Steven think?"

"Steven doesn't care. He knows he's the love of my life. No drink tonight for me. I'm going to have to drive home in a little bit, and if I drink tonight, I'll drink a lot." She paused for a second. "But why won't you go out with Neil? Just once? Those green eyes…"

Rose opened the oak cabinet, found her favorite glass for drinks – the last of a set of small red tumblers that her mother had given her years ago – and reached into another cabinet for the rum. She didn't answer Penelope until she had pushed the glass to the dispenser on the refrigerator and filled about a quarter of the glass with ice. She was deep in thought, trying to decide how to get the point across to Penelope. She finally answered as she was pouring rum into the glass.

"He's cute. A few years ago, I would have dated him in a heartbeat. But now, there's just no point. You know how I feel about men. They're all just a lot of trouble, and the only good they're doing me right now is this whole marriage record thing. Honestly, they'll probably screw me over on that somehow, too. There's still a lot of time for that to happen." The glass was about half full of rum, and she was on the way back to the sofa. She set the glass on the table, sat on the sofa, and poured soda from her can into the glass. Before Penelope could answer, she had picked the glass back up and gulped down almost half of it.

"I know you feel that way, but you'll change your mind. And one date with Neil isn't going to hurt you. Besides, he may be the one to change your mind. He's really a good guy."

"There's no such thing as a good guy," Rose replied. "Is that the only way he'll do it?"

"He really is a good guy, and you know it. They do still exist, whether you want to believe it or not. And yes," Penelope said. "He just got divorced. His ex cheated on him, and he wants to piss her off."

Rose's smirk was obvious, even though Penelope could only see half her face. "So women are worthless, too. Noted."

"Don't even. Every person on this earth isn't evil. I mean, there's me!" Penelope held her hands out and gave Rose a big smile.

Rose was still smirking. "Weren't we just talking about how you used to dump guys for other guys all the time before you married Steven?"

Penelope grabbed Rose's glass and took a drink. There wasn't even a sip left when she finished. It was mostly just ice. "You're hopeless," she said as she set the glass back on the table and fell back onto the sofa.

Rose got up to refill the glass. "Hopeless. I'm pretty sure that's what I've been trying to tell you. Are you sure you don't want your own glass?"

"Screw it. Go ahead and get me one. Steven won't mind coming to get me."

"He may just tell you to walk home. I wouldn't blame him. Find out if Neil will marry me without the date."

"I tried. He won't. Just go out with him! You don't have to do it again if you don't want to."

"Fine," Rose said. She reached for a clear glass out of the cabinet, but smiled to herself and looked to be sure Penelope wasn't watching. She wasn't; she was still on the sofa, looking at her phone. Rose got a cartoon-covered plastic cup instead. She started pouring ice and rum into both glasses. "I'll go, but make it clear to him that I'm not going to enjoy it, and it's only going to be one."

"I already told him that. I believe he thinks he can change your mind."

"Not happening," Rose said bluntly.

"We'll see," Penelope replied, looking up. "Hurry up and get in here. I've got his profile pic pulled up for you."

"Does it really matter?" Rose asked.

Penelope held her phone up, even though she knew Rose couldn't see it from the kitchen. "It might once you see him!"

Rose finished pouring the rum and started walking back to the living room. "I'm not even going to bother answering that. You know what I said."

Penelope looked at the glasses in Rose's hand and frowned. "What the hell is that?" she asked. "Why do I have a kid's glass? And why do you even have a kid's glass?"

Rose laughed at her. "You act like a kid sometimes, and this way you won't break it when you knock it off my table. And I have them because Leann brings the kids over sometimes. You know I've had kid dishes here for years."

Penelope frowned until she took the glass from Rose's hand and took a long drink. "You're a good bartender, even if you are a bitch sometimes."

Rose bowed before she sat down, "My pleasure, dahlin'."

CHAPTER 8

That Saturday, August 22, at 3:00 PM, Rose married Neil in a quiet ceremony outside Penelope's house. Leann had met them there. Neil was still as good-looking as he was in high school. He had short cropped blonde hair and green eyes. He was tall and still built like the basketball player he used to be. Rose was impressed that he had managed to keep his looks, but she still had no interest in actually dating him. When he asked what time he should pick her up for dinner, Rose had to stop for a minute. She had forgotten that she'd agreed to go out with him.

"Penelope explained…" Rose started, but Neil interrupted.

"Yes, she explained. You don't actually want to date. That's okay, but if I'm going to make my ex jealous, I've got to be seen with you in public at least once." He smiled and looked down at her.

"Okay," Rose shrugged. "Where are we going?"

"Wilson's," he replied. Rose could see the victorious smile that reached his eyes. "It's a nice place, and her parents own it."

Rose laughed. "Pick me up at 7. Penelope can give you my address."

She went home, took care of a little work she had brought home, and then changed into a long blue dress and silver heels. She even put on a little makeup. "It's for the show," she muttered to herself as she was getting ready, reminding herself that it wasn't an actual date; it was just her fifth husband, who she'd divorce in a couple of weeks.

Neil knocked on the door promptly at 7:00, and they drove to the restaurant in his dark gray Lexus. They talked about high school and what they'd both been doing since. He really did seem nice. Rose was having a good time – enough that she had to remind herself again that it wasn't a real date.

Rose had never been to Wilson's before, though she heard it was a nice restaurant. When she walked in, she could tell why. It looked like a five-star restaurant. Everything seemed to be expensive, from the black linen tablecloths to the crystal chandeliers. The prices on the menu told her that this place made some major money considering how many people were there, and the first bite of their appetizer explained why it was packed. The food was delicious. Even apart from the amazing food, she was having a great time with Neil. They talked constantly, and she almost forgot to move her hand when he reached across the table to put his on hers.

About halfway through dinner, an older woman approached their table. "Neil, darling, what are you doing here?" she called, holding out her arms.

Neil stood and hugged the woman. "I couldn't stay away from your cooking, Maria." She was average height, with short dark hair and dark eyes. She was very pretty. Rose assumed it was his ex-wife's mother.

She chatted with Neil for a minute, and then turned to Rose. "And who did you bring with you tonight?" she smiled.

"This is my wife, Rose," Neil said proudly.

Rose had never seen a smile turn to a frown more quickly. "Married again already?" she asked, slowly turning to Neil.

"I liked it so much I had to do it again," he replied, still smiling.

"But I thought…" she began, and then stopped. She composed herself, and then spoke again. "But what of working things out with my dear Vicki?" she asked. She turned to Rose again. "No offense, my dear. I'm sure you're perfectly lovely, but Neil can't possibly stay married to you. Didn't he tell you that he already has someone?"

Maria carried herself well, even as she was berating Neil and treating Rose like a homewrecker. Neil kept himself in good humor. "Maria, you know that Vicki and I are divorced."

She gave him a curt nod. "That doesn't have to last," she said.

Neil hugged her again. She hugged back, but without smiling this time. She whispered something in his ear, then let go of him. She turned to Rose again, "I hope you've enjoyed your meal, dear. It was a pleasure meeting you."

"The pleasure was all mine," Rose smiled, and then Maria walked away.

Neil sat down and apologized. "That, in case you didn't figure it out, is my ex-mother-in-law," he said. "That went better than I thought it would, but I'm sure it's not the end of it."

"And yet," Rose said, "you're still smiling."

"Oh, yes. Vicki will be sufficiently jealous." He took a bite of his food.

Rose looked at him for a few seconds, concentrating on what was in her mind. "So are you doing this for revenge, or because you want her back?"

Neil seemed surprised. "I want her back, of course."

"But she cheated on you. You left her." Rose was confused.

"She did cheat, but I didn't leave her. She left me for him when I found out and gave her an ultimatum. They're actually living together now."

It was the end of that conversation. They ate in silence for a couple of minutes as Rose thought about the situation. It was Neil's life, and if he wanted to take his ex-wife back, even after she cheated and left him for another man, that was his decision. She had no place to tell him that, personally, she thought it was stupid, but there may be other factors that she didn't know about, so she just didn't say anything.

Before she could think of something else to chat about over their meal, the server came back to the table. "I trust everything has been satisfactory," he said.

Neil spoke up. "Of course, Eric. Everything's wonderful, as usual."

"Very well, sir," Eric said. He pulled the check out of his apron and set it on the table. "I am ready to take your bill, sir."

Neil had taken a bite, so he chewed quickly and swallowed it. "We were going to order dessert," he said.

"No, sir," Eric said, still smiling and acting as if everything was fine. "I need to take your bill. We cannot serve you dessert tonight."

Rose was almost shocked, but she knew exactly what happened. Maria had gone back to the kitchen and told the server to get rid of them both.

Neil knew what happened, too, but wasn't happy about it. "May I speak with the manager?"

"No, sir," Eric replied. "The manager sent the check for you. I am to escort you and this lovely lady out."

Rose was setting her napkin on the table and getting ready to stand up, but Neil wasn't finished. "We won't be leaving until we finish eating," he said.

Eric began again, in his nice, professional way, to tell Neil that they needed to leave. Neil looked towards the door and smiled. Rose turned to see what he was looking at. A woman their age had just walked through the door and was looking around. She looked very much like Maria, with dark eyes and dark hair, but her hair was longer than her mother's. She was wearing old jeans and a tank top, very unusual in a restaurant like this one. Rose decided it must be Vicki.

Vicki caught sight of Neil and almost ran over. She practically pushed Eric out of the way and bent over the table, almost in Neil's face. "How dare you show up here?" she yelled. Everyone in the restaurant turned to see what was happening. "And with some slut?" she pointed at Rose.

Rose was shocked and embarrassed. She wanted to hide. Neil was still smiling. "Got your attention, though, right?" he said.

Vicki stood up straight and knocked Neil's full water glass off the table. The glass shattered on the marble floor. Rose looked at the puddle of water and then back at Vicki. "You got married?" Vicki yelled again. "How dare you! Were you seeing her when we were married?"

Rose was torn between wanting to witness this horrifying scene and wanting to run out the door. She didn't drive, but at this point, she wasn't sure that she wanted to ride home with Neil. She stood quietly, gave the server a sympathetic glance, and started walking to the door.

When she passed the bar at the front of the restaurant, she turned to look back. Neil didn't even seem to notice that she left, and Vicki was still standing there yelling. The server was standing a few feet back, holding the check, pretending that nothing unusual was happening. Just before Rose turned to walk out the door, she saw Maria running from the kitchen. Vicki turned to look at her mother and slipped on the water in the floor, falling into it. Rose stifled a laugh as she saw Vicki start to stand, the seat of her jeans soaking wet.

As soon as she got into the parking lot, she called Leann, who could barely understand that Rose needed a ride. Rose was laughing much too hard.

Neil tried to call the next day, but Rose ignored his calls. She had no desire to see him or talk to him again.

She got together with Leann and Penelope the night after the wedding. Penelope completely agreed that there would be no more dates in exchange for vows. If the man didn't agree to it her way, she just wouldn't marry him.

Two weeks later, Steven brought her the divorce papers, already signed by Neil. The divorce was final a week and a half after that. Marriage 5 down…25 to go.

CHAPTER 9

Rose's next husband was one of the other lawyers at Steven's office. His name was Phil, and he seemed to be a perfectly nice man, a few years older than Rose. She met him at the ceremony and chatted with him long enough to know that his reason was similar to Neil's. The woman he was seeing had cheated on him. He didn't want her back, though. He just wanted to let her know that she was replaceable.

It was a completely uneventful marriage. They got married at Penelope and Steven's house on September 27, chatted for a few minutes, and went their separate ways. She didn't hear from him after the wedding, which was preferable to her.

At the office Monday, Bianca, Elsa, Terry, and Will threw her a surprise fake bridal shower. They brought breakfast from a local bagel place and anyone in the office who wanted to participate gave her cheap gifts, mostly those that had to do with divorce. She protested, and Elsa told her that it was all for fun, and they agreed to only spend a couple of dollars on the gifts. Someone gave her the same kind of little girl's wedding set that Luke had gotten her fake ring from. Elsa gave her an accordion-style file folder to store her divorce papers, and someone else gave her a candy ring pop. Penelope made a cake and wrote *Happy Divorce!* on it. They all had fun laughing about Marriage Number 6, and someone suggested they take bets on how many times Rose would be married before she grew tired of the game.

Other than the fake bridal shower, the couple of weeks that Rose was married to Phil were completely normal. She worked and hung out with Leann, Penelope, and Luke a few times. Steven joined them once. He said that Phil's ex was sufficiently jealous, though there wasn't a scene like Neil's ex made. Instead, she had called to tell him that he was an idiot and hung up. Phil was smiling when he told the guys in the office about it.

On October 9, Rose received the divorce papers in the mail, signed her name, and filed them the following Monday. The divorce was final on October 23.

CHAPTER 10

"This is taking too long!" Penelope screamed.

"You know my neighbors are going to hear you," Leann said calmly. The three women were sitting in her back yard around a patio table, watching the kids throw water balloons at each other. They all had diet sodas in their hands, because Leann didn't drink around the kids.

The kids turned towards them for a second, but then went back to their game.

"Let them hear," Penelope said at normal volume. "We've been doing this for four months and still have 25 weddings to go. We've only done three."

"Find men to marry me faster," Rose said, barely looking away from the kids.

"Oh, no! This is not my fault. You're married for two weeks. It takes almost two weeks for the divorce to go through. I can't schedule a wedding until one's legally over. I'm getting them lined up just fine. In fact, I've got one for you for next week."

It had only been a few days since Rose got her final divorce papers from her marriage to Phil. Penelope really was getting them lined up pretty quickly. "It's fine. We said to begin with it would be a month or so between each one. We're actually doing great," Rose said absently.

Leann jumped in. "We could make it a little quicker if you only stay married a week."

Rose was still watching the kids. "Two weeks is fine."

Leann and Penelope looked at each other. "It's fine?" Penelope asked. "Rose, since when are you okay with slow?"

"Can't make the judge sign papers any quicker," she said.

Leann nodded to Penelope, then turned to Rose. "Do you want to start dating again and forget this?"

Rose turned to them and shook her head vehemently. "NO!" she said, surprised. "Why would I ever want to do that? I'm just getting started good."

Penelope smiled at her a little. "Because you want kids."

"Maybe," Rose said, a little sad. "But what does that have to do with dating?"

Leann looked at the kids and then back at Rose. "Ummm...you'll need someone to get you pregnant, right?"

Rose shook her head. "Not necessarily. I can adopt. Or do the sperm donor thing. I know my options, and only one of them is to have a man in my life."

Penelope looked at her. "You know it would be easier if you have someone you love helping you with that."

"Love's not happening. That's what I have you two for, right? The aunts?"

"I've got my own kids," Leann laughed.

Rose scowled at her.

"I know. I know," Leann said. "You know Aunt Leann will babysit anytime. But that's not even the issue. How are you going to keep up these marriages and still have a baby?"

"Oh, I can wait to have kids until we're finished with this. Or at least close to finished. At the rate we're going, it'll only take another couple of years. I've got time. Besides, I only need a little bit of time every few weeks to tie the knot. Untying the knot is easy. Mail worked just fine with Phil."

Just then, a water balloon hit Leann's chair, splashing water on the three of them. Leann turned around long enough to tell the kids to be careful, not even concerned with the soaking she got. Rose laughed at Penelope, who was sitting behind Leann and barely got a few drops on her, wiping her face and standing up as if she'd been drenched.

Leann turned back to Rose and Penelope, ignoring Penelope's pouts, and continued the conversation as if nothing had happened. "You can still change your mind and date, you know," she said. "No one is going to fault you for wanting to find somebody to grow old with."

51

"Cats. And you two," Rose said, still laughing at Penelope.

"Ugh," Leann replied, sitting back in her chair and throwing her hands up in disgust. "You don't even have any cats."

"It doesn't take long to get one. It's actually much easier than getting a husband. I'll have 30 cats in no time."

"You're ridiculous," Leann said. "One cat might be fine. I know you love them. But you know you'll never have 30."

Rose ignored her and turned to Penelope. "So who's next?"

Penelope forgot the little bit of water. "Oh, it's Henry!" she said, excited.

Rose and Leann looked at each other. "Henry Watkins?" Leann asked. "As in, the first guy who commented on that Facebook post that started all this?"

"Yep!" Penelope said. "He tried to get a date out of it, but I told him no. He wants to do it anyway. Said he's bored and wants to do something fun."

Rose laughed. "How much fun does he think it is? It's like 10 minutes to get married, and we won't even see each other after that."

Leann smiled a little. "He's always had a crush on you."

"He said he wouldn't mind going out with her, but since she won't, he'll settle for marrying her," Penelope said.

They laughed until Bev walked over. "Mom," she said. Leann didn't hear her, so she spoke louder. "MOM!"

Leann turned around. "Yes, honey," she said.

"Can we eat now? I'm getting hungry."

"Oh, the hamburgers!" Rose said, getting up quickly. She ran the few feet over to the grill and opened the cover.

"Did you burn them?" Jeremy asked from just behind his sister.

Rose looked at him in surprise as she picked up the spatula. "Of course not. They're done, but they'd need a few more minutes to be burned!" She picked up a platter, and started transferring the burgers to it. When she was finished, they walked over to a folding table Leann had set up with the rest of the food and all got their plates ready. Rose helped Bev with hers. They had the burgers, slaw, and potato salad. The kids didn't want to eat with the adults, so they took their plates and cans of soda to the shade under a tree and sat in the grass. The women went back to the patio table and ate while they talked.

"So, Henry. Next Friday. 6:00," Penelope said after she chewed her first bite of burger. "And I'm glad you didn't burn these. They're good."

"That sounds like a date to me," Rose said through a mouthful of potato salad.

"Me, too," Leann agreed.

Penelope shook her head. "He's going out of town right after. Said he's going to visit his sister in Mississippi or something. And he wants to know if you can wait until after he gets back to put it on Facebook."

Rose thought while she chewed another bite. After she swallowed, she answered. "Actually, let's just stop the Facebook posting. I'm getting so many notifications every time I change that damn status, and I'm sick of the messages asking about it."

"I thought you wanted to let people know. I mean, it does help in getting you more husbands lined up," Penelope said.

Rose sat back, stretching. "Yeah, but it's just annoying. I don't want to deal with it for two years."

Leann nodded. "I can see that. How about we do a blog instead?"

Penelope agreed. "That's a good idea. Rose can write a little about each husband. I mean, that Neil story is pretty good."

"Nope," Rose said. "A blog is fine, but I'm not writing it. Work's busy right now, and I've got a list of projects I want to finish around the house."

Penelope said, "Well, I'm not a writer. Numbers, I can work with. I hate words. Well, written ones, anyway. Talking's fine, but I'm not a writer."

"I'll write it," Leann said. "We'd only need to do it every few weeks. I can do that while Brent has the kids. I get bored anyway. Y'all will need to read over it, though."

"Deal," Rose and Penelope said at the same time.

Rose took a big bite of her burger and pulled her phone from her back pocket.

"What are you doing?" Leann asked.

Rose held up a finger to tell Leann to wait as she scrolled and tapped a few times. When she finished chewing, she said, "Relationship status hidden. Now we'll see how many times people ask me if I'm married again yet."

Leann and Penelope kept eating. Before Rose dug into her meal again, she picked up a water balloon she had put under the table earlier and threw it at the tree. When the kids got splashed, they jumped, then shook themselves off, gave her a phony evil look, and picked up their burgers.

CHAPTER 11

Rose walked into Leann's house at 6:00 the following Friday, October 30. Henry was already there. He was 5"10' and had brown hair and brown eyes. He was cute, but he had never been Rose's type. She'd heard he got arrested a couple of years ago for drugs or something, and that wasn't her thing. She noticed he was thinner than she remembered, but it had been years since she saw him last. He didn't have quite the "druggie" look, but was thin enough that it was possible he was still on them.

It didn't matter. Everything was lined up, and Penelope didn't think he'd be any trouble. He handed her a bouquet of flowers. "I know this isn't a real wedding, but I wanted to at least give you these."

"Thank you," she said, surprised.

Leann performed the ceremony. Afterwards, Henry hugged her and said, "Thanks. You just made my week. I hate to rush off. I don't know if Penelope told you, but I have to take a trip. I'll be back next week. Just let me know when the divorce papers are ready for me to sign."

So it was done. She was married to Henry Watkins. She still had an uneasy feeling about it because he'd asked her out before, but she wasn't that worried about it. Everything had gone smoothly so far. There was no reason to expect anything different. She didn't hear from him at all, so she figured her uneasy feeling was wrong.

Two weeks later, Rose sent Henry a message, letting him know it was time. She got out her computer, filled in her name and Henry's name on the divorce agreement Steven had sent her, and printed the papers. She signed her name so they would be ready for Henry to sign.

The next day, she didn't have a response from Henry, so she tried again. When he hadn't answered later in the day, she called Penelope.

"I'll call him," she said. "Maybe he's just not checking messages."

Rose started cooking dinner. She decided to have spaghetti, so she got out a can of tomato sauce and started cooking. She'd only been in the kitchen for about 10 minutes when the phone rang.

"Hey! When am I supposed to meet up to sign these?" she answered.

"Well, there's a problem," Penelope said.

"What kind of problem?" Rose asked.

Penelope took a second to answer. She started talking once, and then was silent, like she was trying to figure out how to say whatever she needed to say. "It's actually kind of funny. I had to call his mom. She babysat me some when we were growing up."

"Okay." Rose was impatient. She didn't think it was a good sign that Henry wouldn't answer when either of them tried to call.

Penelope continued. "You know how he got arrested before. It was silly, really. He had a little bit of pot. He got probation." She paused.

"Yeah?" Rose said, confused.

"Well, he didn't learn his lesson. Of course, his mom said it's not his fault. Something about him being framed. But he got arrested on his way back from that trip. I looked it up online before I called you back. He was transporting drugs. Like, a lot. Your husband's a drug runner."

Rose looked down at the bubbling marinara sauce on the stove and dropped the herbs in her hand into it. "Lovely," she said as she picked up the spoon to stir the herbs in. "So when is he getting out so he can sign these papers?"

"That's the thing. I doubt he'll get out for a really long time. Apparently, he had a gun, too. But it wasn't pot this time, either. That would be one thing, since it's more acceptable now, but it was meth. This isn't going to be some silly little thing where he gets probation. According to the paper, they haven't set bail yet. They're doing that Monday morning."

Rose turned down the heat on the stove, walked over to the kitchen table, pulled out a chair, and sat down. "I mean, not that it's really a horrible thing considering the reasons he's my husband, but what happens now? Not as far as him. That sounds selfish, but whatever at the moment. How do I get the divorce? And can I be in any kind of trouble?"

Rose heard Penelope take a deep breath. "I don't know yet," she said. "Steven's at work. He'll be home in a little bit. I'm going to talk to him about all that when he gets here. I'm assuming we'll just have to find a way to get in to see him and get him to sign the papers, but he's about 200 miles away, in Alabama. And I'm sure there's nothing they can do to you. You two weren't even living together or anything. But I'll call you back when I talk to Steven."

"Okay," Rose said. "Just let me know."

Steven called Rose an hour later and told her not to worry about a thing. He was going to make some calls Monday morning, but she wasn't in any danger. She was clean, and it was doubtful that Henry had even mentioned they got married anyway.

So, for the entire weekend and most of the day Monday, Rose waited. She did worry, even though Steven told her not to. Regardless of the reasons for the marriage, Henry was technically her husband. She really didn't want to be investigated by the police. They wouldn't find anything, and they certainly wouldn't be able to do anything to her if they did, but she didn't want to go through all that. And, of course, she wanted this marriage to be over as quickly as possible.

CHAPTER 12

Monday afternoon, Rose was in a meeting with other managers when her phone rang. She looked at it. It was Steven. She excused herself from the meeting and walked out to the hallway.

"Hello?"

"Hey. It's me. Sorry for calling you during the day. I know you're busy, but I finally got through to Henry's lawyer. He's a public defender in Birmingham, where Henry is right now. We know a couple of the same people. He's a good lawyer. Not that you care about that right now. Anyway, he can get us into the jail to see Henry, but we'll have to do it soon. Bail's too high for him, and he can't get out, but they're going to transfer him to another place Thursday. It'll be harder to get in then."

"The sooner the better," Rose said. "Can he not just get him to sign the papers for us?"

"Well, that's the part I skipped over. I actually talked to him early this morning and emailed him the agreement. He went over to the jail, saw Henry, and Henry refused to sign them. Said something about wanting to see you first. You're going to have to go there to get him to sign."

Rose paced in the hall, knowing that she was probably holding up the meeting. "Do I have to go by myself?"

Steven answered quickly, "Oh, no! No! I wouldn't do that to you. I can take a personal day Wednesday if you want me to go with you. It'll be probably a three hour drive each way. Do you want to get Penelope or Leann to go instead? Or in addition?"

"I want you to go. You know whatever legal stuff we might need if he's refusing to sign. I'll see if one of the girls wants to go, too." She paused and looked in the little window in the door of the conference room. The other managers were looking at the door, waiting for her. She signaled "one minute" and continued pacing. "I'll call them tonight and then call you back then. I've got to get back to a meeting."

"Okay. We'll get this taken care of. The attorney said Henry told him he'd sign when he sees you."

Rose sighed. "Okay. I'll talk to you tonight and we'll figure it out. I'll go ahead and see about Wednesday."

She hung up, took a couple of deep breaths, and walked back into the meeting. They were just waiting for a little information from her so they could make a decision about something Kenneth wanted. She gave them the details she and Penelope had discussed with Kenneth at the last meeting, knowing it could change again within a few days. When it was over, she walked to Jessica's office, explained the situation, and scheduled her personal day.

There were only a couple of hours left in the day. She spent that time answering questions from her team and rescheduling everything she had on her calendar for Wednesday.

She got up to leave a few minutes early. "What's wrong?" Will asked.

She turned and looked at them. She didn't realize until that moment that she had been short with all of them for the last couple of hours. "Sorry. It's been a bad couple of days. It seems that my current husband got himself arrested, won't sign the divorce papers, and I'm going to have to take Wednesday off to go see him in jail."

They all looked at her, stunned. "You're joking with us again, right?" Terry asked.

"I wish," she replied. "Husband Number 7 is definitely a winner, right?"

"Wait, seven? Are you already up to seven?" Bianca said.

"Yeah," she answered.

"Yay! That's a good number. We figure you'll get to at least ten before you give up this nonsense," Bianca said.

She smiled at them. It was the first time she'd really smiled all day. "I'll prove you all wrong, then. This is just a problem that needs to be fixed. One difficult one out of four isn't that bad," she said.

Terry spoke up, "But you didn't post it on Facebook. We've been watching."

"Oh, yeah," Rose said. "I've stopped that. A friend of mine is starting a blog instead. It's too much trouble to do all that on Facebook. And annoying. I'm sick of messages about getting married."

"We need the link!" Elsa said. "This is something we want to keep up on!"

She was surprised. She figured it would lose the novelty after a few weeks, and they'd forget about it. So far, though, they seemed just as excited and curious as they were with her marriage to Luke. There was no harm in that, though. She was trying to do something unusual. Their interest may last for a while yet. "I'll get it to you as soon as Leann puts it up. Maybe the rest of my husbands won't be as much trouble as this one."

"So are you going to get him out of jail?" Terry asked.

Rose laughed. "Hell, no. I'm going to get him to sign the divorce papers, and whatever he's done is on him."

"Good," Bianca said.

Rose went home feeling only slightly better about being married to a man who was in jail. At least no one thought any less of her over it. Jessica was very understanding about the whole thing, and that was good, as long as she didn't have to take time off work to deal with things like this often. She was sure Jessica's mind would change quickly if it happened again. She still had twenty-three husbands to go. Taking time off work every few weeks to deal with a man who was resistant to divorce wouldn't be fun for her or good for her job.

Luke called her that night, and they laughed about the situation she was in. She had never touched drugs except a little pot in college, so the fact that she was currently stuck with a husband in jail for drugs amused them. It was annoying that she'd have to drive to Birmingham, but it would be over in a few days.

CHAPTER 13

On Wednesday, November 18, Rose, Steven, and Penelope all got into Rose's silver Honda. Penelope set the GPS for the address Steven gave her, and they started driving. It took three and a half hours to get to the jail where Henry was being held. They were all tired and hungry, but decided to take care of business before trying to find lunch.

They walked into the lobby. Steven looked around until he saw a man holding a briefcase walking into the door. The man wore a suit and was looking around for something. He was tall with a little bit of gray in his dark hair, but the gray didn't age him. Rose noticed him before Steven did without realizing he was the lawyer they were there to see. Steven walked over to him first, chatted with him for a couple of minutes, and then waved the girls over. Rose was surprised. She didn't expect to meet a handsome man that day.

"Hi," the man said, smiling and holding out his hand. "You must be Rose. I'm Matt."

Rose shook his hand and smiled back at his bright blue eyes. She couldn't help it, even considering the situation. "Hi, Matt. I guess you know the story."

"I do," he said. "It's quite a story, too." He turned to Penelope and introduced himself, then turned back to Rose. "So, Henry is husband number...?"

"Seven," Rose replied. "And in the last few months, the hardest to divorce."

Matt laughed. "Well, he said he'll sign when you show up, so let's go in and see him. Hopefully it won't take long, and then you can get back to your little project."

He walked towards a door at the far end of the lobby. "Have you girls ever been in a jail?" he asked.

Penelope and Rose both told him that they hadn't. Matt explained what Steven had already told them about the metal detectors and the rules for visiting. "Did you leave your phones and everything in the car?"

Steven answered for them, "Yes. I made them leave everything they hold dear."

Matt continued. "Everything's already arranged, but you'll need to sign in. Then, they'll take us to the room so we can see him."

They walked through the gray door and into a hall that was also gray. After that, they walked through a metal detector, signed in at a desk, and the officer led them to a small gray room with a table. The officer left. They had to wait 15 minutes. Rose commented on how gray and dull everything was, and Matt said that it could be a little depressing if you had to spend a lot of time in there. He tried to surround himself with a little more color at home.

Finally, Henry walked in, escorted by a different officer. He led Henry around to the table and let him sit down, then looked at Matt. "Are you good?"

"Yes. Thank you," he said.

The officer left. Steven pulled the papers out of his briefcase and set them on the table, along with a pen.

"Wait a minute," Henry said, crossing his arms on the table and leaning forward. "Do you want me to sign those right now?"

Matt looked at him. "Now, Henry. You said you'd sign the papers when you see Rose. She's here."

Henry smiled. "What if I want to stay married?" he asked.

Rose looked questioningly at Steven, then Matt. They were both looking at her. Steven shrugged, and Matt motioned for her to pick up the conversation. She turned back to Henry. "Why?" she asked.

"I just want a wife," he said. "There's no real reason other than that."

"Did you plan all along not to sign the papers?" She was confused. Everything seemed fine a couple of weeks ago when they got married, and he had been perfectly agreeable for it to last just a couple of weeks. If he had a problem with anything, he should have said so before they even got married.

"No," he said, looking down at the table. "I decided while I was in here. I never thought I'd be locked up, but since I am, I might as well have a wife to tell the other guys about."

"But we agreed," she said.

He looked up at her. "Yeah, we did. But I changed my mind. Stay married to me. Come visit me. When I get out, I'll be good to you."

Steven and Matt were calm. They were used to not showing their emotions. Matt folded his hands on the table and looked directly at Henry. "Henry, we talked about this. You may not get out for years. There's a lot of evidence, and I still say a plea bargain is your best shot. Even then, you'll have to serve time."

Henry kept his eyes on Rose, waiting for her response. He ignored what Matt said, waiting instead for Rose to response.

When Rose realized that Henry wasn't going to answer Matt, she said, "No. I'm not staying married to you. We agreed to the divorce, and that's what I want. You need to sign the papers."

Henry just looked calmly at her, smiling a little, and said, "Well, I'm not divorcing you. So where does that leave us?"

Steven tried then. "Henry, you know that she can get a divorce even if you don't sign. It'll just take longer."

Henry still didn't look away from Rose. "Then she'll just stay married to me longer. I'm not signing." He stood up, walked to the door, and knocked. The same officer opened the door and led him out.

Rose was stunned. She looked around at Penelope, Steven, and Matt. Penelope was stunned, too. Steven and Matt just sat there with their heads down for a minute. Then, Steven reached for the papers and put them back in his briefcase.

"What now?" Rose asked.

"Now, we need to leave. And I think Steven and I need to think a little," Matt said.

"But what are our options? I don't want this to take forever."

Steven shook his head, still looking down at the table. He finally looked up at Rose. "It's going to be more of a hassle than we thought. But we can't stay here to talk about it. They may need the room for other meetings, so they'd kick us out in a few minutes anyway. We need to go."

Matt held his hand to Rose to help her up and then opened the door for all of them. They walked down the hall in silence, signed out, and then kept walking. Rose couldn't bring herself to speak.

In the parking lot, they decided to go to a burger chain down the street for lunch. Rose drove, following Matt.

CHAPTER 14

The restaurant was cheery, especially after the gray décor of the jail. Rose chose to ignore it. She didn't feel very cheery right now. This was almost as bad as when Toby refused to divorce her. She hoped it wouldn't take two years for this one. Or, worse, that she'd have to wait until Henry was out of prison. There was no telling how long that would be.

"So what do we do now?" Rose asked when they sat down at a table by the window. Rose scooted in to the window so Penelope could sit on the outside, then reached up and pulled the shades down. Sunlight wasn't what she needed right now.

Steven looked at Matt, who nodded for him to go ahead. "We can do a contested divorce, or we can look into whether you can get an annulment," he said. "But I'm going to suggest we get a divorce attorney to take care of that. The last few months is all the divorce work I've ever done. I don't know as much about it."

Matt smiled at Rose, "You know it's pretty easy to divorce an inmate, right?"

She felt reassured a little. "Thank God," she said. "Any idea how long it'll take?"

The men looked at each other questioningly. "Not really," Matt finally answered. "It might be a little easier since you've only been married a couple of weeks, but like Steven said, a divorce attorney is your best bet." Neither man had much experience with divorce. Matt's concentration was criminal law, and Steven's was corporate. Matt explained that he had helped a couple of clients with divorces during his job as public defender, but it was minimal – mostly just looking over papers their spouses had sent after they were arrested. He wasn't comfortable really handling a divorce, and he wasn't licensed in Georgia, anyway.

They decided that Rose would call Jim, the divorce attorney she used before, when she was home.

"For now," Matt said, "why don't we just enjoy our lunch? There's no point worrying about it right now. You can't do anything until you see this guy and see what he says, anyway."

They chatted over lunch. Rose found that Matt was easy to talk to. He shared some stories about his work, and she found herself more interested than she cared to admit. He asked about her project and why she decided to do it.

"I've been married three times. Well, really married. I got sick of it. Men are horrible creatures." She stopped long enough to realize she'd just called Matt a horrible creature. She didn't know him well, and didn't know if it would bother him. "No offense."

It didn't bother him. "None taken," he laughed. Penelope and Steven gave each other a smile.

"Anyway, it was a joke at first. That I'd already been married so many times, so I should just try to make a record out of it. We looked up how many that would be. I was kind of thinking about actually doing it, but Penelope's the one who talked me into it."

"And now a few more marriages, and you're thinking about giving it up?" Matt asked.

"No way!" Rose said. "We'll figure this one out, and *someone*," she nudged Penelope, "is going to do a better job of picking from now on."

"Who knows? I may find her one that she actually stays married to one day," Penelope said.

"No," Rose replied.

Matt looked at her questioningly. "Why not? I'm sure there are lots of men who'd want to stay married to you."

"I'm done with men. They're nothing but trouble. I've tried to find the right one, the man of my dreams, whatever. He doesn't exist. This project is the only thing I'm going to have to do with men from now on."

"So, what, women now?" Matt asked with a mischievous smile.

Rose laughed. "Nope. Not interested in women, either. My only relationships from now on will be these marriages."

"Sounds pretty lonely," Matt said.

"Alone and lonely are different. If it's a choice, it's not lonely."

"What if you meet someone?" he asked.

"I won't."

They kept talking about work and Rose's project as they ate. She and Matt had a lot in common. They both liked playing video games, read fantasy adventure, and liked hiking.

When they finished lunch and started walking to the door, Matt gave Rose his card. "Call me if you ever want to talk," he said, smiling. He shook Steven's hand and walked towards his car.

Rose turned the card over. He had written his personal email address and phone number on the back.

When they got into the car, Penelope sat in front. "So, when are you going out with him?" she joked.

Rose opened the console and threw the card in it. She closed it, then started the car. "I'm not. He's nice, but I'm still not dating." Penelope tried for a couple of minutes to change her mind, but gave up when Rose turned the music up to drown out her voice. Penelope looked out the window. She wasn't upset with Rose for refusing to acknowledge the sparks between her and Matt, but she did think it was a shame. After a few minutes, she turned the music down and changed the subject.

CHAPTER 15

Rose was able to get an appointment with Jim, her divorce attorney, the following Tuesday, so that was her lunch break. After a long discussion where he told her how silly the whole record-breaking thing sounded to him, he told her that she would have to file for a contested divorce. She didn't qualify for an annulment based on Georgia's qualifications, and an annulment would be rare even if she did meet the qualifications.

"I thought if you didn't consummate the marriage, you could get an annulment?" Rose asked.

"Well, that's true in some states," Jim said. "But not in Georgia. Unless you're mentally incapable of a contract, underage, forced or tricked into the marriage, related, or if one of you was already married, you're going to have to do contested. Even if you met one of those qualifications, an annulment's really rare. Sorry, hon, but that's how it works here."

At least she'd dealt with a contested divorce before, so she knew what to expect.

She and Jim talked for a while longer. She didn't want anything from Henry, and she didn't want him to have anything of hers. He said the paperwork should be pretty standard. It was just going to be a lot of waiting. If he filed anything in response, they'd need to respond to that. She paid his fee that day and let him start work. There were no assets to divide, so at least the agreement itself would be simpler than what he'd written for her before. He said he would have everything ready for her to look over by the end of the next week, since he wasn't working over Thanksgiving.

She didn't even realize it was so close to Thanksgiving. She was so worried about the divorce and work, she'd forgotten. She only had one more day of work that week, and then she'd want to go to her parents' house for a couple of days. At least there was that break to look forward to.

The next few days really were a welcome break. The office was slow

Wednesday since everybody was getting ready for the holiday. There were no client meetings, and she was even able to let the team leave at 2:00 to start their holiday early. She left at 5:00 after making sure everything was caught up and planned for the following week.

After stopping at her house to pack a bag, she drove the hour through traffic to her parents' house. They were happy to see her. They hugged and caught up over dinner. She didn't mention a word about the marriages and even laughed when her mom asked if she was seeing anyone. "No, Mom," she finally got out, though neither her mom nor dad could figure out why it was so funny. The next day, her brothers and sisters got to the house early and woke her up. They had a relaxing long weekend, several amazing meals, and Rose felt happy when she left Sunday evening.

Work Monday and Tuesday seemed easy. Rose had done most of her planning the week before after the team left, so all she really had to deal with were a couple of client meetings. She knew that wouldn't last long, so she enjoyed it while it lasted. Wednesday, she and Penelope had to meet with Kenneth. That was the most annoying thing all week. After visiting with her family, Rose felt that nothing could get her down. She was sure the divorce with Henry would be over soon, and she could get on with her life.

Jim kept his promise of getting the papers to her quickly. When she got home Wednesday, she had an email from him with the paperwork attached. It was short and simple. She signed and took them by his office on the way to work the following Thursday morning.

Then, she had to wait. Jim filed on Monday. He worked his magic to get everything filed as quickly as possible, but Henry had 30 days to respond. By then, it was the middle of December, and Jim told her it would be a while before the divorce would be final. She would just have to keep waiting.

Leann got the blog running early in December. It took her some time between the kids and holiday hours at the store, but once she got the site set up, she posted regularly. She kept the growing number of readers updated on the drawn-out divorce with Henry. She threw in some stories about Rose when she thought it was getting too boring. It was mostly about trips the girls had taken or things she remembered from when they were younger. It only took about a month for the blog to gain a few hundred followers. Leann was sure that most of them thought it was all fiction, but several people commented regularly. Leann was having fun writing it and keeping up with the comments. Rose and Penelope were having fun reading Leann's blogs before she posted them, and they rarely had anything to add or change. It was a great system, and the girls enjoyed working together on it.

She didn't have to wait thirty days to get a response to the divorce papers. In the second week of December, Jim called laughing to let her know that Henry had filed a response asking for some things out of the marriage, including money to hire an attorney. He said he'd handle it, but wanted to let her know. She should watch for a document to read over the next day.

Rose was on the way back to work from picking up lunch when she got the call from Jim. She parked at the office and dug into the console to find Matt's card. When she found it, she just sat staring at it for a long while. What did she actually expect from him? When she started looking for the card, she intended to email and ask him to try again to just get Henry to sign the papers. Now, seeing his name in print, she was sure he wouldn't even bother. He may not even answer her. Henry was his client, and he had no reason to want to help her. Actually, he probably helped Henry draft the response that Jim was just laughing about.

A knock at her window made her jump. She rolled down the window to see what Elsa wanted. "We're hungry!" she said. She was holding a cigarette, probably taking her smoke break to watch for the food Rose was bringing back.

"Sorry," Rose said. "I got distracted. I'll meet you inside." Elsa walked back to the smoking area to put out her cigarette and go inside to eat. Rose whispered, "Screw it," and took out her phone. She opened her personal

70

email, typed in the address Matt had written on the back of the card, and typed the message she originally got out the card to send. Then, she took the bags of food upstairs and had lunch in the breakroom with her team. They got back to work afterwards, and she didn't check her personal email until she got home.

She was surprised to find that she did have an email from Matt. He had an appointment with Henry that afternoon, so he did check on the papers again. Henry still refused to sign them. He continued by asking how work was going. She replied, happy to know that he wanted to chat. She found out that he wasn't helping Henry with the divorce; another inmate was doing that. He worked into the conversation that he was single, and they switched to texting not long after that.

It wasn't long before they were texting off and on all day. They were just friends, though. It wasn't that Matt asked her out or even flirted that much, but Rose mentioned her belief that love wasn't for her fairly often. She knew it was partly to remind herself, but thought it was worth saying either way. He was easy to talk to, and they soon knew a lot about each other. They talked about their work, families, hobbies, and everything else. Rose was thrilled to have found a new friend, and secretly thought it was a shame that she decided not to date anymore. She thought he might actually be one of the few good ones left.

They didn't really talk about much that other people would find interesting – mostly just how their days were going. Rose told him about the projects she was working on around the house and kept him updated on the husband search, as well as progress on the divorce. Matt told her about his clients, without using their names, and about his fishing trips.

He was easy to talk to, and she felt herself growing attached to him and their conversations. In January, Matt convinced her to meet him for dinner.

They met in a small town that was about halfway between them. Matt found a local steak place that had amazing reviews. After driving an hour and a half, Rose got out to stretch her legs while she waited for him. He was there within a few minutes, and they had a nice dinner, talking and laughing through it. The meal was excellent, and Rose enjoyed herself.

"I guess it's time to go," Rose said when all the other tables except one was empty. She looked at her phone. "It's almost 10:00."

Matt reached for the check. "Let me get half," Rose said as she reached for it, too.

"No, I'll get it," he said. "You drove a long way to meet me."

She laughed. "And you drove just as far."

"Still, let me. It's not that big of a deal."

Rose argued a little bit more, but he insisted, so she gave in. When the server brought his receipt back, they stood and walked outside. He walked towards her car with her.

"I had a really good time," she said.

"So did I." They were at her car. She turned to look at him. "Let me know when you get back?"

"I will," he said. "You let me know, too."

"Of course," she answered.

He reached down and hugged her. She hugged him back, and then stood back. Even as she thought that she shouldn't, she stood on her toes and kissed him. He kissed her back, and that was all it took for her to feel that she might be wrong about love.

She drove home happy. After everything, she felt good about Matt. There was no reason she should, except there was that feeling that it was right. She had had doubts about every other man in her life, but she didn't have any now. She'd wait and see, but she thought this one might be different.

They texted when they both got home, and it seemed that they didn't stop texting from that point on. She loved it.

CHAPTER 16

In early February, Rose went to see her accountant. She had all her paperwork ready and assumed it would go as quickly and painlessly as usual. She didn't have to wait long; Crissy was ready for her when she walked in the door – one of the reasons she loved using her. Crissy started looking over her paperwork. As she did, she asked jokingly, "Did you get married or have any babies this year? I haven't seen you in a while." Crissy wasn't one of her friends on Facebook, so she didn't know about the project.

Rose hadn't thought much of the marriage, other than trying to get divorced. It didn't even dawn on her that it might affect her taxes until that moment. "Ummm…well, I did technically get married."

Crissy looked up, surprised. "Wow! Congratulations!"

Rose slumped in the black vinyl-cushioned chair. "No congratulations. I'm actually doing a thing where I'm trying to break the world record for marriages. I got married 4 times last year."

"Oh, girl! I need to hear more about this. But were you married on December 31?"

"Yeah. Number 7 refuses to divorce me. It's a big mess." She went into the story, at least a short version because she knew Crissy had other clients.

"I'm so sorry. I'm sure you don't want to file jointly with him?" Crissy said.

"No way!" Rose exclaimed.

"Well, we'll have to do married filing separate, then. I'm afraid your taxes may be higher this year."

While Crissy worked on the tax return, Rose told her the whole story and gave her the link to Leann's blog. But, Rose owed $1,500 to the IRS. She usually got at least a small refund, so this was a shock.

"Well, I can try to set up an installment agreement if you need it…" Crissy began.

Rose interrupted her. "No, I can pay it. I just don't want to. Go ahead and have them deduct it from my bank account. You can do that, right?"

"Yep!" Crissy replied. "I'm sorry, girl, but that's how it happens. Make sure you're never married on December 31 from now on unless it's for real."

Rose left Crissy's office and called Leann to complain. They talked about it for a few minutes, then talked about how Jim was doing with getting the divorce finalized. She hadn't heard from him in a few days, but she knew he'd let her know as soon as there was news. When she hung up with Leann, she texted Matt.

Everything was going well with Matt. They still talked every day, and they had started trying to meet at least every couple of weeks. With their schedules, that was the best they could do, but Rose didn't mind, and it didn't seem like Matt did, either. The first couple of times, they met at the same steak place and had dinner.

He called her back. "How upset are you about the taxes?" he asked.

"It's okay," she said. "Just another bump in the road. I hate losing the money, but now I know not to be married at the end of the year anymore."

"Haha. Well, that's a good thing to know. Are we meeting this weekend?"

"Of course! But, do you want to come here? I can cook dinner for us."

"I'd love to," he replied. "But I can take you out instead of you cooking."

"No, I like to cook. Just let me know if you want something specific."

They talked until she got back to the office. She wondered if he would stay the night. She really wanted him to, but didn't want to rush him. They'd talked a little about his past relationships, and he'd had some bad ones, too. She thought it was better for him to make all the first moves.

He didn't, and that was fine with her. They had dinner and talked. She introduced him to her favorite show, and they snuggled on the sofa to watch the first episode. The show had been over for several years, but he'd never seen it, and she still loved to rewatch it. When the episode was over, he said he liked it and looked forward to watching more with her, but he needed to get home. It was late, and he was going to visit his parents for lunch the next day.

He kissed her good night, a longer and better kiss than they really got to have standing in the parking lot at the restaurant they usually went to, and she was smiling and happy when he left, looking forward to the next time she could see him.

That happened a couple of weeks later. He insisted on driving to her house again and taking her out to eat. That time, he stayed. The next morning, she woke up happier than she'd ever been. She still didn't have any doubts about him and noted that it was unusual.

CHAPTER 17

After that night, Rose thought it was probably time to tell Penelope and Leann about Matt, so she did.

"Wait? The lawyer? Henry's lawyer?" Penelope said, thrilled.

"Yep. He's wonderful."

"I knew it!" Penelope shouted, hugging her as they were standing outside the Mexican restaurant, waiting for a table. "Leann, didn't I tell you?"

Leann hugged Rose, too. "You did. I'm glad you were right. So, Rose, tell us all about him. And why didn't you tell us sooner that you don't hate love anymore?"

"I wanted to make sure I wasn't wrong this time. But I don't think I am. He's wonderful. I mean, he lives three hours away, but does that really matter? I'd rather not get to see the right man often than be annoyed by the wrong man."

"Sweetie, if you're happy, we're happy. But I need to meet him."

"Yeah," Penelope said. "Bring him over for games one night. I'll even cook."

Leann and Rose both looked stunned. Penelope almost never offered to cook. "Oh, don't be like that," Penelope said. "Matt's good for her. Steven will like having him over, too. They got along."

"So," Leann began. "Is this love? We want details."

Rose looked down to hide her smile. She still couldn't use the word *love*, but she had a good feeling about Matt. Everything about him made her trust him. He even told her the other night that he wasn't going anywhere. She knew she'd been tricked before, but she didn't get any bad feelings from him at all. Even when he went out to have a drink with his friends, he told her not to worry, and he texted her the entire night so she wouldn't.

The girls had dinner, and Rose told them a little more about Matt. Even though she wouldn't say she loved him, both the other girls knew that she did.

Rose was finally divorced from Henry on March 10. She called Matt that evening, happily telling him the news and letting him know that Penelope already had more lined up. As usual, he laughed at her little project. She was glad that he didn't mind at all that she was constantly married to other men. They talked for a while and made plans for the following weekend.

They were going to Penelope's so Leann could meet Matt. He was as excited about it as they were. Luke showed up, too. Penelope and Steven grilled hamburgers, and they played board games and had a couple of drinks for the rest of the night. There was a lot of conversation, funny stories about their jobs, and even more laughter.

"So, next marriage?" Matt asked, looking at Penelope.

"Oh, yeah. A guy I went to college with."

Rose said, "And will he divorce me? I don't want a repeat of Henry."

"You're not thinking of quitting, are you?" Luke asked. "I'll happily marry you again if you need reassurance that all men aren't going to change their minds about divorcing you."

They had to explain to Matt about the fourth marriage. She had told him that it was Leann's brother, but didn't mention his name, and they hadn't introduced him that night as Leann's brother, only Luke. Once he knew that Luke was Rose's first "fake" husband, he laughed along with them.

"No, not quitting," Rose said after they finished the explanation. "I've gotten this far, and I want to finish it. Henry was a one-time thing. If we have to, we'll start prenups."

Steven didn't think that was necessary. He knew who Penelope had lined up for the next couple of marriages. He'd at least met them, and he didn't think there would be any problems. "We're just glad that Henry thing is over with," he said. "That was a lot of trouble for all of us."

The night was a success. When Matt went home later that weekend, Penelope and Leann came over to tell her that they thought he was awesome. He got along great with everyone, and even Luke thought he was a good guy.

Rose wasn't surprised; she thought they would all like him as much as she did. She didn't say so, but let them continue telling her how great he was because it felt good. There were so many things that they saw with her real ex-husbands that she didn't see to begin with, and they, like her, didn't see anything wrong with Matt. She felt that it was a good sign, and it reaffirmed her belief that he might be the right one.

Rose's next three marriages had a lot less drama, and the divorces were just as easy as before. Penelope made sure to have a rock-solid agreement with them. They divorced her without question, signing the papers just as Luke, Neil, and Phil had done.

Gary was the guy Penelope went to college with. He was an accountant in a small town further outside of Atlanta. He thought the whole idea was funny and was laughing when Leann pronounced him Husband Number 8. When Rose asked him why he was doing it, he said just for the fun of it. He'd been married twice already, so another one – especially a short one- wasn't a big deal to him. They got married on March 12 and didn't see each other again. The divorce was final on April 7.

Rose married Andrew on April 13. He was a younger, rebellious struggling artist who wanted to make his parents shut up about when he would get married. He wanted to meet for coffee to sign the divorce papers. Rose reminded him that she wasn't dating. "Oh, no. I don't mean as a date. I really just want to say hi. I'm actually seeing someone. She's cool with it and wants to come for coffee, too." When they met to sign the papers, he told Rose it was hilarious; his parents vowed never to ask him about getting married again after this "stunt." The girlfriend didn't mind; she didn't believe in marriage any more than he did. They were living together, serious about the relationship, and thought a piece of paper was worthless. Rose and Andrew were divorced on May 6.

Zachary, one of Leann's coworkers at the department store, became Rose's tenth husband on May 15. He said he was just bored and wanted to do something amusing. He told everyone at the store; they all read the blog anyway, and so they were keeping up with Rose's story. On the Saturday two weeks after the ceremony, Rose walked into the store with the papers. It wasn't far, and she wanted to see if Leann had time for lunch. When she walked in, all of the employees at the front of the store applauded. The customers at the registers looked confused. She hadn't been at the store in a while, so she was a little confused at first, too. "Here to divorce Zachary?" one of the cashiers asked.

"Oh, yeah." She smiled at them and walked towards the back of the store where Zachary usually worked the jewelry counter.

He was there and happy to see her. "There's my lovely wife," he said. "Here to get unhitched?"

"Yes, my darling husband," she joked. When she pulled the papers out of her purse, she noticed that other employees were starting to gather around. Leann walked by and gave them a stern look. They ignored her. It was too much fun to watch their coworker get divorced. Rose called out to her, "I'll find you in a minute. Your office?"

Leann nodded and walked on. Rose saw her heading towards the stairs to her office and turned back to Zachary. She was unfolding and straightening out the papers when she heard Leann's voice over the loudspeakers. "All employees, please return to your work areas."

A couple of people walked away, but most of them ignored the announcement. Rose found a pen and signed the papers, then handed the pen to Zachary. He decided to make it a little show, getting down on one knee and faking a sad face. "Come on. Leann's going to be mad," Rose said, but Zachary continued his exaggerated begging. It was all in fun, but Rose didn't want him to get in trouble. She knew that Leann could see the whole store from her office.

It didn't take long to hear another announcement. This time, Rose could hear the exasperation in Leann's voice. "All employees, return to your work

THE SANCTITY OF MARRIAGE

areas immediately."

This time, everyone started moving. Leann was pretty lenient, but the store was busy, and she could see that some of the real customers (other than Rose, of course) were a little annoyed that there wasn't anyone around to help them. Zachary stood and sheepishly signed the papers, giving Rose a little hug when he handed them and the pen back to her. She let him get back to work and walked up to Leann's office.

"Distracting my employees?" Leann asked.

"You know I didn't mean to. They just followed me. Looks like Zachary's been telling them all about it."

"He has. Sorry. Just had a customer cuss me out over a sale we had that ended yesterday. She wanted me to give her the discount anyway. I ended up just giving it to her. I'm in a rotten mood."

"Will lunch help? We can run next door to that deli. Their BLTs are great."

"Sure. Let me just tell Sharon that I'm leaving." Sharon was the assistant manager. She was in her own office next door, so Rose didn't have to wait long. She and Leann walked to the deli and ordered sandwiches. The kids were just starting their summer break, so the girls talked about what the kids were planning to do over the summer until time for Leann to go back to work.

Rose got the final divorce decree for Zachary in the mail on June 7. She had been putting them in the empty drawer of the second nightstand in her bedroom, so she glanced at it to be sure it was in order and added it to the growing stack of papers in the drawer.

Through all of it, Rose continued to talk to Matt every day. She saw him every couple of weeks, whenever they both had time. They started taking turns driving to each other's houses for the weekend. Rose was still nervous about dating, but Matt reassured her over and over that he was around to stay. Usually, the reassurances were unprompted. Rose didn't say much about her nervousness, but she felt that Matt could sense it. His reassurances were exactly what she needed. That, the way he made her laugh, and the way he made her feel that nothing could go wrong, were all she needed out of life. She missed him whenever he wasn't around, but she knew he cared about her, so she didn't mind waiting until the next time she could see him.

Leann and Penelope were happy because Rose was happy. On the weekends in Atlanta, they usually had a fun game night. It became a regular event, and it didn't take long before Matt became close friends with everyone else, too. They all chatted on a regular basis.

CHAPTER 18

It was late Saturday morning, and Rose was lying in her bed. She had woken up a few minutes before and turned to put her arm around Matt. She tried to go back to sleep, but she was enjoying holding him and couldn't. He didn't move. She was afraid he was still asleep, so she didn't, either. It seemed that they did that every morning they stayed with each other – Rose awake and just enjoying being near him, and him either asleep or pretending to be asleep, too.

After a while, she decided they'd both probably want coffee, so she slowly and carefully turned away from him, hoping she wouldn't wake him. She wanted to start the coffee, sneak back into bed, and put her arms around him again before he got out of the bed. As careful as she was, though, it didn't work. By the time she started the coffee pot, he was next to her, getting mugs out of the cabinet so they'd be ready when the coffee finished brewing.

"You didn't have to get up yet," she said. "I could have brought the coffee to you."

"That's okay," Matt smiled. "I can help with coffee."

Rose didn't usually eat breakfast, and Matt knew it. He opened the refrigerator, got a bagel, and walked to the toaster. Several times, she wished she could remember to get up and cook breakfast for him, but since she didn't think about food in the morning, she always forgot. She felt bad about him having to get a bagel when she could have thought to cook, but he said it was fine.

Rose went to the sofa and sat down, then picked up the remote to turn on the tv. She looked through Netflix for something to watch, but nothing interested her that she hadn't already seen. She finally set the remote back down and picked up her phone. There was an email from Elsa about a project she was working on, so Rose typed. She sent the reply just as Matt walked in with two cups of coffee and a plate balanced on top of one of them. He set everything on the table, his black coffee and Rose's with milk and sugar. Then, he sat down to eat his bagel and cream cheese. She set down her phone and picked up the remote. "Here, you find something to watch," she said.

He took the remote in the hand that wasn't holding the bagel and scrolled until he found a show they both liked. It was the same show she introduced him to the first night he was there. They watched other shows and sometimes movies, but this was one of their favorites. They were only just starting the second season, but he vowed to watch the entire series with her. He wouldn't watch it without her.

Matt finished the bagel while they were watching. When he was finished eating, Rose scooted over, he put his arm around her, and she settled into their normal tv-watching position. She couldn't imagine being more comfortable with anyone. He never tried to force her to talk like other men. She didn't know whether it was because he knew she didn't really talk that much or because he just liked silence, too, but it was nice to be able to watch a show with him keeping her warm and not worry about whether they had to talk or not. When they did talk, she always loved the conversation, but it was nice that it didn't feel mandatory.

Just as she was settled, the door opened. Penelope burst in already talking. Rose didn't catch it all – something about "new husband" – because Penelope stopped with her hand on the door to close it. She had seen Matt sitting on the sofa.

It took her a few seconds to stop staring. "Well, what is this?" she finally asked.

"Hi, Penelope," Matt said.

"Hi, Matt," she replied, then turned to Rose. "You forgot to tell me you were having company this weekend."

"Morning," Rose said. "Yeah, I haven't talked to you much this week. Work's been busy." She reached for the remote and paused the show. "So what were you saying when you walked in?"

"Are you sure you want me to talk to you about your future husband when your boyfriend's sitting right there?"

Rose almost said something about the "boyfriend" comment. She and Matt hadn't used that word, so she looked at him to see if he had a reaction. He didn't. He was still sitting there smiling, just as he had been, so she hoped he didn't mind it. In fact, she hoped he liked it.

"Go ahead. I don't mind," he said. "She only has, what, 20 left?"

"Well, after next week, it'll be 19. Rose, you're getting married Tuesday afternoon. His name's Will. You don't know him, and neither do any of the rest of us. He found us through the blog. But we did get Steven to check him out. He'll be good."

"Great. Just great," Rose said sarcastically.

Penelope was quick to reassure Rose that Steven's background check was thorough. Will was a grad student, squeaky clean, and looked like he wouldn't give them any trouble at all. "Plus, you know we'll eventually run out of men you know. We don't want any repeats if we can avoid it, though Luke's willing to marry you again if you want. I'm sure Henry would be, too. And you can always ask Matt if he wants to be number 30 and make it the one that lasts."

They all laughed, though the comment made Rose nervous. She and Matt had talked about doing things together months and even years down the road, but marriage had never come up. She didn't want him to think she was rushing him, partly because she was still scared herself, and partly because she didn't want to push him. She knew he'd had bad relationships, too, and didn't know if the thought of marriage sometime in the future would be too much for him. He seemed fine, though, so she let it go. She thought she was probably silly for letting comments like those make her nervous. They'd been seeing each other for months. Even though they hadn't actually put a name to their relationship, the way he reassured her made her believe the relationship was real.

Leann showed up a few minutes later. She and Penelope had planned to take Rose to lunch, so the four of them went out a little while later. They talked about Rose's next husband, and Matt, as usual, was great with everything.

Rose forgot her concerns about marrying someone that none of them knew when she met Will. They met at a park close to Leann's house, because none of the girls wanted to tell a stranger where they lived. He seemed nice enough. They got married, and two weeks later, he signed the divorce papers and sent them back with a note: *Thank you for a wonderful marriage. I wish you the best.*

Rose filed the papers, and that was it. The marriage to a complete stranger was over, and Rose got back to work on the project.

The next few months went by quickly. Rose married Jake, Carl, Sam, Shannon, and Darrell. Thanks to Steven's new background checks – which he dutifully billed Rose for – all of the marriages were relatively uneventful. Jake was Elsa's cousin, so Rose had to chat about that marriage more at work. The team was a little disappointed that there was really nothing to talk about. She thought she'd explained to them how it all worked, but it seemed that Elsa expected her to at least talk to Jake because she was related to him. Even so, the marriage was the same as the others.

Carl was another marriage from the blog. He messaged Leann, and a few weeks later, he was on Penelope's lineup, cleared by Steven. He was an investment banker from New York. Why he flew to Atlanta for a fake marriage was a mystery to Rose until the wedding. She asked him. He said he had family in Atlanta and was visiting them. He promised that he didn't travel just for a fake marriage. He actually signed the divorce papers at the ceremony, dating his signature for the right day. He said it would take too long to mail the papers to New York and back. Rose kept them in her files for two weeks, signed them, and took them to the courthouse to file. Everything went smoothly.

Sam was slightly more trouble, but not much. Rose had dated him in college, and she had been pretty upset when they broke up. Still, when Penelope told her who it was, she figured it had been long enough that there wouldn't be a problem. When Leann finished the ceremony, Sam kissed her, but not on the cheek like she'd told all of her husbands to do. He wanted a real kiss. They talked about it afterwards, and he seemed to understand that everything was fake.

The next day, Rose was working on some budget projections for Kenneth in her living room, and there was a knock at the door. Sam was there.

"Hey," she said when she opened the door. "What are you doing here?"

Sam looked nervous. "I was hoping I could talk you into going to dinner with me," he said. "I mean, since we're married and all."

"I'm actually working right now. Besides, Penelope explained the deal to you, right?"

Sam looked at his shoes, and then back up at her. "Working on a Sunday?"

"Yes." She was annoyed, and she was pretty sure he could tell. "So you understand the deal from what Penelope said, right? You can't show up here. I'm not dating you. Are you going to have a problem signing the divorce papers?"

"No. It's not that. I'll sign them like I said. But I was hoping we could see each other."

Rose didn't want to hurt his feelings, but this was more like a business deal to her. Plus, there was Matt. She didn't want to date anyone else. "Sam, I'm actually seeing someone. I know that's not a normal thing when you're married, but neither is trying to break a record for the number of marriages. I'm sorry that our breakup was so bad. But you're the one who wanted to break up, remember?"

"Yeah, but I was wrong. The girl I ended up marrying was…not good for me. She was mean."

"But you ended up divorcing her, right?"

"Yes. And I've dated since then. But we had such a good time. I thought we could try again."

"No. I'm sorry. We can't."

"I understand," he said. He turned to walk away, and then turned back to her. "Can I at least get a kiss?"

"No, Sam."

He walked away, looking dejected. She felt a little bit bad about it, but Penelope had explained everything to him. She closed the door, locked it, and went back to her computer.

When she sat down, she realized that she'd forgotten to ask him how he found out where she lived. Oh, well. It was too late now. The best thing she could do now is to hope he signs the papers. She finished what she was working on. Instead of putting away the computer, though, she pulled up the divorce agreement, filled in her name and Sam's, and printed it. She addressed the envelope, found her stamps, and walked out to the mailbox. She had decided to go ahead and mail the papers to Sam now instead of waiting the full two weeks. At least she'd know whether she'd have problems getting a divorce within a few days.

Then, she called Matt to let him know what happened. He asked if she needed him to come stay with her that night. "No, I don't think so. I want to see you, but you have work tomorrow. I've got a good lock on my door and a gun in my nightstand. I'll be fine, though I don't think he'll show up again."

By Thursday, she had the papers back, signed. Sam had even added a short note apologizing for showing up unannounced. She breathed a sigh of relief and took the papers to the courthouse the next day.

Her marriage to Shannon was another truly uneventful one. He was Penelope's cousin. She remembered meeting him once or twice when they were kids, and she actually had a little bit of a crush on him then. But she hadn't seen him in years, and she barely remembered what he looked like until they got married. He was a couple of years younger, anyway. He and Penelope carried most of the conversation after the ceremony, and then he hugged

Rose goodbye and left. A couple of weeks later, they signed the papers over board games with everyone – including Matt – at Penelope and Steven's house, and the divorce was final not long afterwards.

Darrell was one that Rose actually set up herself. She and Darrell had been friends for years. They met at work when she first started at the marketing firm. He got married a couple of years later and moved to Kansas with his new wife. They were divorced now, and he was back in Georgia to be near his family. They chatted occasionally, but there was never anything more than friendship between them. They all hung out for a little bit after the ceremony, which Matt even attended this time, and the marriage didn't change anything in their friendship.

By Christmas, she and Darrell were divorced. They all decided to take a break from marriages until after the new year. After all, she was over halfway there. Darrell was number 16, and she definitely didn't want to be married at the end of the year and have to deal with the tax nightmare again.

Rose was incredibly happy with Matt. She had started to believe in love again, though she still didn't say anything specific about it to him. She didn't want to push him. They did talk about things they wanted to do in the future, though, like trips to take and shows to watch. They made plans to go to a concert a few months later. Rose had known from that first kiss that she loved him, but sometime over the summer, she had decided to completely admit it to herself. He was everything she'd ever wanted, and she knew that she loved him. She even took him to meet her parents for her birthday in August. She constantly wondered if she was good enough for him, but that just made her try to be better. She even started painting again, something she hadn't done since she was a teenager. He loved her paintings, though she felt she needed a lot more practice for them to be good. She started a painting for her parents – one of her and all her siblings together. She knew it would take several months because she wanted it to be perfect. She and Matt never went more than a few hours without talking, and he continued to reassure her all the time that he was staying around.

On December 12, Matt was leaving after a wonderful weekend. Rose stood with him next to the door, kissing him goodbye. She really wanted to try to tell him she loved him, but now didn't seem like the right time. It never did. She'd been trying for a couple of months to tell him. She even thought about it when they were texting, but she definitely didn't want it to be something she said in such an impersonal way. She wanted to see his face when she told him. And, assuming he felt the same way, she wanted to be able to kiss him when he said that he loved her, too. She knew it was never the right time only because she was scared. Even though he acted like he cared about her and told her constantly that he did, she was afraid there was just too much wrong with her, or that the marriages bothered him, and he would just shake his head, smile, and ignore it. Instead of taking the leap and facing her fears, she asked, "What are you doing for Christmas?"

"I'm not sure. How long is it? I barely know what day it is now."

"Two weeks. Maybe you can come see me Christmas Eve?"

"I'd like that. I'll come up after I have lunch at my mom's."

"Perfect," she smiled. She gave him another kiss, told him to be careful driving home, and watched him walk out the door.

CHAPTER 19

Leann was sitting at Rose's house chatting the Saturday before Christmas. They were supposed to go shopping, but Rose was taking her time getting ready. She hadn't heard from Matt in a couple of days.

"I really should just call him, but I'm sure he's busy," she said.

"You know everything's fine. Just text him." Leann was impatient to leave and not hiding it.

"But what if it's not fine?" Rose asked. "It's unusual to not hear from him for this long."

"Don't be silly. You two are fine. You're just being paranoid."

Rose picked up her phone and texted Matt: *Hi. I hope you're having a good day. I'll see you soon!*

Then, she found a coat, and they went to shop. They stopped for lunch after a while and made some plans. Rose would come over that weekend to have Christmas with the kids. She might even bring Matt if he could come up. The kids loved him. Rose checked her phone, but even though it had been a couple of hours since she sent her text, he still hadn't answered. She frowned and put the phone back in her purse.

"Still nothing?" Leann asked.

Rose just shook her head. It wasn't like Matt to take this long to answer.

"Don't worry about it," Leann said. "You know he's probably busy. Maybe he's visiting his parents or something. He'll text you later."

Rose shook it off, and they went back to shopping. By the end of the day, both of them had finished all their Christmas shopping, so it was done for the year.

When they got back a few hours later, Matt still hadn't responded, so Rose tried to call him. He didn't answer. She left a voicemail asking him to call her.

The next day, Rose was starting to get really worried. She thought something may have happened to Matt, so she tried to call again. He didn't answer, so she texted again: *Please just let me know you're ok.*

About an hour later, she finally got a response. It said, simply, *I can't keep doing this. The drive is too much. I'm sorry.*

Rose was standing next to the kitchen table. She pulled out a chair and dropped into it. She couldn't believe her eyes. This was the last thing she expected. Everything was fine. At least, she thought it was. He was supposed to come for Christmas. But if the drive was too much, she could have driven there. *I don't understand. This seems to be out of nowhere. I'd drive more if that would help.*

He didn't respond to the text. She texted Penelope. *He dumped me*, she texted.

She sat there in the kitchen, her head on her crossed arms on the table, crying, until Penelope got there. Then, she moved to the sofa to cry while Penelope, and then Leann, tried to console her. Nothing they said made her feel any better.

CHAPTER 20

Rose didn't go to work Monday. She called Jessica instead and asked if she could work from home for a day or two. Jessica agreed.

Rose did work, but only as much as was absolutely necessary. She called into meetings, chatted online with her team about projects, and didn't move from the computer for 8 hours both days. As soon as it was 5:00, though, she closed her laptop, walked into the kitchen, and got the bottle of rum out of the cabinet. No glass. Just the bottle. She continued watching her favorite show – the one she and Matt had been watching - wondering if he would ever finish it now, but she barely saw it, because she was drunk.

On Wednesday, Rose went to work. She was on auto-pilot. She took care of everything that needed to be done, cried with her office door closed between meetings, and made sure to fix her makeup before she opened the door again. That, along with the nightly drinking, continued for three weeks.

Christmas was hell. She went to her parents' house, exchanged gifts, pretended to have a great time for a few hours, and then went home to drink some more. Her parents tried to get her to stay for a day or two. They knew she was hurting, but there was nothing they could do about it. She wished every second that Matt would call and tell her he changed his mind.

Leann and Penelope messaged her periodically to check on her. She had known them long enough that she didn't lie to them. They knew that she woke up every morning in pain, and it didn't get any better during the day. "This isn't like with my husbands," she said when they asked. "They didn't make me feel the way he did. I'm not saying I didn't love them, but not like this. This is different. I just knew he was the right one. He made me feel safe. I could trust him completely. No one else ever made me feel like that."

"Just text him and cuss him out. You'll feel better," Leann said.

"He won't answer. I've tried to text him. I think he blocked me. Besides, I can't cuss him out. I'm not mad at him."

"Why the hell not?" Penelope asked.

"I'm just not." She left it at that. She did try to be mad at him for breaking it off so abruptly, but she couldn't. After all, she was the one who fell for him. She was the one who wanted to see him on a major holiday. She was the one who was marrying other men every few weeks while they were dating. She still didn't know exactly what it was that made him change his mind. She actually didn't even care. If he'd tell her, she'd fix it. All she knew was that she wanted him back.

After Leann and Penelope left that day, Rose wrote a letter to Matt. She figured that, if he did have her blocked on the phone, maybe he would at least read the letter. In it, she told him that she loved him. She told him that she was sorry she didn't say it sooner, even if it wouldn't have made a difference. She also said that she wasn't mad at him, and if he changed his mind, all he has to do is let her know. The whole time she wrote, she wondered if it would make any difference at all. Whether he'd read it, know she loved him, and call her. Or at least write back and explain. She decided it didn't matter. He needed to know how she felt, even if it was too late. If it was better for him to not make the drive, or if he was seeing someone else who made him happier, or if he just couldn't handle her string of marriages, she'd just have to accept that, but she needed for him to know what she'd been trying to tell him for the last couple of months. Maybe if she had told him instead of being scared, things would be different now. Maybe they wouldn't be different, but she had nothing to lose at this point. She'd already lost him. So she wrote the letter and prayed that he would read it. She mailed it the day after Christmas.

CHAPTER 21

On January 2, Rose married a guy named Freddie. He was another one who had messaged Leann from the blog, and they met at the park. He told Rose that he knew Crissy, her accountant, and that he had gotten the blog information from her. "I was actually surprised it was for real. The blog looks like it has a lot of followers, and I assumed it was something Leann was just writing out of her head. When I messaged, I thought I'd get a laugh out of it. I didn't think I'd actually get a wife!" He had a nice laugh, but Rose was still in shock from her breakup with Matt, and she was less than enthusiastic with the automated laugh she gave in response.

Penelope pulled her away from him. "I know you're hurting, but you're almost being rude. What the hell?"

"I can't help it," she explained. "Besides, we're already married. I'm going home. Tell him I'm really not this bitchy."

She left and let Penelope make her excuses. On the way, she got another bottle of rum. She was almost out.

She walked in, pulled the brown paper bag off the rum and threw it in the trash can, and went to the sofa. She turned on the tv and checked her texts. Still nothing from Matt, but she did have a text from Crissy: *Congrats! Hope you and Freddie have a good non-marriage! BTW, did you see this article?*

There was a link to a news article from a newspaper out of Atlanta. She didn't even bother looking at the name of the paper, but the headline read *Local Woman Well on Her Way to Marriage World Record!*

How did this happen? I mean, there was the blog, but there would probably be someone trying to call her, Leann, or at least Penelope if they were writing an article about the marriages. She looked at the byline before she started on the article. It had yesterday's date, and the reporter was William Kennedy. The name sounded familiar, but she didn't place it right away. She started reading the article and remembered the name before she finished the first paragraph. Will. Husband Number 11. It seems that Will had only volunteered to marry her to get information, and he had definitely been following the blog, which the article noted had over 8,000 followers. He described the marriage perfectly, though. "All business, Ms. Wilson chats with her husbands for a few minutes after the ceremony, but not at all during the marriage. After exactly two weeks, I received divorce papers to sign, and I have not heard from her since." He also had some quotes from a couple of her more recent husbands – Carl and Shannon. She thought he actually did a good job on the article. It was simple, factual, and had a lot of good information. She just wished he had told her upfront that's what he was doing. She might have even helped him with some information. It didn't seem that was necessary, though, because he did a decent job of covering it himself.

She threw her phone onto the sofa next to her, and then picked it up again. She replied *Thanks* to Crissy, and then texted Leann and Penelope the link to the article. It was annoying, but she was sure it would blow over soon. The girls agreed.

Wow! You're famous now! Lol Penelope texted back, then called Leann into a group call.

"Seriously? Famous?" Rose asked.

"Oh, you know I'm joking. That paper doesn't have many subscribers. But it is funny. You were trying to be all quiet about this, and Facebook's not your problem. Husbands are." Penelope said.

"It won't last long," Leann said. "I'm looking at blog comments now, though, and someone put the link to the article in it. They're talking about it a little, but they don't think it's that big of a deal."

"The article said the blog has 8,000 followers now," Rose said.

It took a few seconds for Leann to look. "Yeah. 8,300. Not bad for a little blog from some girls in Georgia."

Rose took a drink of the rum. "Yeah. Not bad." The other girls talked for a couple more minutes, and Rose answered when she needed to, but she wasn't really into the conversation anymore. She was starting to zone out. They hung up, and she found a show on TV that had nothing to do with love or sadness or anything resembling emotion. It was some action sci-fi show about people flying around in space fighting with other ships. Something. She barely remembered what it was about, only that it was something to occupy her time.

A couple of hours later, Steven called her. "You don't have to talk to anyone."

"Huh?" she asked. She had finished half the bottle of rum and didn't know what he was talking about.

"The article. If a reporter or anyone else tries to talk to you, don't talk to them. Say 'no comment' or whatever. But you don't have to talk to them. I mean, unless you just want to."

"Why wouldn't I? It doesn't really matter." She knew she was slurring a little, but didn't really care. She didn't think it was enough for Steven to notice.

"Are you still drinking a lot?" he asked.

"I'm fine." Rose knew what he was getting at, and she didn't want to talk to him about Matt. She got the feeling he thought she should be over it by now. She tried to get over it, but that hadn't happened yet, and she didn't want to try to explain that. She didn't have an explanation.

"You know things are going to be okay?"

"Whatever."

"You're drunk. I'll call you tomorrow." He hung up. She thought for a minute that he was mad at her for being drunk, or for being pathetic over Matt, or something, but then decided that it didn't really matter if he was mad at her. Or disappointed, or irritated, or whatever he was. This was the best way she knew to feel better at the moment. The rum didn't really help her forget anything, and she was still crying more than she'd like to admit to anyone, but it did sometimes make her feel numb about it anyway. She took another long drink from the bottle, set it back on the table, and settled onto the sofa to sleep, adjusting the *Love* pillow under her head. She turned onto her side so she could see better and started to adjust the pillow again. When she noticed the word on it, she was disgusted and threw it across the room, hitting a glass on the kitchen counter. She started to get up to sweep up the broken glass and decided it wasn't worth it. She'd get it later.

The next morning, Rose overslept. Not a lot, but enough that she would have to rush to get to work. She stepped over the broken glass in the kitchen, vowing to sweep when she got home, and made it to work only 5 minutes late, which was still actually early for most of the office.

Steven did call again later that day. He thought it would probably turn out to be nothing. After all, it was a local paper, and the article was written by a grad student. But it had a lot of comments already. "I'm just saying. You don't have to talk to reporters if they come by. I just want you to be prepared. That Will guy has never had anything published before. He either spent a lot of time writing it, or he shopped it around for a while before he found someone who would publish it. But still, there's a chance that other reporters will want to do a story. Just be prepared in case it happens."

"Okay," she replied. "I need to think about whether it even matters. I should have known it would get out eventually, especially with the blog. Most of the people following that think it's made up, anyway, but there would probably be some announcement when I actually break the record. I didn't even think about all that."

"True. I don't think any of us really thought that far ahead." She didn't answer right away, because she was still working on her computer while she was talking to him. She was currently answering an email from Penelope about one of their clients' accounts. "How are you doing?" Steven asked, after waiting a few seconds.

"Fine. I'm at work."

"You know what I mean. Have you heard from Matt?"

"Nope. I guess he forgot that I exist already."

She could hear his sigh. "I doubt that. I was just wondering if he had given you any better explanation. We could all tell that there was something there."

Rose took her hands off the keyboard and leaned back in her chair, staring at books on the shelf on the other side of the office. She was frustrated, not only with Matt's silence, but with herself for feeling the way she did. "I know there was something more to it. If it was just the drive, we'd have had a conversation about that before. Nothing was ever said. I don't know what it was, and it looks like I'm never going to find out. I want to, but I can't exactly do that when he won't talk to me, can I?"

There was no mistaking the irritation in her tone. She knew it was there, and at the moment, she didn't really care. Steven and everyone else could just deal with the mess she was right now. She'd apologize to them later. "I'm sorry," Steven said. "I shouldn't have brought it up. I'm just concerned about you."

"Rightly so," she admitted. "But you have more important things to do than to worry about me."

Steven changed the subject back to the article. He was a good friend, but he wasn't great at consoling women after a heartbreak, so he left that up to Penelope. "We'll watch for another article, and let me know if anyone starts hassling you. Reporters, I mean. I still think it's probably nothing, but we should at least be prepared if I'm wrong."

She hung up with him and got back to work, thinking he was probably right that it was nothing. She went on about her day, dealing with clients and avoiding her team, because they were still asking her what was wrong. She already told them that Matt broke it off with her. They just seemed to think she should be over it already. Everyone seemed to think that. She wasn't.

When she got home that night, she dutifully swept up the glass in the kitchen, chastising herself for not doing it the night before. She usually kept the house clean, keeping everything picked up every day. She even dusted, cleaned bathrooms, and everything else once a week. The last few weeks, though, she had barely done any cleaning. For the most part, she'd still been keeping up with the big stuff – running the dishwasher and doing laundry every few days. There were a few dishes in the sink, and she needed to take the trash out. "Screw it," she said, and then loaded the dishwasher and took the trash out before getting out the bottle of rum she'd bought on the way home. She opened it as she walked to the sofa to turn on the TV.

She looked around at the house. The floor definitely needed to be swept, and she could see some dust on top of the entertainment center. She looked up at the ceiling fan and grimaced when she saw the dark layer of dust on the edges. She got up long enough to turn on the fan so she at least wouldn't see that and settled back down with her bottle and the show she was watching.

The next few weeks, just like the few weeks before, went by slowly, but Rose barely noticed anything that actually happened. She went to work every morning, did what she needed to do, and avoided unnecessary conversations. She closed her office door a lot when she wasn't needed. When it was time to leave, she left. Some days, she stopped at the store for more rum or wine. When she got home, she tried to eat, but couldn't eat much. She drank instead, watching tv shows she'd already seen. She finished rewatching the show she and Matt had been watching and cried at the final episode, just as she'd always done. But that wasn't a big feat, because she was crying a lot anyway.

Freddie divorced her without a problem. She married Xander on February 7. He was a friend of Luke's, who was also at the ceremony. She hung out there longer than she usually did, talking with Luke and catching up with Xander, since they had met when they were younger, but even Xander noticed that she wasn't herself, and Luke said something to her later about how fast she was drinking. She answered Leann and Penelope when they texted, but didn't talk to anyone other than that. She did check the mail and her phone every day, hoping to have a response from Matt. Nothing but bills. She thought he probably just threw the letter out without opening it.

She talked to Steven a little about it again, because she knew he had kept in touch with Matt. "Nope," he said. "I haven't heard from him, either, and I don't know what happened. We never talked about relationships. Mostly just work. Let me know if you need anything."

But she didn't need anything from Steven. Or anyone else. Right now, she just needed her rum, her tv, and to hear from Matt. She only got two of those things.

CHAPTER 22

Leann and Penelope showed up the Saturday after she married Xander, and they brought Luke with them. It was 5:30. She had been trying to wait until later in the day to get out the rum, but was in the kitchen getting the bottle out of the cabinet when they walked through the door. They knew she'd been drinking, but she didn't want them to know how much, so she took down a glass when they walked in.

"Drinking so early? Pour me a glass, too." Luke walked over and got himself a glass, setting it on the counter.

Rose picked up the glasses, turned to the refrigerator, and pushed the dispenser for ice. She filled both glasses halfway, set them on the counter again, and asked, "Girls? Drinks? Do you need anything?"

Penelope piped up. "Wine for me!"

"Sure, I'll take rum and diet coke," Leann said.

"Anything in yours?" Rose asked Luke.

"I'll take a regular Coke in mine, if you even have one." He opened the refrigerator and pulled out two Diet Cokes and a Coke, along with a bottle of wine, while Rose reached for another tumbler and a wine glass. She poured the alcohol, and Luke added the soda to the glasses with rum. They each took two glasses and walked into the living room to join the girls.

"I didn't know y'all were coming," Rose said.

"We decided you needed a break from being all pouty and sad," Penelope said. "We're here to cheer you up."

"Oh," Rose answered. "I figured you were sick of hearing me whine. I am pretty pathetic lately."

Leann gave her a little smile that seemed slightly patronizing, but Rose thought it could have been her imagination. "We're your friends, silly. Listening to you whine is what you keep us around for."

The girls took their drinks. Rose sat on the chair and let the girls and Luke have the sofa. She sat back and sipped her diluted drink. It didn't taste the same with the soda in it anymore. She was getting used to not mixing it with anything. Penelope found Rose's music playlist on the tv and randomized it. They sat in silence for a few minutes.

"So, how *are* you doing?" Luke said.

"Same," was all Rose replied.

"You know that was a jerk move, right?" Luke asked. "I mean, just texting you like that and then ignoring you?"

"Doesn't matter."

"Aren't you mad?" he asked.

"Nope."

She saw the three of them look at each other out of the corner of her eye. Clearly, they had been talking about her. She wasn't upset about it, though. They could say whatever they wanted. She couldn't help how she felt. She'd lost the best thing that had happened to her in a very long time, and she didn't know when she would get over it. Instead of acknowledging their looks, she stared at the tv, even though all it was showing was the lyrics for the song currently playing.

"So you're saying you'd seriously just accept his apology and see him again if he came back?" Leann asked.

Rose sighed. She knew they didn't like her short replies, but it was all she had right now. "Yes."

"No questions asked?" Leann asked.

"Nope. If he wants to tell me what really happened, that's fine, but I don't care."

Luke changed the subject then, hoping to help her stop thinking about it. He didn't like seeing her upset, and he clearly thought she should be mad at Matt. He couldn't force her to be mad, or to be less sad about it, so he did the next best thing he could think to do. He tried to get her mind off that subject. "So, there's another reason we're here."

Rose looked over at him. "Okay?"

"Xander called me today. He said a reporter was calling him this morning, wanting him to answer questions about your marriages. He wouldn't talk to them. He said he would with your permission, but didn't know how you felt about publicity."

Rose hadn't thought about the article for a couple of weeks. The blog was one thing, since Leann was writing it, and Leann didn't use her own name or anyone's last name. She knew Leann wouldn't say anything negative about the whole project or about her. Anything negative about the husbands was only if it was well-deserved, like Henry's refusal to sign the papers or the scene Neil caused at the restaurant. Rose didn't really care much about the article, or about publicity, other than it meant she'd have to tell her parents what she was doing. And right now, she didn't even care that much about that. "I don't know. What do y'all think?"

Leann was the first to answer. "I think it's going to get out there anyway. If reporters are asking around, the story's going to be written whether you want it to be or not. Xander's a good guy. He'll be nice. I think it's better to just let it happen. At least if we don't discourage him, maybe whatever reporter is working on it won't have anything bad to say."

"I was hoping to keep it from my parents."

"Yeah, but you still can. They don't really pay much attention to that kind of news. It was probably a local reporter, so the story would be small. Or it may have been that Will guy doing a follow-up. Chances are, they won't hear about it."

The others nodded in agreement. Rose leaned forward and took another sip of her drink. What she really wanted to do was gulp it down and get the bottle, but she didn't want to do that with them there. "So, we let it go. If they come asking questions, we answer. And we forget about it."

They all agreed. Luke texted Xander and told him it was fine to talk to the reporter.

Leann also wanted to talk about timing. "Why don't we do a week at a time now? We've been doing this for something like 18 months now. You've only got 12 left. We can have them over with sooner."

"Fine." Rose sat back in her chair again, still sipping the drink. She thought back to the conversation they'd had at Leann's house when they were hanging out with the kids. Penelope had wanted to speed up the timeline then, and she'd refused. How long ago was that? A year, maybe? She couldn't remember, and it really didn't matter all that much. Nothing really mattered that much right now. She'd still go through with this. She was way too far into it now to give up. Leann said she only had 12 husbands left. She actually had started hoping that the last one would be Matt. She signed without realizing it.

"You okay?" Luke asked.

"Oh, yeah. Sorry. I was in my thoughts again. Were y'all saying something?"

Penelope repeated what she'd been saying. "I've got the next couple of husbands lined up. And actually, I was thinking it might be fun for you to marry Luke again."

"Okay," she said.

"No objections?" Penelope asked.

"Nope. Do whatever you want. I'm in."

They were all surprised. Rose usually had opinions about these things, and, at least with them, she never hesitated to voice those opinions. It wasn't that she was rude or anything. They had discussions and figured out a solution that everyone agreed to, at least mostly. She wasn't necessarily being *too* agreeable, because Rose was up for most things after they decided on something. It was more that she just didn't seem to care. She'd let them make all the decisions, and she'd go along. That wasn't her.

"Are you sure you're okay?" Leann asked.

"Yeah," she said. She looked at her glass and took the last sip. She thought she'd drank that glass slowly enough. She walked into the kitchen. Since they couldn't see her through the counter and Luke wasn't next to her watching, she poured a lot more rum into this glass than she'd poured into the last one. She filled it the last quarter with her diet soda and walked back to her chair, taking a sip as she went.

"So, who's the next one?" she asked, making an effort to sound somewhat like her old self. She didn't really think she was completely fooling them into thinking the normal Rose was back, but pretending was a good start.

"His name is Doyle. Bianca came to my office one day and gave me his information. He's a friend of hers. I think she actually said an ex she's still friends with."

Rose remembered the name. "Yeah. They met on some dating site and went out once or twice. There was something she didn't like about him. I don't remember what. But they're still friends. Why didn't she say anything to me?"

Penelope looked a little uncomfortable, like she didn't really want to answer. "Ummm…your office door has been closed a lot lately," she finally said. "Your team has noticed that you're not talking much."

"Oh, shit," Rose said. "I didn't realize it was that bad. Well, maybe I did and just didn't care. Are they mad?"

"Oh, no!" Penelope said quickly. "They get it. They're just waiting for you to come back to the land of the living."

Rose leaned forward, actually concerned about something other than her own thoughts for the first time in a couple of months. "And Jessica? Has she noticed?"

"Your work's fine. Jessica said something about you not socializing as much, but you know she's barely in the office anyway. And she doesn't care much whether everyone chats, anyway. She's all business, and your business is still pretty much perfect."

"Good. So does everybody hate me for being quiet? How much are they talking about me?"

"No, honey," Penelope answered. "The only thing they said is that you've seemed a little distant. I just told them you were going through some personal stuff. Don't worry about them. No one wants anything but for you to do what you need to do to feel better."

They were back to talking about Rose's feelings, which she really didn't want to talk about, so she thought quickly of a way to get things back to something a little less depressing. "So, this guy? What's his name again?"

Luke answered this time. "Doyle. I met him last night. Seems like a good guy. No trouble. He's ready whenever we get you unhitched from Xander."

"Speaking of which," Leann said, "why don't we go ahead and start that? Get this one-week timeline going? Luke, do you think Xander will mind?"

"Nah. He won't care. Rose signs the papers, and I'll take them to him. I'm supposed to golf with him and some other guys later in the week."

Rose got out her computer, filled in the names on the agreement, printed it, and signed it. Luke set the papers on the table with his keys. They kept talking for a while, and Rose thought she did a good job of pretending that everything was okay, at least after those first few minutes. She did drink, but saved drinking straight from the bottle for after they left.

On Sunday, Rose got a call from a reporter. Thankfully, it wasn't long after she woke up. She was drinking her second cup of coffee and thinking about getting out the painting she'd started for her parents. She hadn't worked on it in several weeks. If she was going to finish it before Mother's Day or Father's Day, she needed to work on it at least a little bit.

When she saw that she didn't recognize the number, she almost didn't answer. After the second ring, though, she decided that getting rid of a telemarketer wouldn't be the worst thing that could happen, so she tapped the button and raised the phone to her ear. "Hello?"

"Hi! This is Jane from the Atlanta Times. Is this Rose Wilson?"

"Yes," Rose answered, waiting.

"I'm looking into an article that was originally printed in another paper.

It's about your effort to break the record for the number of marriages. Did you happen to see it?"

"I did."

"I was wondering if you mind getting together to answer some questions for me. I want to do my own article, but from your perspective. I think it's a great story."

"Sure. I don't mind answering questions."

The reporter was enthusiastic. They agreed to meet the next evening for coffee. Rose wasn't as excited about it, but figured it was best to get it over with. And she decided she'd better tell her parents soon, too. Her parents still got the Atlanta Times delivered to their home, and they usually read it as far as she knew.

She texted Leann and Penelope. *Reporter called. Meeting tomorrow. Want to join?*

They both agreed. At least she wouldn't be alone in this. They'd be there to help her figure out what to say. They decided to meet an hour early to talk about what to tell the reporter. Though, there really wasn't a lot to it. There was nothing Rose felt she needed to hide.

CHAPTER 23

Rose was the first to arrive at Joe's, a local coffee shop she and the girls had always liked. She ordered coffee and pastries and found a table. Penelope got there in time to help her bring everything to the table. They were already starting on the pastries when Leann walked in a few minutes later.

"No waiting for me?" she asked as she sat down.

"Sorry. I didn't have time for lunch today," Rose said. "I may actually get something else before the reporter gets here."

"Fair enough. I may, too. I came straight from work, and had about five minutes to eat a chicken sandwich today. The store was busy for some reason."

Penelope was nibbling. "Am I the only one who actually got a real meal today? Steven picked me up for Italian."

"You could have brought me something back," Rose whined.

"If I had known you weren't eating, I would have. But anyway, who's this reporter?"

"Her name's Jane something from the Atlanta Times. I looked up some of her stuff. She does mostly human interest stuff, but it doesn't look like she puts much of a spin on it. I think we're safe with having her write it."

Leann agreed. "I looked her up last night, too. I think we're good."

They tried to talk about what they'd tell the reporter, but there really wasn't a lot to it. Almost everything was in the blog, so there wouldn't be any surprises. None of them thought there was much they needed to leave out of the story.

Jane arrived on time in black slacks and a stylish top. Rose introduced her to the girls. "Oh, this is great! I'm so glad you brought your friends. Are they helping you out with this?"

Rose answered, "Yes. Penelope's kind of being a manager. She arranges everything. Leann became a minister so she can perform all the ceremonies, and she also writes our blog."

Jane was impressed. "I've read the blog. It's very good. Leann, you have a gift."

Leann was as embarrassed as Jane was impressed. "All I do is tell what's happening."

"No, no. You tell it in way that it's engaging. You know what details to add and how to add them. You make it a real story, not just an account of the truth. If I'm being honest, I'm a little jealous. I'm a pretty good reporter, but I'm not a storyteller. I report. You really write."

After that, the girls warmed up to Jane even more. They all knew that she may be simply using flattery to put them at ease and get more of the story, but it still made them feel good about talking to her, especially since they already knew there was nothing to hide.

"Is everyone okay with me using your full names?" Jane asked, pulling out her phone. "And do you mind if I record our conversation?"

They all looked at each other. None of them cared about recording; they figured she would want to do that. Names was something they hadn't really talked about, though they realized now that it should have been the first thing they discussed. Rose shrugged. "Sure," she said.

Penelope and Leann agreed. If Rose used her name, there was no reason for them not to use theirs. Everyone who knew them would know exactly who her friends were, anyway. Jane started her recording. She asked for some more details about Penelope and Leann's work behind the scenes. That was one thing that Leann didn't cover a lot in her blog. The blog was more about the marriages and the fun times they had, usually related to the marriages. She tried to keep it entertaining and didn't think the planning and everything was as interesting. Rose was interested, though, so they talked about it.

To begin with, Penelope had to search a little more for husbands. At this point, though, since most of the people they knew at least knew what they were doing, and many followed the blog, most of the men came to her. Some of them were through Leann and the blog. Her work was a lot easier now than it was before, though she and Steven did add in the background checks and a little more legwork on making sure the husbands wouldn't cause any trouble. She gave Jane the highlights of her work, as did Leann. Leann thought her job of performing the ceremonies was a little simpler. She had everything memorized at this point, so she showed up, did her 10 minutes, and then wrote about it. She didn't consider writing the blog that much work. It was fun for her. She had her normal chats with the girls, so she didn't have to do any research. At least, not what she would consider research. She enjoyed writing and always had. Literature was her favorite subject in school, and she excelled at writing reports. She even loved writing essays and the occasional short story or poem they had to do back then. She loved the blog as much as she had loved writing when it was homework.

"So, why aren't you trying to make money off the blog?" Jane asked.

"I'm sorry?" Leann asked in return. That was something the girls had never even considered. They all knew somewhere in the back of their minds that it was possible, but this was all for fun, not for a side job.

"Well," Jane said, "You can put in ads and make some money. You have enough followers to do it. When I checked this morning, it was around 10,000. Or you can make it a subscription service. You girls could have a real side job. I'm sure it would at least cover paying for the marriage certificates and divorce filings, if not be a good bit of pocket money."

"We never really thought of that. When we started it, it was just an alternative to me getting questions from people on Facebook," Rose said.

"Did you get a lot of them?" Jane asked.

"Yeah. My friends were really curious. I think we stopped putting anything on Facebook after the first couple of marriages. It was a hassle looking at comments when I changed my relationship status, and there were messages every time, too. Some of them were male friends asking if they could be next, but most were just from people who wanted details. It wasn't long after that

that Leann got the blog running."

"Did you know then that you'd end up with 10,000 or more curious people who want details?"

Penelope answered that one. "We had no idea. We just figured it would be mostly our friends who were asking anyway and maybe a few other people. We had no idea that many people would want to read it."

Jane laughed. They were getting pretty comfortable with her, and she was easy to talk to. That was probably one of things that made her a good reporter. "Well, I have a feeling you'll have even more after I write my article. What does it feel like to be famous?"

"Famous?" Rose asked. "I hardly think we're famous."

"Give it time. You've got a good story, and you're well on your way to breaking a world record. Not just that, but it's one that is very difficult to break. People are going to want to know everything, including how intimate you are with these men."

"Oh, it's nothing like…" Rose began.

"I know, dear. That's very clear from the blog, and I'm not even going to mention it in my article. You do need to understand that people are going to ask anyway. They're going to want it to be true so they can try to get all the juicy details of your encounters with these men. Thirty husbands and not even a sleepover will sound unusual to them. Speaking of which, are you dating anyone?"

Rose thought about Matt. She wished she was still dating him. "No," she answered, thinking it best to leave him out of the story completely. Leann hadn't even put him in the blog, because that relationship wasn't part of the marriages, and Rose wanted to keep that part of her life private. "That's kind of how this started. I don't really believe in love or relationships anymore. I started doing this sort of as a joke about how marriage isn't for everyone. Instead of becoming a nun, I'm marrying as many men as possible, but not dating any of them, and not trying to fall in love."

"Interesting. So do you think you'll date when all this is over?"

"No," Rose replied. "I won't."

Jane tried to dig a little more into why Rose felt that way, but the girls changed the subject, knowing Rose didn't want to talk about it. Jane moved to other questions, most of which were already answered in the blog. They chatted with Jane for almost two hours and didn't realize how long it had been until they walked out of the coffee shop. The three of them decided to go out for dinner, so they did. Then, Rose went home to her sorrow and her rum.

Jane told them it would be a couple of weeks before she finished the article, and she would let them know when it would be printed. Rose decided she needed to tell her parents about the project the next weekend, and she thought she needed the girls there to help her. Before she went to sleep, she texted to let them know that, and they both agreed to make the trip with her.

CHAPTER 24

Everything was pretty normal for the rest of the week. Well, at least the normal for the last couple of months. Rose went to work and did her job. She did try to be a little more outgoing. She knew it was forced but hoped that no one around the office noticed that. She did think that if she kept faking it, eventually she'd be back to her old self. Work at least kept her mind off of Matt, so she dove into it while she was at the office. She found herself checking her phone to see if he had texted her a little less, so that was good. At night, though, when she was home alone, it was still hard, so she kept drinking.

The mornings were even worse. For months, she had texted him as soon as she woke up, often before she even got out of bed. She reached for her phone every morning, realized that she wouldn't have a text from him and he wouldn't answer a text from her, and pulled her hand back. Even though it had been weeks since she talked to him, she wished almost constantly that he'd show up and tell her it had all been a horrible nightmare. In her daydreams, he was there to wake her up and let her know that everything was fine. But she knew it wasn't a nightmare. So, in the mornings when she felt it the worst, she pulled herself out of bed, dressed hurriedly for work, and did everything she could at the office to occupy her mind for as long as possible.

That was her life now - trying to keep her mind on other things as much as possible. When she couldn't, she analyzed everything, trying to figure out where she went wrong. There were so many things, and she couldn't find any one specific conversation or action that changed Matt's mind.

So she went on. She tried. She faked it. She decided it was better to let other people think she was happy, so she tried to do that. Inside, she knew she wasn't.

Saturday morning, Rose got dressed, thankful that she had something to do that day. She'd read almost all the books she had on her shelf and started ordering more. She still hadn't gotten out her painting stuff, but it didn't keep her mind busy as well as books did. She'd watched every good show and movie she could find. Now, she was binge watching old shows like *Buffy the Vampire Slayer*. She enjoyed them, and they did a decent job of keeping her from overthinking, but reading worked better.

She got in her car and picked up Leann first. Brent had the kids that weekend, so they could take all the time they needed. They headed to Penelope's.

"You seem more cheerful," Leann said when they were about halfway there.

Rose knew better than to lie to Leann. She'd figure it out sooner or later if she did. "It's fake. But I'm trying."

"I get it. Better to fake it 'til you make it, right? But how are you really feeling?"

Rose turned the music down. She knew this wouldn't be an easy conversation, especially for her, and she didn't want to be distracted by the music. "I'm the same. It's not getting any better. I still think about him all the time, and I don't know how to stop."

"I wish I could just tell you to stop and it would happen. Or that I could make him call you," Leann said.

"Me, too. Especially the calling part. I've been thinking about it a lot, and I think maybe it's just a punishment."

Rose glanced at Leann when she said it, and Leann obviously didn't like what she heard. "What the hell? Why would you be punished?"

"I'm in the middle of a big 'screw you' to marriage and relationships and love. The whole record thing. I said that love doesn't exist for me. I said I was finished. Then I met Matt. I fell for him. Then, I thought maybe God sent me exactly what I had been waiting for my whole life. Like maybe my curse or search or whatever was over. But it wasn't over. Matt is a punishment. Well, not him specifically. Not being with him is a punishment."

"That's silly," Leann said. "What you're doing is not enough for you to be punished. It's a silly project that we're doing for fun."

"No, Leann," Rose said. "I know you don't understand, but it's karma. I told love to go screw itself because I hadn't found it. I said the words. You were there and heard them. So, I got love. And then I lost it to teach me a lesson."

"This isn't a lesson. I don't know what happened with Matt, but either he'll come back because it's true love, or you'll find someone else."

Rose had to stop at a red light. She looked at Leann. "No. If he does come back, it'll only be when I've felt enough pain. When I've learned my lesson. That's what I wish for every day. But if he doesn't come back, I won't find anyone else. I'm done."

"You've said that before."

The light was green, so Rose turned left towards Penelope's house. "Yes, and I meant it. Matt happened by accident, and I let it happen. But not again. I'm not dating anymore. I'm going to finish these marriages because I started them, and then I'm not dealing with men anymore."

"So women?" Leann asked jokingly.

Rose was still serious. "Nope. Not women, either. I'm finished. No more marriages after number 30. No more dating as of now. If I'm being punished, I'm just accepting it. I'll learn my lesson and never try to tell fate it's wrong for leaving me out again. I've had love, and it's not worth the pain. I finally got my love, and I really, really loved him. But then I lost him. I'm not trying again."

Leann tried to tell her again how ridiculous she thought it sounded, without exactly saying the word *ridiculous*, but Rose pulled up in Penelope's driveway. "I'm sorry, but I'm right," Rose said as she opened the door to the car. They knocked on the door, chatted with Steven while Penelope finished getting ready, and all three girls got in the car. Rose and Leann pretended the conversation on the way there never happened, and Leann chose to believe that Rose didn't really believe what she was saying, though they both knew she did.

They drove the hour to Rose's parents' house chatting about work, the marriages, and Leann's kids. They all knew why they were going and knew that it wouldn't be an easy conversation for Rose. The girls wanted to keep her as cheerful as possible. Her parents wouldn't like what she was doing. They were noticeably disappointed after her first divorce, though they understood. They were even more understanding after the second and third, but Rose always felt she disappointed them with her marriages. She knew they loved her and wanted the best for her, but didn't like the feeling of disappointing them. They had been married so long, and her brothers and sisters were all happily married. She was probably exaggerating it in her mind, but she felt like a failure sometimes, at least in the area of marriage.

When they arrived, Rose's parents greeted them all just as warmly as ever. They walked into the house and sat, watching a documentary about aliens and chatting about work. Rose's mom asked about Leann's kids.

"They're great. Growing like weeds." She pulled out her phone and showed pictures of the kids. It had been a while since they visited, but Leann promised they'd visit again soon. Rose's mom had lunch ready soon after they got there, and the girls were grateful. They were all hungry.

After lunch, the girls helped clear the table and wash dishes, and then they sat outside on the patio, enjoying the sunshine. Rose thought it was as good a time as any to bring up the topic of her marriages.

"Mom, Dad," she began. "I need to tell you something. I've been doing this project, and you should know about it." She took a deep breath. "I'm breaking the record for the number of marriages."

They thought she was joking and started laughing. That wasn't surprising. She joked with them a lot about how many times she'd been married. They just thought the number was still three. "I'm serious. I've now been married 18 times. I'll be divorced again in a couple of weeks, and then I'm going to get married 12 more times."

They spent the next hour or so talking about the marriages. Her parents asked a lot of questions, which Rose, Penelope, and Leann answered for them. She made it clear that the marriages were real, but weren't *really* marriages, so they knew exactly what was going on. She didn't want them thinking that she was, to use the word that she and the girls had made fun of several times, consummating every marriage.

In the end, they thought it was silly, but didn't think it was that big of a deal for her to do it. She was relieved. They gave her a lot more questions than she'd anticipated, and none of the judgement.

"Why did you decide to tell us now? You've been doing this for almost two years without a word," her dad finally asked.

Rose took a deep breath. "I knew you'd think it was silly. I meant to tell you eventually, but it never really came up. But now, I'm telling you because a reporter is writing an article about it. I didn't want you to see the article before you knew."

The conversation was over, and it was painless. Rose wondered why she hadn't told them sooner, but she knew. She was worried they wouldn't like it. Her worry wasn't justified, though. Other than laughing about their goofy daughter, they seemed to actually think it was kind of cool. They wanted to know about the husbands so far and what she planned afterwards. She, Penelope, and Leann told them everything they wanted to know.

Then, they turned to other topics. They went inside and watched more alien documentaries, still chatting some as they watched. When the girls left, everything was fine, and Rose's parents wanted to watch for the article and were excited to read it.

CHAPTER 25

Sunday, Rose woke up just as heartbroken as she had every morning for the last couple of months. She did have a text when she looked at her phone, though. Unfortunately, it wasn't from Matt.

Got your papers signed. Lunch with the girls to hand them over? Leann's. 11. Luke had sent it. She looked at the clock on her phone. It was already 10:00. She really didn't feel like going anywhere, but she'd need to take the papers to the courthouse tomorrow at lunch, so decided she didn't really have a choice.

She texted Luke back. *I'll be late. Just now waking up.*

She stayed in bed for another minute, trying to put on her fake smile for the day, before she went to start coffee and get a shower. Luke had texted back something that included *sleepyhead* and *hurry.* She didn't answer, but instead drank a cup of coffee before pulling on jeans and a short-sleeved shirt. She grabbed a jacket in case it was chilly outside, refilled her mug, and went out to her car.

She got to Leann's at 11:15. It was a nice day, so she left the jacket in the car. She heard the kids outside so didn't bother with the front door. She walked around to the side and climbed over the wooden fence instead. She could have used the gate, but it was old and tricky. It was easier to just climb over.

"Aunt Rose!" Bev cried as she ran to her. Rose gave both the kids big hugs and looked around for the adults. Leann and Luke were at the patio table.

"Where's lunch?" she asked as she walked over.

"Penelope's bringing it. We're having takeout. Luke wouldn't cook."

Luke looked sternly at her. "You know cooking's for the women. I'll cook when it's time to grill again." He never meant his sexist jokes, and the girls usually laughed at them. They knew he could, and did, cook at least as well as any of them. "Seriously, though, Penelope offered, and neither of us argued. She's running a little late, too. She just texted that she's got the food and on her way."

It didn't take long. A few minutes later, they heard Penelope trying to open the gate. Jeremy ran over and opened it for her. He had more practice with it than she did. She walked over with a couple of pizza boxes and set them on the table, along with plates. "You know, it wouldn't really take that long to replace the latch on that gate. I feel like an invalid having to get the kids to open it for me."

"Just climb over," Rose said. "It's easier."

"Of course you would. But not me."

Luke promised to fix the gate the next time he was over, then sent the kids in to get drinks. When they brought them out, everyone dug into the pizza.

"How'd the visit with Mom and Dad go?" Luke asked Rose.

"I'm surprised Leann didn't already tell you," she said. "Everything's good. They think I'm goofy for doing it, but they're behind me on it. It went a lot better than I expected."

"Awesome. And I owe you," he reached into his back pocket, "this." He had folded the divorce papers, but Xander had signed them. They were ready to be filed as soon as Rose added her signature. She checked everything, folded them back the way they were, and put them in her own back pocket.

"Thanks," she said. "I'll take care of it tomorrow. How's Xander doing?"

"He wanted to know if he could talk his ex-wife into a real date."

Rose shook her head almost violently.

"I guess not. I'll let him know. Are you ever going to go out again?"

"No," she said. "Y'all can try to talk me into it as much as you want, but it's not happening."

They all knew better than to argue with her when she was this adamant, so they let the issue drop. Leann changed the subject. "I have to go out of town for a couple of days. There's this training at the store headquarters for all the managers. Brent can't take the kids. He's going to be out of town, too. Rose, can you watch the kids for a couple of days? It's in two weeks."

Rose pulled out her phone and checked her work schedule to make sure she didn't have anything those days and then agreed. She'd love to spend some time with the kids. At the very least, having fun with them would keep her mind occupied. She put it into her calendar and told Leann to just drop them off at her house when she left that Sunday.

Not long after that, Jeremy asked them to play baseball. The girls kicked off their shoes, and they started a game with the kids. Luke, Penelope, and Bev played against Rose, Leann, and Jeremy. Bev was getting to be pretty great at bat. Rose helped her a little, but she didn't really need it. Jeremy was a good pitcher. They played for the rest of the afternoon. When it was starting to get dark and Leann announced it was time for the kids to go in and get showers, they were tied 4-4. The kids were happy with themselves, and the adults were sweaty in spite of the cool February breeze. It was Georgia, after all, where a cool February breeze could be anywhere from 30-60 degrees. Today, it was around 50. Rose didn't bother walking all the way to the patio chair after she handed Jeremy her glove to put away. She lowered herself to the grass, laid down, and looked up at the darkening blue sky. She felt better right then than she had in weeks.

Until she got home an hour later. Then, she started thinking too much again. About kids she might have one day had. About things that might have one day been. And she got out her rum instead of cleaning the house.

CHAPTER 26

For the first time in a while, the rum wasn't helping. She'd been home for a few hours. She was in an alcohol-induced fog, but still felt all of the emotions that started forming when she was driving back from Leann's. She loved the kids, especially Leann's, but she still thought often about having children of her own. She had thought that was possible for a while, but now she had doubts. Yes, there were alternatives to having kids in the traditional way, but that wasn't how she'd always envisioned having them.

And then, there was the fact that she was alone in general. She hadn't cared before. Between her "real" marriages, she'd always felt happier alone. It was better to be alone than with the wrong guy. Always. Now, though, she wasn't with who she thought was the right guy, and that felt different.

She'd gone to bed about 30 minutes before, deciding that sleep was her only option since the rum wasn't helping. Now, she was wide awake. She opened her eyes and turned to look at the clock she still kept by her bed. She rarely used the alarm, setting her phone's alarm instead, but the clock stayed. 11:10. She needed to go to sleep soon. She had meetings scheduled all day on Monday.

She threw the blankets to the side and sat up on the edge of the bed. Maybe a cup of tea would help. She thought there was some chamomile in the cabinet.

Rose walked to the kitchen and ran some water in the tea kettle, then took a mug out of the cabinet and started rummaging through the pantry for tea. She had to crouch to see into one of the bottom shelves.

No chamomile, but there was a nighttime blend that probably had chamomile in it. She held the box of tea in one hand and used her other hand to steady herself as she started to get up.

Pain. That was weird. She sat down on the floor instead of raising herself to her feet and looked at the palm of her hand. There was blood and a triangle of curved clear glass. Thankfully, the glass hadn't gone far into her hand – just enough to give her a nice cut, but it was sticking out of her hand.

It was probably a good thing she had been drinking at that moment. She didn't feel the pain as intensely as she would have otherwise. She sat on the floor for what seemed like several minutes, just staring at the glass sticking out of her hand. It was probably only a few seconds. When a drop of blood fell onto her favorite blue pajama pants, she shook her head, dropped the box of tea she was still holding in her left hand, and clumsily stood up.

She turned to the sink and held her right hand over it, silently thanking herself for loading the dishwasher before she started drinking. Still watching the blood begin to pool in her palm, she reached for the paper towels with her left hand.

"Do I need stitches?" she asked the air around her, thinking she'd need to leave the glass where it was if she did.

"No," she answered herself. "It's not very deep. Glass is only like an inch long, and not much of it's in there. Just pull it out and stop the bleeding."

Then, in spite of her hand hurting, Rose laughed. "Talking to myself is one thing, but now I'm answering myself. I should probably stop before my ghosts around here think I'm insane."

She was still laughing as she carefully folded the two paper towels until they were only a couple of inches wide. She thought that should be thick enough to staunch the bleeding. She carefully held the bandage with her right index finger and thumb. Bracing herself in case the glass was deeper than she thought, she pulled the glass out with her left hand, dropped it in the sink, and held the bandage to the cut with her left fingers. She stared at the glass for a moment. As she thought, only about a centimeter of the point was bloody. She probably didn't need stitches.

She started walking towards the sofa when the tea kettle whistled. She stopped, drunkenly maneuvered almost a military about-face, and walked to the stove. The tea was out at this point. She didn't know how long she'd have to hold the bandage to stop the bleeding. After turning the dial on the stove awkwardly with her right fingers, she walked into the living room. She found the remote and figured out how to push the buttons while still holding the paper towel bandage to the cut. Then, she sat back and watched tv. After a few minutes, she pulled the paper towel back to check on the cut. It was still bleeding.

It took a while for her hand to stop bleeding enough that she felt comfortable bandaging it. She hoped the bleeding would stop overnight, since she had to use thickly folded gauze and didn't want to show up at work with it on her hand. It would create questions, and she didn't want to answer, "I got drunk and cut my hand."

She finally went to sleep after taking 10 minutes to put on the bandage without use of her dominant hand. The clock said 1:05 when she laid down.

The next morning, she surprisingly woke up on time. The pain in her hand was worse in the morning, but she had time to replace the huge bandage she'd fashioned the night before with a Band-Aid, throw away the glass she'd left in the sink, and put away the box of tea that was still in the floor.

She was still trying to figure out how the glass was in the floor. It finally dawned on her when she was sitting in traffic halfway to work. It wasn't that long ago that she'd thrown one of the pillows on the sofa and knocked over a wine glass. She must have missed that piece when she swept.

She hit the side of the steering wheel, not thinking about the cut.

"Dammit!" she yelled, looking at her palm. It still looked fine, but it hurt. She decided right then that she couldn't drink anymore. She broke a glass, didn't sweep it all up, and cut her hand – all because she was drinking. No more. She'd have to find another way to keep her mind off the topic of Matt.

CHAPTER 27

That night, Rose was exhausted again when she got home. She wanted to take a nap but had things to do. She decided during the day that burning things was therapeutic. Of course, there wasn't much. Matt had left a shirt, which was hanging in her closet. There were some ticket stubs from when they went to a movie. She'd look around the house for anything else that might remind her of him, but that was all she could remember.

It didn't matter. There were trees in her yard, which meant she could pick up some fallen branches and have a real fire. She changed into jeans and an old t-shirt and walked out the back door. The back yard was half an acre, and there was plenty of shade. She walked around under the trees, picking up a couple of armloads of branches. She did this every few months anyway, so she already had a spot ready for burning. Last fall, Matt had gone with her to pick up a few large stones and arrange them in a circle around the area she usually burned the limbs. It was too bad she couldn't burn the stones, but she'd just have to deal with a couple of things around the house that reminded her of him.

She arranged the limbs in a pile that was almost as high as her waist, then walked back into the house. The ticket stubs were in a small platter on the kitchen counter. She grabbed them and then took the shirt from the hanger in her closet. She had washed it the day after he left it. It still smelled of her lavender-scented fabric softener. She looked around to see if there was anything else. Nothing.

Rose walked towards the back door and then remembered that she had the week's local newspaper on the kitchen counter, and she would need a lighter. It was in the same platter she took the ticket stubs from. She grabbed both the newspaper and lighter.

"Notebook," she said to herself. She walked to the sofa and set everything she was holding on it. She kept a notebook on the end table, and it still had the first draft of the letter she'd sent to Matt weeks ago in it. She found it and pulled the pages out of the wire binder. Then, she picked up everything she'd dropped on the sofa and went back outside, setting everything down again outside of the circle of stones.

She sat on the ground next to the circle. First, she separated the pages from the newspaper and crumpled them, pushing them under the limbs. She reread the letter draft, starting to cry about halfway through it. Now, knowing that he wasn't coming back, it seemed stupid. Weak. Pathetic. How could she have thought telling him she loved him would do anything? He didn't want her, and it didn't matter if she wanted him. But she thought he didn't read it anyway, so at least he didn't have to see how pitiful and ridiculous she was. She imagined him seeing the letter and dropping it directly into the trash can, never to be thought of again. Instead of making her feel better, that thought just made her silent tears turn to sobs.

When she finished reading the letter, which was almost exactly what she sent him, she crumpled it and pushed it under the limbs along with the newspaper. She stood up and used the lighter to start the letter burning first, then walked around to the other side, lighting a page of crumpled newspaper.

It only took a minute or two for the fire to get started. The dry limbs caught easily. When it was going pretty well, she picked up the ticket stubs and held them above the fire, looking at them for a second before she let them float down to the flames.

Last, she picked up Matt's shirt. It was a nice blue dress shirt. He'd probably worn it to work that Friday before coming to the house. It looked good on him. The blue was almost the same color as his eyes. She thought she should just mail it to him, but he had probably already forgotten about it. It was better to burn it than to mail it and have any hope that he'd see her name on the package and think about her. She especially didn't want to sit around hoping the package would inspire him to call or show up at her door. She couldn't have hope anymore. She knew it would always be there, and if he did get in touch with her, she wouldn't even question whether to take him back. She would, without a doubt. What she couldn't do, though, is try to get him back. She would just have to wait. She could wish and pray, but the letter was enough. Whether he read it or threw it away, she tried. There was nothing more she could do. Anything at this point had to be completely up to Matt.

She held the shirt above the fire much longer than the ticket stubs, but finally let it fall, too. The ticket stubs were already nothing but ash, and it didn't take long for the shirt's fabric to be engulfed in flames.

After a few seconds, anything of Matt's that was flammable was gone. Rose stayed, sitting on the ground a few feet away, and watched until the fire was nothing but cold gray ash. The sun was starting to set. It had been a while since she'd seen the sunset, so she decided to stay lie down on the grass where she was and watch it before finding something for dinner. When there was barely any light left and a few dark clouds were starting to fill the sky, she stood up slowly, stretched, and walked back inside. There was no rum that night, only a sandwich, the tv, a light thunderstorm, and tears.

CHAPTER 28

Rose really did think she would feel better after burning the things that reminded her of Matt, but it didn't help very much. She didn't know whether it was that the last parts of him were gone from her house or that she didn't have alcohol as an escape from her thoughts. It may have been a combination of both. Maybe she shouldn't have decided to eliminate both from her life at the same time, but it was done now.

Tuesday night, she cleaned her house completely for the first time in weeks. She did everything she usually did when she cleaned. She dusted, vacuumed, swept, and mopped. She washed the windows. She cleaned the bathrooms until they almost shone. The spare bedroom didn't take long, but it was perfectly clean, too. When she finished, she poured the mop water down the bathtub drain, unhooked the shower head and used it to rinse the tub one more time, and put everything away.

She needed a shower. It took almost four hours to clean the house. She also needed to eat, but she didn't really want to do anything else for a little bit. What she wanted was a drink, but she had decided not to drink at all for a little while. The alcohol was still there, taunting her in the cabinet, but she wouldn't touch it except maybe when the girls came over.

She sat on the sofa and picked up a book that was sitting on the end table. It was a book of short stories, and she had only read half of it. She read a short story and then took a shower. She took the book to the bed with her, turned on the lamp on her nightstand, and read until she was tired enough to go to sleep.

The next morning, she went to work as usual. It was a boring day. The team wanted to talk, but she wasn't in the mood. She pretended for a couple of minutes, but couldn't remember later what they'd talked about. It was something about Elsa's new boyfriend, she thought. And that was something she really didn't want to hear about. She was happy for Elsa. She didn't begrudge her. She hoped that it would work out for her. She just didn't want to hear about it. She was mostly tuned out for the couple of minutes she stood there before making an excuse about a report she needed to turn in.

When it was almost lunchtime, she remembered that Luke had given her the signed divorce papers from Xander. What had she done with them? She put them in her back pocket when Luke gave them to her, meaning to go to the courthouse and file them Monday, but she had completely forgotten, distracted instead with what she now thought of as her silly little ritual of burning the only things she had left to remember Matt by. Now that they were burned, she wanted them, but it was too late.

It didn't matter right then, because she needed to file the papers. She couldn't stay married to Xander. It would have to wait until she got home. She couldn't remember whether she took them out of her pocket that night or left them in her jeans. If she'd taken them out of the pocket, she would have seen them when she cleaned the night before. She hadn't, so they must still be in her jeans. She would need to find them that night and go to the courthouse on her lunch Thursday.

When she got home, she went straight to the hamper. The jeans she wore Sunday were there, but there wasn't anything in the back pocket.

"Hello," Leann answered when she called.

"Have you seen the divorce papers? I can't find them."

"I figured you already filed them. It's been days. No, I haven't seen them."

"Dammit. Look in the back yard. We played baseball, and I was laying down out there after."

"Going," Leann said. "And I haven't heard from you since Sunday. I tried to call yesterday."

"Yeah. I burned Matt's stuff the other night and haven't felt like talking much."

"Rose! You burned his stuff without Penelope and me? That is a drinking event!"

Rose wasn't in the mood for this conversation. She just wanted the papers. "Yeah. I'm also not drinking for a while."

"Finally decided it was too much?"

"You noticed?"

"Honey, we all did. What was it, every night? Or at least most nights. We didn't want to say anything. Figured you'd work through it."

"Yeah," Rose said sullenly, surprised and embarrassed that her friends noticed the drinking.

She didn't need to continue the conversation about drinking, though. "Well, I found the papers, but I don't think they're going to do much good. Remember the rain Monday night?"

"Yeah, wasn't it more of a storm?"

"True. I remember thunder. Anyway…" Leann started.

Before Leann could finish her sentence, Rose realized what had happened. "They're drenched, aren't they?"

"Dammit. Yeah. Kind of mushy still, too. There must have been more rain than I thought. They were in the shade, so the sun didn't even dry them up."

Leann tried to see if the papers were salvageable, but they fell apart when she tried to open them. Rose hung up and called Luke.

"I need you to call Xander."

"Well, hi to you, too, Rose. How are you? I'm good, thanks for asking."

"Ugh. Luke. I love you, but this is important. The papers fell out of my pocket the other night and then it rained. We need Xander to sign again."

"Oh, damn," Luke said. "I'll call him."

Ten minutes later, Luke called back. "He said it's no problem, but it'll be a couple of days. He's on a work trip. Somewhere in Kansas or something. He did say it's boring. He'll come over with new papers as soon as he gets back Friday. He'd mail them, but it'd take longer than just bringing them by."

"Lovely," Rose said sarcastically. "I guess I'm married to Xander for a little longer. Next time, I should just put the papers in my car instead of my pocket."

Rose spent a couple of minutes whining to Luke about how horrible she felt about ruining the divorce papers. He told a couple of jokes to make her feel better, reminding her that at least Xander wouldn't get arrested on his way back.

She laughed at him and did feel a little better as she emailed him the divorce agreement so he could print them before Friday.

Friday night, Rose was reading the newest Stephen King book when there was a knock at the door. She was a little irritated that she had to stop in the middle of a paragraph, but turned the book upside down on the coffee table and went to the door. Luke and Xander were standing there.

"We have come with divorce papers, madam," Xander said with an exaggerated bow. "And to see if you wanted to come out for a drink."

"I was just reading a book," Rose answered. She really didn't want to go out. She wanted to stay home and just be alone with the monsters in the book.

"We called Leann and Penelope on the way. They're meeting us," Luke said.

"So, you're not giving me a choice."

Xander piped up again. He acted like maybe he'd already had a drink or two. "No choice. Put on some shoes, and let's go." They walked in, and Xander set the papers on the kitchen table. They stood there waiting. Rose was still in her work clothes, which today consisted of a long skirt and lacy top. It was a little chilly outside, so she went to her closet and found a jacket that matched, then found the shoes she was wearing that day.

She was putting on her shoes as she walked back into the living room. "Man, I've got a hot wife," Xander said when he saw her.

"Soon to be ex," she responded. "And how much have you already had to drink?"

"A little," he said. "I had a couple of drinks on the flight and made Luke pick me up at the airport. Just landed about an hour ago."

That explained how he was acting. After she put on her second high-heeled shoe, she picked up the papers from the kitchen table and checked to make sure he signed them. The signature was a little sloppy, but readable. That was all that mattered. She set them back down, picked up her purse that was sitting next to them, and they all walked out to Luke's car.

Leann and Penelope were already at the bar when they arrived. They found them at a table in the corner and sat down.

"It's about time," Penelope said. "We've been waiting *forever*."

"Five minutes. Leann texted me when you got the table," Luke replied, playfully swatting at her arm.

Penelope tried to pout, but the server arrived with their drinks. She and Leann had ordered for everyone. Rose sipped her rum and Diet Coke, promising herself she would really only have one or two. Drinking with her friends was fine, but she wasn't going back to how much she'd been drinking the last couple of months.

They did all have a good time that night. They laughed about Rose losing the divorce papers. Xander hit on her more than once, but she brushed him off. She knew he was harmless. Penelope said she'd found Rose's next husband, a guy named Pete. He was at Penelope and Steven's wedding, but Rose didn't remember him. He was patiently waiting for his turn as husband of the week.

Rose did only have two drinks. When she finished those, she ordered Diet Coke without the rum. No one commented on it. Leann had probably told the others that it was a sensitive subject right now.

Luke didn't drink much because he would be driving, but Xander had several more drinks. He didn't really get more drunk than when he showed up at Rose's door that night, but he definitely maintained his heavy buzz. When Luke pulled into Rose's driveway, Xander insisted on walking her to the door.

She already had her keys out before she got out of the car. Xander walked beside her to the door, chatting about his work trip on the way. He had gone to a convention where he was supposed to learn more about the business. Rose wasn't exactly bored, but she knew he was making small talk and getting ready to hit on her again. She turned when they got to the door and said, "Thank you for walking me up. I'm good now." Then, she turned and unlocked the door.

Xander waited until she had her hand on the doorknob. "Rose," he said. Rose turned to look at him.

"I know that Luke asked you about going on a real date with me, but I wanted you to know that I'm serious. It's not the alcohol talking. I really want to go out with you."

At another time, Rose might have said yes. Now, though, she didn't want to go out with anyone. She just wanted to sit at home, read books, and be alone. She was determined that there wouldn't be another man in her life. "I'm sorry, Xander. You're a great guy, but I just really don't want to date right now."

"What can I do to convince you?"

"Nothing. It's not you. I'm not dating. Period. No one can change my mind."

"What about Luke? Are you waiting for him to ask you out?"

Rose's shock at the question was obvious. "Luke? He's like a brother." She took a moment to let her face soften from the confusion that must be showing. "Look, I know it's hard for some people to understand, but I'm just done with dating. It's not you. It's not anyone."

"Well, if you don't want to date, what about being friends with benefits?"

"No. No dating. No benefits. No anything. I'm going to be alone."

Before she realized what was happening, Xander bent down and touched his lips to hers. She jerked back, put the hand not holding keys on his chest, and pushed. If he hadn't been drinking, he probably would have barely moved. In his current condition, however, he stumbled back a couple of steps.

He composed himself and stepped forward again. "Come on. You know you need *something*. No strings. Just let me spend the night. We're married. Maybe you lost that first set of papers for a reason. Fate or something."

Rose knew he wouldn't do this if he was sober, but it didn't keep her from getting mad. She wished that Luke could see the front door from the car, but it was off to the side a little, and she was sure he couldn't see. She grabbed Xander's arm and pulled him along the walkway to the driveway. Luke was still sitting in the car. As she almost dragged Xander, still pleading, towards him, she motioned for Luke to come to them. He did, wondering what was happening. Rose dropped Xander's arm.

"Take your friend home. He's drunk."

Luke looked at her and then at Xander. "Huh? What did he do?"

Xander slurred with his hands in his pockets, "Just trying to make her happy."

"Trying to make *you* happy," she said angrily, looking at Xander. Then, she turned to Luke. "He just continued the hitting on me that he was doing at the bar. Take him home." She turned and walked back to the front door, knowing that Luke would take care of it.

She slammed and locked the door when she walked in, threw her purse on the table, kicked her shoes off towards the wall, and decided she needed a cup of coffee. She made half a pot and drank it while she finished her book. By the time she drank the last sip of the first cup, she was calm and wished she hadn't yelled at Luke and Xander.

Rose was up most of the night reading. When she woke up at almost noon, she had a text from Xander, apologizing for how he acted the night before. She had another one from Luke, apologizing for Xander and asking her to call and tell him what happened. It seemed that Xander was too drunk to really remember everything.

She made a pot of coffee and sat down with a cup before she called Luke.

She went through the details of what Xander did. "How's his arm? I'm afraid I pulled him pretty hard."

"He's fine," Luke said. "Bruised his ego a little. And he's embarrassed. You know he'd never usually do anything like that."

"I know. And he texted he's sorry. I'm not mad anymore. Just don't want him to think anything's going to happen."

"Oh, he knows that. He slept on the sofa here last night. Just left. He feels awful."

"It's fine," Rose said. "Tell him not to worry about it."

CHAPTER 29

Rose really didn't have any hard feelings about Xander, but she did go ahead and sign the divorce papers and put them in the mail. She figured it might add a day or two to the time it took her to get divorced, but that was fine.

The next Sunday, Leann brought the kids over on her way to the airport. It was about 4:00 in the afternoon, and Rose was already working on making pizza dough. Jeremy and Bev loved making their own pizzas.

"They just had a snack, so you might want to let that sit for a while," Leann said as she walked through, taking the kids' bags to the second bedroom.

"It still has to rise. And you know, they can carry their own bags," Rose called back.

Leann took the bags into the bedroom and walked back out before she answered. "They can, but I'm spoiling them today."

Jeremy and Bev had already plopped on the sofa. Jeremy was scrolling through Netflix, trying to find something they could agree to watch. "How about this?" he asked Bev.

"No. I hate dinosaurs."

"Ugh," he said and kept scrolling.

Rose looked at Leann. "Are you all packed? Got everything you need?"

"Of course. I think I overpacked. For me and the kids. Their bags were heavy."

Rose laughed. "It's three days, and I have a key to your place in case they need anything."

"I know, but you know how I get sometimes."

"What time's your flight?"

"Not until 7. I thought I'd hang out here for a little bit. I just need to get to the airport by 6. I've got an hour."

"You'll have to leave before pizzas are ready. Want us to save you one for when you get back?" She set the timer on the microwave so she could check on the dough.

"I'll grab something at the airport."

Rose looked over at the kids. "Do you two want to play a game while we wait?"

The kids jumped up and ran to the cabinet where Rose kept board games. They quickly agreed on Clue and set it up on the kitchen table. They finished the game just as the timer went off for the dough, and Leann needed to leave shortly after. Rose pulled a container of her homemade pizza sauce and several toppings she had gotten ready earlier out of the refrigerator and shaped the dough into three small circles so they could each have their own. She, Jeremy, and Bev piled toppings on their pizzas and picked a movie while they waited for them to cook. They spent the evening watching dinosaurs, which Bev agreed to if she could pick the movie the next night.

The next couple of days, Rose had fun with the kids. She dropped them off at school before work and picked them up from after school care when she left. They loved helping her cook, so they did that Monday night. Tuesday, Rose took them out to eat and then to play miniature golf. She loved hanging out with the kids, and it did help occupy her mind.

She was sad to see them go Wednesday evening when Leann picked them up. Her flight got in late, so it was almost 10:00 when she finally got to the house. They said their goodbyes.

When they left, Rose was sad again. She'd been busy the last few days playing with Jeremy and Bev, and she wished they were still there. She wanted a drink, but resisted and read a book instead.

Her divorce from Xander was final on March 11. Penelope was quick to schedule the next wedding. Rose and Pete met on the afternoon of March 12. It was a rainy Saturday. They got married in Penelope and Steven's living room, and everyone was planning on hanging out for dinner and a couple of drinks. Rose didn't want to stay. She had more books to read, and it was a bad day for her emotionally. She was thinking a lot about Matt that weekend, so she went home. She didn't find out much about Pete, just that he was distantly related to Steven and had been divorced for a couple of years. He had dated some, but wasn't currently dating anyone. He heard about Rose's record project from his parents and called Steven to find out more. From there, he decided he'd be in on it.

Rose was out of books she hadn't read yet, so she found a book she hadn't read in a few years. Before she started reading it, she got out her laptop and ordered a few books that looked good. Maybe they would keep her occupied for a little while.

The book she chose was a good one, and it was the first one in a series of seven. She had all of them, so she knew she would have plenty to read until the new books came in the mail. She turned on some music and lost herself reading. Before she knew it, she looked up and saw that it was dark outside.

She heated some leftover soup and continued reading. When the book was finished, she went to bed and didn't wake up until Leann called her the next morning.

"Hello?" she answered.

"Did I wake you up?" Leann asked.

"Yes. It's early."

"It's 11. The kids woke me up hours ago. I guess you didn't get the email from Jane."

"Huh? Jane?"

"Yeah. The reporter? She sent us an email. The article's going to be in the paper Tuesday."

Rose sat up. "I thought she was going to let us read it."

"Yeah, but she explained that in the email. And the article was attached. She said we can ask her to change stuff as long as we do it today."

Rose sleepily pulled back the covers and swung her legs off the side of the bed. "Ok. Did you read it?"

"Yeah. Nothing to worry about. Just the facts. Penelope's got Steven reading it, too, just in case."

"Then I'm not going to bother." Rose got up and walked to the kitchen to make coffee, chatting with Leann as she did. Rose wasn't concerned about the article as long as Leann and Penelope thought it was fine. She really just wanted to ignore the whole newspaper situation - ignore it and hope this was the last of it. She didn't want to have attention called to her, especially right now. She knew there may be something when she broke the actual record, but she didn't want to think about it until then.

She and Leann hung up just after she poured a cup of coffee, and she spent the rest of the day relaxing with another book.

She couldn't ignore the article anymore Tuesday evening when Leann and Penelope showed up after work, though. Penelope had stopped to buy a copy of the paper, which she held up for Rose to see. Rose was front page news.

Rose let them in and went back to the kitchen, where she was heating leftover soup again.

"Aren't you going to read it?" Leann asked.

"Don't care. What else is up with you two?'

"Read the article!" Penelope squealed.

They spent the next couple of minutes talking Rose into reading the article, as they heated the rest of the soup and made sandwiches to go with it. With the sandwiches, there was just enough food for the three of them. They ate while Rose read the article.

She finished it and handed the paper back to Penelope. "Nothing new. Looks like the facts. I'm surprised she got a quote from Henry, though."

"Yeah. Isn't it cool that it's front page, though?" Leann asked.

Rose shrugged and took a bite of soup.

"You really don't care, do you?" Leann asked.

"Not really. I don't want the attention. The front page kind of annoys me.

I know most people don't read the *paper* paper, but that means it's obvious on their web site, too."

Penelope was already finished with her food, so she pushed her plate away from her on the table and sat back. "But the attention might be good. Leann and I were talking about the advertising thing Jane suggested. Maybe we should put ads on the blog. Make some money."

"I'd rather not. We don't really need the money, do we?" Rose hadn't eaten much of her soup while she was reading the article, so she was trying to eat it before it got cold.

"Not really, but it would be nice. I mean, when is more money not good?" Leann said.

"My vote is no," Rose said, "but if y'all outvote me, go ahead."

Leann finished her food, too. She picked up her and Penelope's dishes and took them to the sink. "Good, because I've been doing some research. I can set it up pretty easily. We probably won't make a lot, but maybe enough to pay for a dinner every once in a while."

"Yes!" Penelope exclaimed.

"Fine. I'll accept any money handed to me. Just don't be surprised if we lose some followers."

Leann added the ads to the blog the next day and texted the girls that when she checked, they had gained another 2,000 followers. That was more than they had gained in a month before, and it was in just one day. Rose hoped it would all blow over soon and that would be the last they would hear from reporters or anything about media.

Steven and Penelope brought over divorce papers with Pete's signature the following Thursday night. This time, Rose carefully put the papers in her laptop bag so she wouldn't lose them. Friday morning, she checked to be sure they were still there before she left for work.

Work was pretty easy that day. She didn't have any meetings, and the team was mostly caught up with projects. They were testing a couple of web sites they had built that week to make sure they were ready to send to the clients Monday. She did have to take a call from Kenneth – their least favorite client – but he was just calling to ask about a deadline. When she hung up with him, she realized that he had been easier to deal with the last few weeks. He didn't argue about the budget as much, and he seemed more pleasant overall.

Penelope came by her office just after she hung up with Kenneth and asked if she wanted to go to lunch.

"Sure. We just need to stop at the courthouse. I have papers to file."

"That takes what, 5 minutes?"

"Yeah. Not long. And things are slow around here today. If we're a couple of minutes late, it should be fine."

They talked about Kenneth a little at lunch. "Have you noticed that he hasn't been as difficult lately?" Rose asked.

Penelope didn't have to think about it. "He hasn't. It's you."

"What?"

"He called me a while back. After that article from Will. He tried to get me to put him on the list," Penelope said matter-of-factly.

"Like, the marriage list?" Rose was the one who practically screamed in the restaurant this time. She heard how loud she was and looked around, but everyone else was chatting, so the little noise she made was barely noticeable.

Penelope nodded. "I told him no and made excuses about work relationships and everything. I was afraid he'd go directly to you, but it doesn't sound like he did."

"No. I would have said no, too. Jessica wouldn't like me marrying a client very much."

Penelope just laughed in response.

"Though, him just thinking about it apparently makes him more reasonable. Maybe it'll stay this way for a while. I kind of like the new Kenneth," Rose said.

Penelope smiled slyly. "Oh, so you like a man again now?"

Rose waved her off. "You know that's not what I mean. I wouldn't date him in a million years. And that's not just because he's a client, or just because I don't want to date anyone."

They finished lunch without talking about Kenneth or any other man except Steven. They dropped the divorce papers at the courthouse and were only 10 minutes late getting back to the office. No one noticed.

The divorce took about the usual amount of time. Rose's divorce from Pete was final on March 30. When she got the mail that day, she went to throw them in the drawer of her nightstand where she had been keeping them and decided it was time to organize all the divorce papers. The drawer was almost full. She found the accordion file that Elsa gave her for the fake bridal shower and spent a couple of hours adding the papers to the file in order. She even found the papers from her first two marriages in a box at the back of her closet and added them to the file. 19 marriages down. 11 to go.

CHAPTER 30

The next morning, Rose got to work early. She had a meeting at 8:30 and wanted to get some work done before it started. Penelope texted her before she even pulled into the parking lot: *Wedding 6:30 tonight at Leann's.*

Rose answered it right after she parked. *Seriously? On April Fool's Day?*

None of the team was there yet. That was actually a little of a relief. She didn't feel like chatting much that morning. But Penelope's office wasn't far, and she was waiting at Rose's office.

"Yes, on April Fool's Day!" she called out as soon as she saw Rose walk around the corner.

Rose quickened her step down the walkway between cubicles. As she opened her office door, she asked, "Who?"

"Surprise."

"And you know how much I *love* surprises. Really, who is it?"

Penelope still wouldn't say. "All you need to know is that he'll be no trouble at all."

"You know how much I hate when you do that. What's up today? You're in this meeting with Kenneth this afternoon, right?"

"Yeah. He wants to talk about adding another page to his web site. Something about an offer he's giving his customers. So today should just be him telling us exactly what he wants. We'll send a quote for him to argue about later."

"Good. Maybe it'll go quickly, then. I'm hoping to get out of here by 4:30."

"Any particular reason?" Penelope's phone beeped, and she looked down at it.

Rose was setting her stuff on her desk and getting her laptop out of the bag. "Only that I'm here before 7:30 this morning, so I want to leave early, too."

Penelope typed a reply to the text she got and looked up. "Oh, I thought you might have a date or something."

Rose laughed. "First of all, it's too early to make me laugh. Second, if you thought for one second that I'd have a date, you wouldn't have scheduled me a wedding tonight."

"Oh, it'll be fun," Penelope replied. "April Fool's Day marriage. It fits the theme. And that was Leann just now. She said she's cooking tonight, so you have to stay for dinner."

"Ugh. I wanted to read tonight."

"Well, you're getting married instead. You can read afterwards, for your honeymoon."

They chatted until Rose got her laptop turned on, and then Penelope went to her office. Rose worked until she had to what was supposed to be the first of two meetings that day. During the hour she was stuck in the boring 8:30 one, three more got added to her calendar. She ended up not having even a second to herself all day except the hour that morning. When she finally saw Penelope that afternoon for the meeting with Kenneth, she whispered as they walked in, "Any way we can reschedule this wedding? I'm exhausted."

"Sorry. No can do. It's the only day the groom's available."

"Dammit," Rose breathed and then put on a fake smile for Kenneth, who was already in the conference room. Everything went smoothly, just as things had been with him for the last several weeks. She was starting to get used to it and hoped this was a permanent change.

What he needed was a little more than just one web page, though. "So, we'll need three new pages, additional shopping cart features, and you want full marketing for these new products?" Rose asked at the end of the meeting.

"Sounds right. Email series, social media, everything," Kenneth replied.

"We can do it," Rose said. "Penelope and I will work up pricing and get it to you by the end of the week."

"I'll approve it."

Kenneth was facing her, so he didn't see Penelope's look of shock.

"Perfect. Anything else you need today?" Rose asked.

"Well, I asked Penelope about your whole record-breaking thing. Now I want to ask you."

It was Rose's turn to be shocked, and she knew Kenneth could tell. "Kenneth, you know I can't. You're a client."

"Are you sure? I mean, I read the article, and I'm following the blog. It's not like I expect anything. I just think it would be fun. Would Jessica even know?"

Rose shook her head. "If she reads the blog, she will, and I think she might. I really don't want to get fired."

Rose sat still, waiting for Kenneth to get mad. He'd been known to lose his temper in the office on the few occasions they'd had to tell him they couldn't do a project for him. She didn't know if this would be any better.

"But it's just a joke, right? It's not like it's a real marriage. What if I talk to Jessica and explain?"

Penelope jumped in. "Kenneth, you don't need to do that. Jessica and I already talked about it after you asked me. She doesn't like the idea. She said she doesn't care what Rose does in her personal life as long as it doesn't affect her job, and she would consider marrying a client affecting Rose's job, even if it isn't a traditional marriage."

Kenneth looked down. When he looked up again, he was smiling. "Okay. I guess if that's how it is, we have two options. Rose can refuse me, or I can offer her a job if Jessica fires her. More money than you're making here."

Rose looked at Penelope, who was shaking her head, before she looked back at Kenneth to answer. "I really can't. I'm sorry, Kenneth, but I think it's best if we don't add you to the list. I just think it would be unprofessional."

Kenneth nodded curtly, stood, and walked out.

"Oh, shit," Rose said. "I'm glad you talked to Jessica."

"Oh, honey, I didn't. I'm going to have to run talk to her in just a minute.

But do not back down if he tries to ask you again. And I hope to God that he doesn't start being a jerk again now."

Penelope was already almost to the door before she finished talking, and she didn't wait for a reply. She was practically running to Jessica's office so Kenneth couldn't get there before her.

It was 4:15. Rose thought she should probably wait for Penelope to talk to Jessica before she left, but Jessica had already said she could leave when the meeting with Kenneth was over. She was tired, and she knew Penelope could handle the Jessica situation, so she packed her things, told the team bye, and went home.

She had time to try to nap for an hour before going to Leann's, so she laid on the sofa and closed her eyes. She heard the tone on her phone when she was almost asleep and looked at it. *All's good. Jessica will handle Kenneth,* Penelope had said.

Rose replied: *Good. Napping. See you at 6ish.*

Thankfully, Penelope didn't reply. Rose still only slept for about 20 minutes, though. She was thinking about Matt, so it was hard to fall asleep. She wanted to just push him out of her mind, but as much as she tried, she couldn't. She was laying there most of the time thinking things like, "Don't people say it gets easier? That time heals all and all that bullshit?" When she woke up at 5:30, she felt even groggier than when she left work. Oh, well. There was nothing to do now but go to Leann's and get married. Hopefully, whatever man she was marrying wouldn't care that she was half asleep. She brushed her hair, checked her makeup, grabbed her keys, and walked out the door.

The kids were with Brent, so it was just Leann and Penelope when she walked in the house. "So is this an April Fool's Day joke and I'm not really getting married today?"

"Nope. You're getting married. He's just not here yet," Leann said. Rose and Penelope filled Leann in on the situation with Kenneth while they waited.

They weren't quite finished telling her what happened when Luke opened the door. "I'm here for a wedding!" he yelled.

"Shh, Luke. We're talking about something important," Leann said, annoyed.

"Is Luke my April Fool's husband?" Rose asked.

"Leann, hush. You can continue the conversation. Rose, I am not. I'm just here for the fun. Actually, Penelope and I talked about us getting married again, but I think maybe we should limit repeats. It'll make it harder for someone else to break your record of 30 marriages to *different* men later. Though if you don't care, I would marry you again in a heartbeat. You're the best wife ever."

"Good point," Rose said. "I hadn't thought about the repeat thing. It would make it better if they're all different men. The current record holder had a couple of repeats in there, I think. Fine. 30 different men. I might make you Husband Number 31, though."

"That works. Now, what were you ladies talking about that was so important?"

Penelope sighed and started the story over again. Leann listened quietly until they got to where she was hearing new stuff.

They had just finished the story and were talking about how Kenneth might act when there was a knock at the door. "That's your hubby!" Luke called out and went to get the door. He was awfully excited today.

Luke kept the door open while he talked for a minute, and the way Leann's living room was arranged, the girls couldn't see around the door to see who it was. "Luke, are you going to bring him in or just let Rose sit here wondering all day?" Leann asked.

Luke told whoever it was to come in and laughed when Rose jumped up and yelled, "Kurt!" The other girls stood, too, and they all walked over and took turns giving him a hug.

"I haven't seen you in years," Rose said. "I thought Luke said you were dating Jennifer again?"

As Kurt was giving Leann a hug, he answered, "She dumped me again. Luke said he wasn't going to tell you I was going to be your husband for this April. How do you feel about being my future ex-wife?"

"I think it's a great idea," Rose said.

Luke piped up. "You girls actually suggested it. I just had to wait until he and Jen called it quits again."

"Man, why do you have to say it like that? Like you knew it would happen?" Kurt asked.

"I'm sorry. I know it's probably not a good time to joke about it. But Jen keeps doing this to you. I'm sick of it."

Leann changed the subject. She had talked to Kurt about the marriage, and they had talked a little about Jen. She knew it was a sore subject for him. "So, dinner before or after we do the wedding? It's ready whenever. I've got soup on the stove."

Kurt was standing next to Leann. He put one arm around her shoulders and gave her a small thankful squeeze. "Doesn't matter to me. What do you think, wifey?" he asked, looking at Rose.

"Let's go ahead and get it over with," she said. "It takes like 2 minutes, and then we can eat and catch up."

"Sounds good to me. Leann, are you ready to marry us?" Kurt moved to stand next to Rose. "How's this work? Do we need to do the whole music and walking down the aisle thing?"

Penelope answered. "Nah. Just stand there, and Leann will do her thing."

"It's simple, really. I just ask if you take each other to be man and wife, and then we're done. There's no point in going into the whole *dearly beloved* and doing full vows and all that. You just have to say you do and sign the certificate."

Kurt nodded, and Leann continued.

"Do you, Kurt, take Rose to be your wife?"

"I do."

"Do you, Rose, take Kurt to be your husband?"

"I do."

"Then I pronounce you man and wife. You do not need to kiss the bride." She started walking over to the coffee table as Kurt laughed at the last line of her ceremony. "You do, however, need to sign this certificate." She motioned to the table, where the certificate and a pen were already out.

Kurt, Rose, and Leann signed the certificate. Leann would take it to the courthouse for them the next day, because she was off work. When they were finished, the girls helped Leann get bowls and spoons out, and they had dinner while they talked for the next couple of hours. Rose didn't feel as tired. She had a good time catching up with Kurt. They had hung out some when they were younger, when she was with Leann and Luke. She thought it was a nice surprise. Other than remembering that he really was a good-looking man and a generally good guy, she still didn't want to date anyone, including him. And that was good, because she caught him looking at Leann a lot that night.

CHAPTER 31

First thing Monday morning, Jessica walked into Rose's office and closed the door. "Hi, Jessica," Rose said when she looked up from her computer. "Is this about Friday?"

"Yeah," Jessica said and sat down. "I just wanted to tell you that Kenneth called me this morning. Everything's fine. He understands now what kind of situation it would put me in, and he's agreed not to ask you again."

"Oh, thank God. I was worried about it."

"I know. I'm just glad he's the only client who's said anything. I know more of them probably know about it, but they're keeping everything professional."

"So," Rose said, "how does this affect my job?" What she was worried about wasn't so much Kenneth himself, but whether Jessica would be upset with her.

Jessica was still smiling. "It doesn't. You did exactly what you should have done. You told him no, and you and Penelope made sure I knew what was going on. I'm even glad Penelope lied to him about talking to me. As long as you're doing what you're supposed to do here, I don't care about your weddings, just like I said."

"Is Kenneth going to be a jerk about it?"

"Nope. And you're still handling him. He still wants you and Penelope working with him. Just get those estimates for the new stuff to him by tomorrow to show him we're not upset about it, and we're going to pretend it didn't happen unless he becomes a problem."

"Perfect. I'm actually working on them now."

"Great. And maybe he'll still be as nice as he's been the last few weeks." Jessica laughed and walked out. Rose was glad that Jessica had noticed the change in Kenneth, too.

Rose got her part of the estimates to Penelope before lunch and coordinated with the other managers to get their estimates in. By the end of the day, true to his word, Kenneth had responded to Penelope's email with approval for the cost. Rose scheduled a short meeting with her team for the next morning to go over the new project.

That night, Rose called Leann. She had let the looks Leann and Kurt gave each other slide over the weekend, but she wanted to know how much Leann had noticed. "Yes, I saw him looking at me," Leann said when she asked. "And he saw me looking at him. Actually, I was going to ask how you felt about me sleeping with your husband."

"Please do!" Rose said happily.

"Good, because I already did. He stayed Friday night when y'all left."

"Oh, you homewrecker! I'm divorcing him right away! And I want to know all about it."

"It was great. He and I have been talking some lately anyway. He came over with Kurt after Jen broke up with him, and we've been chatting ever since."

"That's great! He's a good guy. How long has that been, though? I don't think I even asked him how long it had been since Jen broke up with him. He didn't seem to want to talk about it."

"No, not really. He's done with her, though. This is the fourth time she's broken up with him. It's been a little over a month. She's already doing what she always does – calling and texting to see if she can get back in."

"Wow. Really? Why does she do it?"

"He and Luke did some asking around. Looks like she wants a fling and breaks up with him to have it, and then wants him back. I just hope I'm not getting myself into a situation where he dumps me to go back to her."

"Do you think he will?"

Leann let out a long sigh. "I hope not. Kurt and I have always gotten along since he's Luke's friend. I do like him, but I'm preparing myself just in case. I'm not telling the kids anything about it, obviously."

"What's Luke think?"

"Kurt told him last night. He gave him the whole 'you'd better not hurt my sister' speech. But we've both explained to him that it's nothing serious, at least for right now. But we are seeing each other, and we wanted to be the ones to tell him."

"Good. That's the best way to do it. Neither of you wants Luke mad at you. I hope it works out. But you're still a homewrecker. Can I call him and tell him I want a divorce?"

Leann laughed, "No. You're doing that anyway. But in a few weeks, we'll have a game night or something."

"Sounds good. I'm going to get back to my book. Give the babies kisses for me. I'll see you soon."

"You know they hate when you call them babies. But they are my babies, so I will. Bye!"

Rose was happy for Leann. Kurt was a good guy, and she really hoped that things would work out for them. They'd known each other almost their whole lives, and it would be great if they could be happy together. They both deserved it, and she knew they would be good for each other.

That Friday night, Luke, Kurt, Leann, Penelope, and Steven met for dinner at Rose's house so she and Kurt could sign the divorce papers. They all had a good time except for a 2-minute conversation about husbands.

"I've got you a new one lined up. One from the blog," Penelope said over dinner.

"What's his name?" Rose asked.

"Ummm…." Penelope didn't seem to want to say.

"What's wrong? Did you forget?" Kurt asked.

"His name's Matthew. He's a mechanic from Atlanta."

"No," Rose said and got up to refill her wine glass. "And I'm not discussing it. Just no. Find someone else."

Kurt looked confused and started to speak. Luke shook his head at him, and Leann whispered that she would explain later. She didn't think Rose heard her.

"I heard that, Leann. I'll explain. Kurt, I was dating a guy named Matt. He dumped me. I'm not marrying someone with that name. And I think that's all the explanation needed right now."

Kurt nodded. "Agreed. That's enough. And I don't blame you. I wouldn't do it, either. It sounds like it was painful. But, who wants dessert? I'll cut that pie Leann brought."

He got up and walked to the counter to cut the pie, starting to tell everyone about something that happened when he was at work that day. Rose, thankful for his subject change, mouthed across the table to Leann, "He's a keeper."

The rest of the night went smoothly, and Penelope quickly found a new man for the list. Rose never asked what she told the Matthew who was supposed to be next, and she didn't care to know. She figured he might be disappointed, and she was sorry for that, but she just didn't feel like she could do it.

Rose and Kurt's divorce was final on April 18. Kurt called her when he got his copy of the papers to congratulate her on their divorce. "Should I get you a divorce present?" he asked.

"You're as silly as Luke. He got me a Ring Pop for our fake engagement. No presents are necessary. You were a good husband. I didn't have to make any prison visits or get a lawyer involved."

"That's always good. I hope the rest of them go as well. How many are left again?"

"10," she replied.

"Oh, wow. That's two thirds of the way. Are you guys not celebrating? I didn't think about being Husband Number 20."

"I haven't really thought about any kind of celebration."

"Well, that's just boring," he said. "You should have done something."

They hung up so Leann could go to a meeting. When she got home that night, everyone was there with a cake. On it, they had had the bakery write *Happy 20th Divorce!* They even made her blow out candles. She told Leann again later that she definitely approved of Kurt.

CHAPTER 32

On April 23, Rose met Leann and Penelope at the park so she could marry the next husband. His name was Sean, and he was a web developer. Rose thought about telling him that she was, too, but thought it would be best not to get to know him too much, just like she did with all of the husbands she didn't already know. So far, she felt that being friendly only got her in trouble somehow. Sean was great, though. He seemed nice and everything went smoothly. They were divorced on May 10.

On May 13, Rose married Eddie. Eddie learned about the project from the blog and also didn't cause her any grief. He owned an herbal medicine shop and let her know that as long as they were married, she could have a 25% discount at the shop. She didn't take him up on it, but thought the offer was nice. Other than that, they didn't talk. He signed the divorce papers without a fuss, and the divorce was final on May 31. Rose filed the marriage certificate and divorce agreement away with all the others.

The day after she got the final divorce papers for Eddie, Rose got a call from Jane, the reporter. "Hi, Rose! How are you?" she said.

"I'm good, Jane. How are you?"

"Great! I was just wondering what husband you're on now."

"I'm in between at the moment, but the next is 23. Why?"

"Well, that one will tie you for a record, right?" Jane said.

Rose hadn't been thinking about the separate record for the woman with the most marriages. She had only been thinking about the end goal, but Jane reminded her that there were two records she was actually working to beat. "Well, yeah, I guess so."

"Great. I'm doing a follow-up article. Can we talk for a few minutes about what's been happening since the last one?"

"Sure. Most of it's on the blog, though. I don't think there's really anything else that's been going on."

"I understand that. Are you going to register the record for 24 when you get to that one?"

"I don't know. Do I need to register it?"

Jane got excited. "Oh, yes! I'll help you if you want. And is there any way I could be at the next couple of weddings to get some pictures? I think it would be great for the article."

"Well, let me talk to Penelope and Leann. I'll have to make sure they're okay with it. And, of course, the future husbands."

"That works. Just let me know in the next couple of days. I'll need to make arrangements here for the photographer."

"Just so you know, we don't do any kind of big wedding. It's basically just saying 'I do' and then we usually go our separate ways. There won't be a lot to take pictures of."

Jane didn't hesitate. "Oh, yes, I know. That's fine, hon. Try to get some photogenic ones, though. I know you'll take great pics, but we'll need to make sure these guys look good next to you."

They talked for a few more minutes, but Rose didn't really have much to tell her that Leann hadn't already written.

Rose called Penelope as soon as she hung up with Jane. "First, Jane's going to call you and Leann at some point to do another article. Also, she wants to know if she can take pictures of the next couple of weddings."

"Leann's here. You're on speaker," Penelope replied.

"Do I need to repeat it?" Rose asked.

"Nope," Leann said. "We were actually just talking about the next one. He's a police officer named Brandon. He comes into the store sometimes, so I kind of know him. He's good-looking enough for a photo, if he's okay with it."

"Are we okay with it?" Rose asked. "Really, though. I didn't want publicity, and I think Jane will understand if we say no."

Penelope called out, "Yes, we do want the publicity!"

"But why?" Rose asked.

"Well, that's another thing we were talking about. We've made almost $1,000 on ads for the blog since I set them up. I actually came over here to get Steven to help get some kind of paperwork drawn up for a partnership or something so we can do a bank account. You were busy at work when we talked about it, and we were about to call you anyway. I don't want the money going into my account if it's that much. But publicity will make that more, so I say let's do it."

"A thousand? That's way more than we thought it would be."

Penelope said, "Yeah, but that's good. Steven will be home in a few minutes. I was about to see if you want to come over so we can talk about all this."

They kept talking as Rose got into her car. "So we want the publicity according to both of you. That means I need to dress better for the next wedding, at least."

"Yeah. Ratty jeans and an old t-shirt won't cut it for pictures. Not a wedding dress, but at least something nice. And you should meet Brandon ahead of time so you can actually talk about something while you're there," Penelope said.

"If you're trying to fix me up..." Rose began.

"No," Leann interrupted. "It's not a fixup. Brandon likes being single, anyway. He's just doing it because Zachary told him it's fun. But if Jane's going to take pictures, you should at least be somewhat friendly with him, right?"

"Okay, okay," Rose answered. "I'll do it for the pictures. But make it clear that it's not a date. Coffee or something, and at least one of you has to be there, too. I guess if we're making money on doing this now, we can buy coffee and expense it."

"That works," Penelope said. "And I've got Joey down for Husband Number 24."

"Joey who?" Rose asked after she screamed at the driver in front of her to stop being so slow.

"You know they can't hear you, right?" Leann asked.

"Yep, but it makes me feel better. If they ever do hear me, it'll probably be someone with road rage. I'll die, and I'll never get to yell at anonymous drivers again. Joey who?"

"Pender. You know him. Used to be in my department. Now he's got his own accounting firm."

"Okay. He'll do for pictures."

They decided that Penelope would call Joey, and Leann would call Brandon. They'd set up meetings and see if both the guys were okay with pictures and some publicity.

"This is starting to be a lot of trouble," Rose said as she walked into Penelope's house and hung up her phone.

Steven was right behind her. "What's trouble?"

"Marriages," Rose answered.

"Well, didn't you already know that?" Steven asked, grinning at Penelope.

"Well, it's more now. The blog is making money off ads, and the reporter wants to do another article and take pictures of weddings. And hi, honey. I'm glad you're home," Penelope said and gave him a kiss on the cheek.

"Uh oh. I'm getting a kiss. I think I'm about to get asked to do some work."

"Well, we want to make it an official business, and we need help," Leann said.

The rest of the night, the three of them worked on making plans while Steven drew up a partnership agreement. They made him a partner, but he insisted on taking less than the rest of them since he wasn't doing as much work. They decided that each of the girls would have 30% of blog profits, and he would get 10%.

After ordering a pizza, they kept working. By the end of the night, they had a partnership agreement signed, with Steven volunteering to file the correct paperwork to make them a limited liability company. Brandon had agreed to have photos taken, but Joey didn't want to, so Penelope moved him on the list and called John, a bank clerk she knew from college. He wouldn't mind being in the paper, and according to Penelope, he was "Hot, hot, hot." The next two nights, they would meet with Brandon and John so Penelope could learn a little about them. Jane was planning to attend the wedding Saturday afternoon in the park with her photographer. Everything was set. When Rose got home, she climbed into bed exhausted and fell asleep immediately for the first time in months.

CHAPTER 33

Rose thought she would hate meeting Brandon and John, but knowing that it was clear that the meetings weren't dates made it a little easier. She decided before she went that she would treat it as business, just as she had been doing with the marriages all along. Both men were funny and easy to talk to, especially with Leann and Penelope along. When they were leaving, John did ask about the possibility of an actual date.

"I'm sorry, but no," Rose said.

"John, we talked about this," Penelope reminded him.

"Yeah, but that was you telling me before I even met her. Now that I have, I didn't think it would hurt to ask. And don't worry, Rose, Penelope told me all about your problems in the past. There won't be any here. I just couldn't leave without asking."

When John left, Penelope said, "You know, he really is a nice guy. You two seemed to hit it off, too. When you're ready to date, I could call him for you."

"Not happening," Rose answered. They left it at that.

On Saturday, they all met at the park for Rose and Brandon to get married. Rose even bought a new dress. She decided on a casual black floral print. It did have some red and white flowers on it, but it was obviously not a wedding dress. Brandon didn't really dress up, either. He wore black jeans and a white polo. They both looked good enough for a few pictures, but made it clear that the wedding wasn't a huge affair.

Jane loved it. She asked Brandon a few questions and promised to send pictures after the photographer had them retouched. They could use them for the blog, too, with credit to the paper.

As usual, the ceremony only took a few minutes, and Brandon needed to leave. He was on duty that night. Jane's photographer left, too, but she stayed for a few minutes.

"Rose, I need to work with you on getting that application in. I'm thinking we can have a rep from the record organization at the next wedding to certify it right away. Will that work for you?"

Leann answered for her. "That's fine with us."

"And, I have a colleague at a local television station who wants to be there to do an interview. It'll run on the evening news. About three weeks, right?"

Penelope answered this one. "Yes, that's fine."

Rose didn't even get a chance to answer. She was fine with letting the other girls make the decisions, as long as all she had to do is go along with it, and as long as it didn't take up too much time. When she started all this, she thought it was just going to be saying "I do" and signing papers. While it had evolved a little since, she still hoped the media part would die down.

"So, how long do you think it'll be before you stop wanting to do articles and interviews and everything?" Rose asked, smiling as sweetly as she could.

Jane laughed. "Hon, you're in it now. I'm not stopping. If you'll let me, I'll be at all the rest of your weddings. This is actually a pretty big story. People are sick of the bad news. You're doing something unusual and fun and happy. Even if people are a little saddened by your reason behind it, it's a good story, and the paper's readers love it. We've been getting emails asking for an update. That's why my editor let me come back."

Rose knew that some people thought her reason was sad. Love wasn't going to happen for her, so why not get married 30 times? She didn't think it was sad. It was just something she accepted. She felt a little pathetic about love and relationships now, but it had nothing to do with the marriages. She couldn't tell Jane anything about Matt, partly because it made her feel weak and partly because she just didn't want to bring him into it. If this attention was going to keep going, she would just have to pretend even harder to be completely happy in other areas of her life.

Jane did ask a few minutes later if she was seeing anyone, and she repeated that she wasn't dating anymore. Jane didn't press the issue. They had already talked about that the first time they met. Rose knew, though, that other reporters may keep asking. They would ask if she ever dated her husbands, what current boyfriends thought of her project, and a lot of other questions about relationships.

But none of that mattered. What mattered was her project, her job, and her friendships. She would concentrate on those and find a way to push everything else out of her mind and ignore the questions she would get that weren't about the project.

The paper published the article a lot quicker this time. It was posted on Monday when Rose got home. It was a nice article, *Local Woman Ties the Record for Most Marriages*, and the photo looked really good. Jane had even tried to get in touch with the current record holder, but apparently couldn't reach her. She checked the blog. Leann had already added a new post. It had a different photo and a link to the paper.

The next Thursday after work, Rose met Brandon at Leann's store to sign the divorce papers. They stayed outside because Rose didn't want a repeat of when she went to have Zachary sign the papers. Rose folded the papers and put them in the console in her car. Then, she went in to get Leann to go to dinner as Brandon left.

"Sorry! I can't go tonight. Brent just called. Jeremy's running a fever and wants me to come get him. I'm waiting for Zachary to get back from his break, and then I'm leaving him in charge."

"Oh, I'm sorry! Tell Jeremy to get better. I am going to look at clothes, though. I should probably wear something different for the next wedding since we're going to have photo evidence of them now."

"Good idea," Leann said. "Call Penelope. She'll probably go to dinner."

"That's okay. I'll eat something at home. If you need anything, call me."

Rose went to the clothing section and found a couple of dresses she liked. It only took a few minutes, but Leann was gone when she got back to the front to check out.

When she got home, she realized that she really didn't have much in the refrigerator. She would have to go to the store, but decided it could wait. Instead, she got online and put in an order at her favorite Chinese place. They were there within twenty minutes with her sweet and sour chicken, and she enjoyed it as she watched a new comedy that Penelope had told her about. Then, she got out one of her new books and read until she couldn't keep her eyes open. She didn't feel like getting up to walk to the bed, so she laid down on the sofa, pulled the blanket she kept on the back of it over her, and closed her eyes.

A couple of minutes later, she was wide awake. This happened far too often lately. She used to be able to fall asleep quickly. Now, it took forever. She knew why, but pushed it from her mind. Instead, she made a cup of chamomile tea, this time without cutting her hand on glass. Moving around didn't help. If it was possible, she was even more awake by the time the tea was ready to add honey to the cup. She took the tea and her book to bed and settled in to read a few more chapters.

After a while, she reached for the tea. The little that was left was cold. She looked at the clock. 3:33. It figured. She needed to be at work by 8:15 to get ready for a meeting, and she still couldn't sleep. Well, the alarm would wake her up anyway, and tomorrow was Friday. She could catch up on sleep over the weekend. She drank the rest of the cold tea and set the cup on the coaster on her nightstand. She read another few chapters. An hour later, she was asleep with the book on her chest.

She hit snooze when her alarm went off at 6:15. At 7:00, she finally slowly got out of bed, took a shower, and got dressed for work. By 7:45, she had a second cup of coffee in her hand and was walking out to the car. The day was exhausting, and coffee wasn't helping much at all. She figured that she drank enough on a normal day that the caffeine didn't really do much to her anymore.

The meeting went well. It was with Kenneth, and he was still being much nicer than in the past. She and Penelope both wondered if he would bring up the marriages again, but so far, he hadn't. That day, she took Brandon's divorce agreement to the courthouse and took a nap when she got home.

The divorce from Brandon was final on June 21. Other than the cameras at the wedding, everything had gone as smoothly as any of her other marriages so far. She filed the papers away with the rest of them, ready to get the next seven marriages over with so she could be finished with everything, especially the new addition of reporters. That would stop when the marriages were all done.

CHAPTER 34

On June 25, Rose was just starting to get ready to meet everyone at the park for the next wedding ceremony. She wore one of her new dresses – this one with black and yellow stripes. Jane called while she was putting on makeup.

"I have a surprise for you today, hon," Jane said.

"Oh? What kind of surprise?"

"Well, you know how I was going to help you with the world record registration?"

Rose had thought about asking Jane about that before, but work had been pretty busy. She knew they needed to meet to file the application and get everything started, but she also figured they needed to wait until after they actually broke the record. "Yes," she replied.

"Someone from Guinness will be there today. I just heard from them. I know it's late notice, but is there any way you can bring copies of your marriage certificates? They'll need them."

Rose didn't think she would have time to make copies before she left. The copier-printer combination she had at home didn't have an auto-feed, so she would have to manually change out the papers. It would take forever. She told Jane as much.

"Don't worry about that. Can you get here early and bring the papers? I'll get the copies taken care of while you're getting married."

So Rose finished her makeup and got another cup of coffee. Before she left, she grabbed the accordion file. Jane was already there and ready. She had Charlotte, one of the paper's assistants, with her. Charlotte took the papers and went to the nearest office supply store to make copies while they waited. The photographer started taking pictures of Rose while she and Jane chatted.

Leann and Luke arrived next, but only a couple of minutes before a representative from the Guinness World Book of Records. Hal introduced himself, and they chatted for a few minutes. Charlotte showed up with copies of the papers. She handed the copies to Hal, who immediately started looking through them, and Rose took the originals to her car. Rose didn't have time to even think that day, because the television reporter got there while she was locking the car.

"Hi, Rose. I'm Marty, your interviewer for today," a man in a suit said and held out his hand.

She shook it. "Hi, you must be Jane's friend."

"Yes. She helped me get this set up. You'll be all over the southeast later today. Are you excited?"

Rose laughed. "Actually, I kind of wanted to avoid all this. But since you're here, we'll make the best of it."

"I hope you're ready. Our station is everywhere here in the South. If you didn't want to be on the news, it's too late for that." He was smiling, but she thought it was already too late. She'd already agreed to the interview, and he was here, so she couldn't change her mind now. "Where can I set up?" he asked.

She looked around and pointed towards a community garden area. "We usually end up over next to the garden. It's really not a big deal, and the wedding will only take a couple of minutes."

Marty glanced over. "It's perfect." He walked towards the back of the van a few feet to find his cameraman. "Jeff, we'll set up over next to the rose bushes. I think we'll start with a quick interview." Turning back to Rose, he asked, "Where's the groom?"

"He's not here yet. I'm sure he'll be here soon. We were supposed to meet at 2:30." She looked at her watch. "It's just 2:20 now."

"Good. We've got time," Marty said, then walked off to help Jeff get everything set up.

Rose went back to where Jane, Charlotte, Leann, Luke, and Hal were waiting, but it was only a couple of minutes before Marty walked over and quietly asked her to come over for an interview. Before he got in front of the camera, he took a compact out of his back pocket and added powder to her face. "Sorry," he said. "The lights can make your face shiny. I'm not really a makeup artist, but you're lucky we have similar coloring." He was smiling and made her feel comfortable, which is probably why he had his job. As he applied the powder, he told her a few of the things he would ask. It was just the basics – questions Jane had asked the first time they met. They stepped in front of the camera, and the interview took several minutes. She was obviously nervous, but Marty stopped a couple of times and let her answer questions again. "We'll cut all this out in editing. I promise you'll look great when we put it together."

When she finally walked back to the group, Penelope and John were there. Marty took John for his interview, and Hal from Guinness was still looking through her marriage records. John's interview took less time than hers, but it was still after 3:00 by the time they were finally able to have the ceremony. This time, it was in front of Jeff's camera. Leann was amazing. She didn't even acknowledge the extra people or the fact that they were being filmed. The ceremony was perfect. John kissed Rose on the cheek when they were finished, and then he shook her hand and walked towards his car. Rose was a little surprised, but Jane told her later that it was the perfect touch, emphasizing the fact that Rose didn't really associate with her husbands during the marriages.

Marty and Jeff packed up, shaking hands all around before they left. He reminded Rose of when the segment would air and handed her a card.

Hal shook hands as well. He let them know that it would take some time for him to certify the record, but the papers seemed to be in order. He congratulated Rose on potentially breaking the record and then quietly left.

Jane was the last of the extra people to leave. They were all starting to feel comfortable around her, and Rose even collapsed on a bench with her there. "I'm so tired," she said. "This has been exhausting."

"Oh, hon, get used to it," Jane said. "I think Marty wants to film some more weddings, and he'll definitely want to be here for the last one."

"He didn't say anything about it," Rose said.

"I can tell. Just don't be surprised if he contacts you again."

They chatted for a few more minutes, and then Jane left. Rose, Luke, Leann, and Penelope met Steven for dinner a little while later. The crowded restaurant had televisions on. While they were eating, the segment about Rose aired. The server and several customers came by and asked Rose if it was her. She didn't like the attention, but Penelope encouraged her to talk to them.

They finally finished eating, and Leann took care of the check out of the earnings from the blog. When Rose got home, she was too tired to read, even though it was only 8:00. She changed into pajamas and crawled into bed, falling asleep almost as soon as her head touched the pillow.

CHAPTER 35

The next Monday, Rose didn't get much work done. The team had seen the television segment on the news, so they wanted to talk about that for a few minutes. She didn't mind; it was looking like it would be a slow day. She didn't have any meetings scheduled for once, so she thought she would have the day free for project planning, something she needed to catch up on. Elsa let her know that her cousin Jake wouldn't mind marrying her again if she needed someone else. They thought the media attention Rose was getting was exciting and all wanted to attend a wedding or two so they could be on the news, too.

The conversation took longer than she thought initially, but at least she was talking with the team a little more again. They had noticed her isolation the last few months and wanted to catch up now that she was starting to be more talkative again. They did talk about some current projects in the hour it took, so Rose didn't feel bad about taking the time.

When she got to her office, though, she had a couple of emails from the receptionist, Willa. She didn't really remember doing it, but she had mentioned where she worked during the interview. A couple of men called the main line asking how to get in touch with her. She called Willa and told her that if anyone else called, she should tell them to just go to the blog. She wasn't going to be disturbed with that topic at work. Then, she went to Jessica's office to let her know and apologize.

"It's okay, hon. We've had a couple of calls to the sales line, too. You've actually gotten us some new business. Just don't let them keep you from doing your job."

"I won't. I promise. And I'm sorry again. I hate that Willa's being bothered with it."

"I know. But I think we'll be okay."

Kenneth called her direct line that day, too, asking for status on his new projects. "We're on target," she said.

"Awesome. And I saw you on the news. I'm not going to push it, but I do want to remind you that my offer stands, including marriage and a job offer. But that's all I'm going to say. I don't want you to get in trouble, and I don't want another call from Jessica."

She hung up with him after telling him no again, as politely as possible, and tried to get back to work.

She had barely gotten started in the project planning app when Willa called. "I just wanted to ask if you want me to send reporters to the blog, too."

"Yes. If there's anything dealing with my marriages, I don't want to deal with it here." She was really starting to get annoyed. When she hung up with Willa, she closed her office door and set her phone to Do Not Disturb.

Throughout the day, several people stopped by and knocked on her door, wanting to talk about the news. It was annoying, but by 5:00, she thought he had told almost everyone in the office that if they wanted to talk about anything other than work, they'd have to talk outside of the office.

The rest of the week was better. At least not many people from the office asked her anything. Penelope said she'd had a similar problem, but she did the same thing Rose did. Willa did send her a few messages, but the calls had dropped off by the end of the week. She was glad that Jessica seemed to be understanding about it.

On Friday, Penelope met John after work to get his divorce papers and brought them to Rose's house.

"John said he's been getting about as much attention as we have. He said it's crazy. At least he's got his own office and doesn't have to explain to anyone but his assistant."

Rose was making a salad and stopped chopping vegetables to get a glass of wine. Penelope already had one, and she thought it had been long enough since she'd had anything to drink that it would be fine. "I hope it stops.

Remind me not to say anything about where we work in any more interviews."

"Yeah, that would be a good idea. I think we learned a lesson there. I can't imagine how many calls you got this week. I only got a few, but it was still annoying as hell. But on the bright side, Leann said the blog numbers have gone up. We're starting to make more money on ads, too."

"Nice," Rose said. "At least that will help cover buying these new dresses. But the next one should be a little more sane. We've got a record broken now, so it shouldn't be a big deal again until Number 30."

"True. Just six more to go, though! You're so close."

The salad was finished, and Rose was taking chicken out of the oven. She and Penelope got out plates as they talked. "Did you really think when we started that we'd get this far?"

Penelope got Italian dressing out of the refrigerator. "Actually, yeah. With my encouragement, of course!" She nudged Rose with her elbow. "You couldn't have done it without me."

"That's actually true. I mean, I would have tried anyway, but I don't know how you've found some of these guys."

They took their plates to the living room to eat while watching TV. "I was mostly joking, but seriously, it has been some work," Penelope said. "You definitely could have done the organizing, but just filing all those papers and saying 'I do' has been a lot for you. But it's been even easier lately. Jane's stuff has made these guys just fall into our laps."

"Good. Maybe it'll be easier to take care of the last few."

"I think it will," Penelope said through a bite of chicken. "I've already got most of them lined up. Joey's next, and then some guy named Arthur from the blog. Leann sent me a couple more from the blog, too. I may have to get her to do a post soon that we're full, unless you want to just keep getting married after 30."

"Hell, no!" Rose laughed. "I think 30 is plenty. The only way I'll get married again is in a few years if I need to hold onto the record."

"Sounds good. We'll talk to Leann about telling men to stop asking, then. That'll take some of the work off us, anyway."

"I know it's taken longer than we thought. It's already been two years, and we've got a few more months. But at least it's almost over. Maybe by Christmas?"

"Maybe, if things keep going as well as they have lately. Here's to a few more months of good husbands!" She held up her wine glass. Rose picked up hers and tapped Penelope's with it.

CHAPTER 36

Rose took John's divorce papers to the courthouse Monday during lunch. There was a new clerk who recognized her and wanted to talk about her marriages. She chatted for a minute to be polite, but then told the girl that she needed to get back to work and paid the fee. She picked up lunch on the way back to the office and ate at her desk.

The next day, she and Penelope went out to lunch. A couple of people in the restaurant recognized them and wanted to talk. After the second one, they asked for to-go boxes and finished their lunch in the breakroom at the office.

The divorce from John was final on July 13. That Saturday, Rose and Joey got married at Penelope's house. Jane called that Monday to ask about the next wedding and was disappointed when Rose told her it had already happened. She promised to keep her updated and invite her to the rest of them. It would annoy her a little, but she figured that there weren't many left, and they could do the rest at the park.

But she heard from Jane again sooner than she expected. Wednesday, she got a text from her: *Guinness called. It's important. Call me after work.*

So, Rose called her when she got in her car at 5:15. "What's up?"

Jane seemed exasperated. "They need the marriage certificate to Joey so you actually have the record. There's a problem."

"What kind of problem? Why would I need 25 marriages for the record?"

"Well, you don't. But there's a guy, Gary?"

Rose was turning onto the street. "Yeah. That name sounds familiar. That was a while ago."

"Gary doesn't count. He was already married."

"What? None of them were married."

"Maybe they all said they weren't, but that was part of Guinness's check. Gary was still married to his second wife. It looks like the divorce was in progress, but it wasn't actually final."

"Dammit. What do I need to do?"

"Well, Hal said Gary's really divorced now if you want to marry him again. It was final a couple of weeks after you got married. It was in another state, which is probably why the clerk's office didn't find out anything when you filed the marriage certificate. But you're on number 24 now – not 25."

By the time Rose finished talking to Jane, she was almost home. Instead of turning onto her street, she kept going and turned towards Penelope's house instead. She figured Penelope would be home by the time she got there.

She was, but barely. Penelope was just getting out of her car.

"We have a problem," Rose said before Penelope could even close her car door. She explained what Jane had told her.

They walked inside, where Penelope found Gary's number and called him. The call took about ten minutes, and part of it was Penelope basically yelling at him.

In the middle of it, Penelope muted the phone and turned to Rose. "He apologized. He said he thought it was final already, but I don't know if I believe him. He's volunteered to do it again, but that's up to you."

"Tell him he owes me the money for the filings. If he'll pay for everything this time, we'll go ahead and do it again."

Penelope unmuted the phone and put Gary on speaker so Rose could hear. By the time she finished the call, Gary was lined up to be the next husband – again – and she and Rose were both annoyed. Neither of them believed that he didn't know his divorce was final, but they just wanted to fix everything and be done with it.

Rose called Jane and they both updated her. Jane thought it would make for an excellent follow-up article, and she wanted to be at the second wedding to Gary. They agreed. Penelope called Gary again to let him know that there would be reporters there. When she got home, Rose scanned her copy of the marriage certificate she and Joey had filed at the courthouse and sent it to Jane. Jane was going to send it to Guinness so they could finish approving the record.

Thankfully, everything with Joey went well. They were divorced on August 3.

Three days later, Jane and Marty were both present at the wedding to Gary, who apologize profusely for the problems he'd caused. Before the ceremony, Jane and Marty pulled Rose, Leann, and Penelope to the side.

Jane started, "I've done some research for you. He knew it wasn't final. The papers weren't even filed until a few days before he married you. I talked to his ex-wife. They were still talking up about the divorce while he was married to you. He even told her about it."

Marty jumped in. "We have her on record telling us that he thought it was all a game. She doesn't think he really meant to do anything dishonest, but since he didn't think of it as a real marriage to you, he didn't think it mattered that he was still married to her. Please let us interview him."

"That's up to him," Leann said. "From the way he was apologizing, I think you're right that he didn't really mean any harm, though we're all pretty annoyed. Just don't be too mean to him if he lets you interview him."

"Will do," Marty said. "I'm thinking we do it as part of a group interview. He can explain, and you guys can say that you forgive him, but hate that you have to do the whole thing over. That'll make you look good, Rose, but also remind the viewers that you're serious about this. And we'll be nice to him. I promise. Jane, do you want to be on camera with me?"

"Sure."

Jane and Marty talked to Gary. They explained what they already knew, and he started apologizing again. When they told him that he could have a chance to explain on camera and make sure everyone knew it was just a mistake, he agreed. After the ceremony, they took a short break while Marty and Jeff moved some benches where they could all sit together for the interview, including Leann and Penelope. Jeff reset his equipment in the new location, and they were ready to go.

Marty introduced everyone, and then Jane started the questions. "So, Gary, it looks like this is actually the second time you've married Rose. Is that right?"

"That's right. There was a mix-up the first time, so we're having to do it over again."

"What kind of mix-up?" Jane asked him.

"Well, my divorce from my second wife wasn't final when I married Rose. I didn't think it mattered, since it was just going to be a short thing for her record. I didn't realize that I was making things difficult for her." He turned to Rose. "Again, I'm really sorry I caused you trouble. If I could do it over, I wouldn't have done it that way."

Rose answered, "That's okay, Gary. We're fixing it now."

Marty asked the next couple of questions. "Rose, how do you feel about having to repeat a marriage?"

"Well, I can't say that it's not annoying. But Gary said he's sorry about it, and he's trying to make it up to us. I'm glad we could work it out with him."

The rest of the interview went well. Gary apologized again. Jane asked Penelope and Leann how they felt about the problem with Gary. "Well, we started doing more thorough background checks after the original wedding with Gary," Penelope said. "If we had started them sooner, we'd have caught this before it became a problem. I'm glad we learned our lesson, though. This just means it'll take a few more weeks for Rose to break the record, but like Rose, I'm glad we could work it out."

Jane turned to Leann, "I agree with Rose and Penelope, and I think we all accept Gary's apology. I can see how he could make the mistake, but now he knows that everything has to be perfectly legal."

Jane turned back to Rose, "You've broken a world record! What do you think of that?"

Rose replied, "Well, if not for their checks, we wouldn't know that I needed to marry Gary again. And we're still waiting for them to approve the record, so it's not official yet, but it feels great."

Marty asked Rose, "You're now on your 25th marriage, so you have six left. How do you feel being so close to the second record you wanted to break?"

Rose laughed. Since this was her second time interviewing on camera with Marty, she was starting to get a little more comfortable with it. "I can't wait for it to be over. In the beginning, it was just going to be fun, but it's turned out to be more work than we thought. I'll be relieved when we're finished in a few months."

"I know that Jane and I love being here when you get married. Are you going to let us be here for the other six?"

"Sure. If you want to be here, you can."

"Is there anything else any of you would like to say before we finish up here?"

Everyone shook their heads to tell him no.

Marty turned to the camera. "Okay, folks. You heard it from her. We'll be here through the rest of Rose's journey to break the record, updating you along the way. I don't know if the others will have a twist like this one, but I'm sure you're just as excited as we are to be here with Rose, Leann, and Penelope as they work towards this goal. Only six left, and we can't wait to be here for every one of them!"

With that, Jeff turned off the camera and started packing up. The girls shook hands with Gary, and he left.

"I think that was good," Marty said when he was gone. "And I'm glad you brought up that you've started doing more background checks. That'll keep anyone else from trying to do the same thing."

Jane also let the girls know that she'd been contacted by some other reporters who wanted to know how to get in touch with them. "One paper out of New York said they'd tried to contact you at work, but you never called them back."

"Yeah," Rose said. "I had the receptionist tell anyone who called not to call there. I'm trying to work, and it's not the place to talk to me about getting married."

"Who do I send them to, or do you want me to just handle it? I don't mind, though I kind of like Marty and me having exclusive access to your weddings." She laughed as she said the last part.

"If you could handle it, I think that would be awesome," Penelope said. "I think we're all starting to get a little overwhelmed. Leann's having trouble keeping up with the comments and messages on the blog."

"Hire someone," Marty said.

"I don't think we can afford to do that," Leann answered. "I mean, we're making some money on ads, but not enough to hire anyone."

"If you get the right person doing it, maybe someone who can handle publicity, too, it'll be worth it. You'll start making more on ads, and maybe they can get you some speaking gigs, too. You may be able to make more money."

Rose didn't really want anyone else involved unless it was absolutely necessary. "We'll hold off on that. In the meantime, I think that Penelope and I will just jump in and help Leann. Or at least me. Penelope may have her hands full getting weddings set up."

"We'll all help," Penelope said. "Most of the weddings are set except the actual dates, and those depend on how long the divorces take."

"If you need help, just let me know," Jane said. "If I'm on the inside, I'll just have more material for updates."

They agreed to let her know if they needed any more help, but they would handle it themselves as long as they could. It didn't take long for Marty and Jeff to finish packing up equipment, and they wanted to get the interview on air in the next couple of days, so they left.

Jane offered to take the girls to dinner, but they all wanted to get home and rest. It had been a long day. Rose wasn't really that tired, but she wanted to go home anyway. She'd had enough of people for the week and just wanted to curl up with a book and pretend the outside world didn't exist for the rest of the weekend.

Guinness called Jane on August 8. The record was official: Rose was the woman who had been married the most times. She would be included on their web site and in the next record book. There would also be a press release. Jane wrote another article and tried again to get a comment from the original recordholder, but she didn't want to be disturbed. She was finished with that record and didn't want anything to do with it, not even a comment about her record being broken.

Jane also looked into contacting the man with the most marriages. She wanted to see how he felt about someone being so close to breaking his record. Unfortunately, he had passed away several years before. His family wished Rose luck, but they didn't want to be involved, either.

Gary signed the papers on August 11, which was a Thursday. Rose went to the courthouse to file them the next day, the same day Jane's new article was published. It was also the same day she got a call on her cell phone from a television station in New York. They wanted her to fly there to be on a national television show, and they would pay her to be on it, plus pay for her travel expenses. She politely refused, letting them know that she couldn't take off work. They promised to find her a spot if she changed her mind and congratulated her on beating the record.

Rose was officially divorced from Gary, really this time, on August 24.

CHAPTER 37

Rose and Penelope started helping Leann take care of questions on the blog. They stopped keeping track of how many followers they had, but the number was steadily growing. Penelope took care of questions from men who wanted to be husbands, and Rose took over replying to reporters. There would be an additional two television stations and three reporters at the next wedding. One of the three reporters was Will, Husband Number 10. Originally, he was Husband Number 11, but they'd had to change most of the numbers after the debacle with Gary. She called him to chat about his article instead of just replying to his message. After his article, the newspaper that published it had hired him. He told her he was sorry that he didn't tell her what he was doing when they got married, but thanked her for helping him to get his first job out of college. He told her that it was a great job, and he wouldn't have gotten it if not for the article about her. He'd been doing some human-interest stories, but hadn't let him do a follow-up on her yet. After she actually broke one record, they finally let him work on her story again.

Penelope scheduled the next wedding for another Saturday, August 27. The man was another one from the blog, so the three girls met with him the night before. His name was Jeremy, and he was actually a reporter from the girls' hometown. He had moved there a few years ago because he got a job at the local paper. He, like Will, wanted to get the story from the husband's side. The girls were fine with it. Rose was starting to get used to the attention. She still didn't love it, but it was just part of her life for the moment, so she went with it.

It was raining that Saturday, so Penelope found them one of the smaller covered picnic areas for the wedding. It worked out pretty well. There was just enough room for everyone.

The girls caught up with Will before the ceremony. He was excited to be back and asked if he could cover all the weddings. They looked at Jane, who nodded. She didn't mind. His paper was smaller, and she already had the coverage from readers that she needed. She was also on the inside, because she and the girls had gotten pretty comfortable with each other.

All of the reporters wanted to do an interview, so they did it all at once. Jane helped coordinate. She and Marty acted as the primary reporters, which was good for them, and pointed everyone else as to where they could set up. They helped the girls and Jeremy field questions from the other reporters. Jeremy did let everyone know that he would be doing his own article. They asked questions about what he planned to include, but he wouldn't give any details.

The next few days were even more hectic than usual for the girls. It seemed that reporters were really good at finding phone numbers. They all had to turn their cell phones off at work, and Will was busier at the front desk than she'd been. She begged Jessica to get her some help answering the phones and complained to Rose, who apologized again.

Jessica did get in touch with the temp agency they used someone and started the process of hiring someone to help Willa. Wednesday afternoon, she called Rose into her office to let her know.

"That's good. Again, I'm so sorry. I had no idea this would happen," Rose said.

"I know you didn't, and that's what makes this so hard," Jessica replied.

"What do you mean?"

"Well, we can't keep working like this. You're still definitely doing what you're supposed to be doing, and you're amazing at your job, but Willa's going crazy with all the calls. There have been reporters showing up, too. I can't have that. I'm going to have to let you go."

"But you said everything was fine."

"I said that it was all fine as long as it didn't affect the workplace. And it's doing it now. I saw how many reporters were at your last wedding. I'm happy for you, and I'm glad you're getting to your goal. We've even gotten a few new accounts, but I can't keep dealing with all this. These reporters are asking my employees questions, catching them as they're leaving the building. I'm surprised you haven't noticed."

"I haven't," Rose replied. "They must not be watching the door I use."

"That's good for you, but I've got to do something. I hate it. When this all dies down, I'd be happy to hire you again, but for now, I think it's best if we can just tell them you don't work here anymore so we can get our jobs done."

"What am I supposed to do?"

"Well, I'm giving you a severance package. Legally, I don't really have to, but I think you deserve it. You've been here forever, and it's not like you've actively tried to disrupt business. I'm paying you for the next three months. That should be enough time for you to figure out what you can do and maybe even for everything to die down."

"Why can't I just work quietly from home? We can tell people I don't work here anymore, and that wouldn't really be a lie if I'm not physically in the building."

Jessica did consider it for a few seconds. "I'd like to, but I think it's better if you just don't work for me for now. I'm sorry, Rose, but this is really what's best for the company. You can take the rest of the afternoon to pack your personal things and even meet with your team. I'll be handling managing them for now. Do you have a recommendation on who can help me? I'll give them a promotion to team leader or supervisor or something. I'll wait a little bit to hire another manager. Hopefully things will calm down and I can hire you back later."

"Bianca, I guess. She's caught up on everything and is the best developer."

Jessica nodded. "Good choice."

"What about Penelope? Is her job safe?"

"Penelope's fine. They're mostly not calling for her. I think things will be quieter after you leave. Again, I hate it, but it's my decision."

And that was the end of it. Rose went to her office and packed up. She texted Penelope and Leann. Then, she met with her team and let them know what was happening. They wanted to meet her for lunch soon, so they decided to get in touch the next week. When the day was almost over, Rose went back to Jessica's office. She signed papers, Jessica made copies for her, and they hugged before Rose handed over her key card and badge and walked out with her boxes.

Leann and Penelope were waiting in the yard when she got home. Jessica had let Penelope leave a little early, because she knew they'd want to talk.

"Guys, what am I going to do?" Rose asked as they helped her get the boxes out of the trunk.

"Jessica said she gave you some severance?" Penelope asked.

"Yeah. Three months. I've got that long to find another job."

"Maybe you'll go back?" Penelope asked. "Jessica talked to me for a while this afternoon."

"Do you really think I want to go back? I love the people there, but she just fired me. I mean, I understand why, but I don't know if I want to go back after that."

Leann spoke up. "Maybe work for Kenneth? I'll bet that job's still open."

Rose balanced a box on her hip to unlock the front door. "I don't think so. He might try to get me to marry him as a condition. Besides, he'd probably make me deal with Jessica or the other people at the agency. I really don't want to. I mean, you," she looked at Penelope, "wouldn't be a problem, but if they don't have to deal directly with him, I'd bet other people would do the meetings."

Rose dropped her box next to the entertainment center, and the other girls gently set theirs down next to it. Rose walked over to close the door.

Leann said, "Well, it might be time to call those people in New York back. You can do that talk show now."

"Did I even tell you about that?" Rose asked.

"No, but they sent a message through the blog page the other day. They said the offer still stands."

The girls chatted for a while and then decided to order Chinese for dinner. Penelope got online with her phone and placed the order.

The next morning, Rose called the show in New York. They said they would make arrangements for her to fly in the next Tuesday and do the show Wednesday. She wanted at least one of the girls to go with her, and the station said they would take care of expenses, but Leann couldn't get off work, and Penelope didn't want to do anything to affect her job considering what had just happened. Rose completely understood.

This was something she wished she could talk to Matt about. The girls were at work and couldn't talk much during the day, and so was Luke. She thought about calling Kurt. He had been hanging out with them some, and he and Leann were going great, but she didn't really know him well enough to whine to him about her life. Just after lunch, she decided that losing her job was grounds for a little afternoon drinking, so she dug out the bottle of rum that she hadn't touched in a couple of months and had a few drinks. She did, however, at least use a glass and mixed it with Diet Coke.

CHAPTER 38

It had been a couple of months since Rose was as depressed as she was for the rest of that week. She didn't have work to keep her busy. She did create profiles on some job sites and applied for a few positions, but there wasn't much open in her field right then. She knew she had some time, so she did what she could every morning and drank again in the afternoon. Every time she got out the bottle, she knew she shouldn't, but she also knew that she needed to have something to do.

Jeremy mailed the divorce papers to her, and she got them Saturday. She signed them and put them in her purse so she could take them to be filed Monday morning. As she was leaving the courthouse, she got a call from one of the companies she'd applied to.

"Hi! Yes, this is Rose."

"My name is Yolanda. We received your application for the lead web developer position. I was wondering if you have time for a few questions."

"Sure."

"Why did you leave your last employer?"

"Ummm…I got laid off."

"Okay. I hate to ask, but are you the same Rose Wilson who I've seen on the news?"

Rose hesitated, but she knew she needed to tell the truth. She just hoped Yolanda wasn't going to ask about her record. "Yes, I am."

"Did that have anything to do with the layoff?"

Rose sighed. "Yes."

"Thank you for your time, Ms. Wilson. I hate to say this, but I think this isn't the best time for you to interview with us."

"Thanks," Rose said and hung up.

Well, that was two employers who didn't want her working for them because of her project. She went home and applied for some more jobs before packing for her trip to New York. At least they were going to pay her to be on the show, so that was something. It was a few hundred dollars, plus she didn't have to pay for her trip. She had to keep receipts for anything she spent, and they would reimburse her.

Her flight left the next morning just before lunch and only took a couple of hours. She did have some fun in New York, and that made her especially wish the girls could be there with her. She went sightseeing a little by herself before she met with the producer at the television show. His name was Alex, and he was all over the place. She knew he had to be good at his job to be working on the show, but he was so bubbly and talked so quickly that she had to concentrate to follow him. All of the questions they wanted to ask were the same ones she'd answered several times before, so that would be easy. She was supposed to be at the station at 4:30 A.M. – which sounded horrible to her – so they could do makeup and hair before she had her interview. He led her to a dressing room and knocked on the door. "Come in," a voice called.

Nancy, the show's host, was reading some papers. She seemed to be annoyed by the interruption. "So Alex has filled you in on the timeline and what kinds of questions I'll ask?" she asked.

"Yes," Rose replied. "I'm really excited to be on."

"I'm sure you are," Nancy said. "And we're happy to have you." Though, Rose, thought, she didn't really look or act like she was happy that Rose was there. In fact, she didn't seem to care much at all, as she kept glancing back at her papers while they talked.

"Great. So is there anything you want to know before tomorrow?"

"No. Alex sent me a report that has everything I need. Good to meet you. Alex can show you out, and I'll talk to you in the morning." She gave the papers her full attention. After they didn't move for a few seconds, she waved to them, basically telling them to get out.

As they walked away from the dressing room, Alex kept talking. "She's busy, but she did want to meet you. Don't worry. She's not as bitchy as she seems."

Rose didn't believe that. She'd watched the show a couple of times after she agreed to do the interview, so she knew that Nancy would be friendlier on the show, but it was hard to believe that the woman really cared about her being there. It didn't matter, though. She was there and had agreed to do the interview, so she would. Jane had thought it was an excellent idea and promised she'd be watching. Alex talked for a few more minutes and then escorted her to the front door where he had a car waiting to take her back to the hotel.

She really tried to go to sleep in the hotel room that night, but ended up falling asleep only after taking a couple of bottles from the minibar. It was still almost 11 when she finally fell asleep. That was early for her, but pretty late considering she needed to get up at 3:30 in order to get dressed and be at the television station on time.

She barely made it, showing up right at 4:30. Alex met her in the lobby and walked her to a dressing room, where people helped her with her hair and makeup. They even made it look like she'd actually had a decent night's sleep. She was happy with how she looked.

She didn't see Nancy again until she walked on the stage and sat down. The woman was super friendly on air. Rose was almost bored with answering the same questions yet again, but figured that she would have to just deal with it. She managed to keep a smile the whole time. Jane told her later that she was perfect.

After the show, they ran into Nancy when Alex was walking her down the hall. Nancy was just as uninterested in Rose as she had been the day before. She said the right things, like "It was great to have you on the show," but the excitement and approachability she showed on air were completely gone.

Rose went back to the hotel and packed, ready for the airport. Alex had arranged for another car to take her. By the time Rose got on the flight home that afternoon, she was exhausted. She tried to nap on the flight, but people were talking too much, so she read a book she'd brought instead. When they landed, Leann, Penelope, and Jane had all left messages for her. She called them back, one by one, on the way home. They all said basically the same thing, that she was great on the interview and were looking forward to seeing her again after she was rested.

She hung up with Jane just as she was throwing her bag onto her bed. She went to the kitchen and poured a glass of rum. She looked at the clock. 4:40. She'd been awake for almost 13 hours, which really wasn't that long, but she felt like she'd been awake for days. She drank her rum and went to bed without bothering with dinner. It's not like she had anything else to do anyway.

CHAPTER 39

The next morning, Rose woke up to her phone ringing. It was 8:30. She quickly calculated that she'd actually gotten over 15 hours of uninterrupted sleep before she even looked for her phone. She had to get up, because it was still in her purse in the kitchen. It looked like the same number had already called once that morning, and she didn't recognize it. She answered sleepily.

"Good morning, Rose," a male voice said.

"Ummm...good morning?"

He heard the question in her voice. "It's Kenneth."

"Oh, hi Kenneth. What can I do for you?"

"I won't keep you long. Jessica told me what happened. I'm sorry you got laid off."

"Yeah, me, too," she said. She waited. There had to be a reason he was calling other than to tell her that.

"I just wanted to let you know that my offer still stands if you need a job. You don't even have to marry me."

"Thanks, Kenneth. I'll think about it."

"You do that. If you work for me, I'll just pay you what I've been paying the agency for all this web site work. It'll be easier anyway."

"Thank you," she said.

Kenneth seemed to want to talk a little more, but she was still half asleep. "I'm sorry, Kenneth," she said. "I'm just now waking up. Can I think about it and get back to you later?"

"Sure. Just keep me in mind. Or let me know if you want to do some contract work, even. Have a good day."

She hung up. At least there was that. She had a job if she wanted to work for Kenneth. She didn't, but it was there if she couldn't find anything else. She started coffee and got her laptop out, determined to apply for every web development job she could find. She spent the morning doing that and then got out the rum after lunch. As a lazy unemployed slacker, she felt that afternoon drinking wasn't a big deal.

Over the next couple of weeks, she did get several calls about her resume, and she went to two interviews. All of them knew who she was. One of the hiring managers just wanted to talk about her record. There weren't any real interview questions at all. The other interview was with the owner of a small marketing agency. They'd just lost their one web developer and needed another one. She thought the interview went well, but she got a call a couple of days later that they were going with another candidate, and it was because they'd talked to Jessica. They didn't want the same problems that had happened there.

Rose was starting to get worried that she wouldn't be able to find anything else at all. She kept applying, but everyone she actually got to talk to had concerns about how her now very public project would affect their business.

The divorce with Jeremy was final on September 15. That night, she was talking to Penelope and told her how frustrated she was getting with the job search.

"You've still got a couple of months of severance. That'll help. Maybe something will work out before then. But that reminds me. Joey called me yesterday. I completely forgot. He found out from somebody here what happened. He said to tell you that if you're interested in contract work, he needs someone to do some quick work on his web site."

"Yes!" Rose shouted. "You know, Kenneth suggested contracting when I wouldn't answer him about the job. That's actually a good idea. It won't affect their businesses, and it's something I can mostly do from home."

"So do you want me to tell your ex to call you?"

"Oh, God, yes. I need some work. I'm going crazy sitting here. I've gotten some calls from reporters, but I can't get a job right now to save my life."

Rose got a call from Joey the next day. He told her everything he wanted done as she looked at the existing web site. She promised to work up a quote for him and hung up. She started estimating right away. She figured she could use the same rates as the agency, because she knew them and knew that they were a good average. It only took a couple of hours for her to get together an estimate and send it to Joey. He replied that he'd see if he could work it into his budget and let her know by Monday.

Saturday, they repeated the media-filled event at the park. Even though it wasn't raining, they used the picnic area again. This time, Rose married a man named Arthur. He was older and retired from owning several businesses of his own, but was a perfect gentleman. He was a widower and thought it would be fun to marry a young woman for a little bit. He was great in front of the cameras, telling the reporters that he was lucky to marry a pretty young woman like Rose. He gave her a gentle kiss on the cheek before he left, promising to send her divorce papers on time.

Monday morning, she got a call from Joey. He was ready for her to start and would send her a contract to sign. She was glad he had thought about a contract, because she hadn't. She figured that she should probably do some research on what she needed to do for contract projects. That afternoon, she signed Joey's contract and started work. She felt better knowing that she had something to do, and she didn't drink that afternoon.

Rose took some time the next morning to do a little research on what she needed to do. After a couple of hours, she picked up the phone and called Crissy. They made an appointment for her to come in later that week to talk about contract work as well as figure out what she, Leann, and Penelope needed to do for their business earnings. She figured it would be better to figure it all out at once, and it was easier for her to do it now than to drag Leann and Penelope along.

That week, she got the basics done for Joey and sent them for his approval. He had someone working on the copy to add to the pages and would send that to her the following week.

The meeting with Crissy took a while, but Crissy had blocked off all of

Wednesday afternoon. She wanted to ask about the marriage project, too, so she made sure she had plenty of time and charged Rose only a flat rate for the consultation. By the end of the day, Rose had all the information she needed and tons of papers. Crissy even sent her a standard contract that she could use for her clients. She'd build her own web page and start doing a little marketing for her own web development business. If nothing else, it would at least keep her busy.

She also scheduled a morning show in Atlanta. It was the same deal as the one in New York. They'd take care of any expenses and pay her a little for being on the show. It wasn't a lot, and there wouldn't be expenses other than driving down, but it was something.

Thursday evening, she got a call from Penelope. "Hey. Don't bother sending divorce papers to Arthur."

"Why?"

"I just got a call from his daughter. She's going to have her lawyer call you. He passed away yesterday."

"Wait, what?" Rose screamed. "What happened?"

Penelope was matter-of-fact, but Rose knew that she really felt pretty sympathetic for Arthur's family. "I'm not completely sure. His daughter said it happened while he was taking a nap yesterday. She was there. It was in his sleep, and it was something she wasn't surprised about."

"Okay," Rose said. "But why do I need to talk to a lawyer?"

"Well, he didn't tell us, but apparently he's got a lot of money. Some big house and a lot of stock in the business he still owned. She basically wants to beg you not to take everything."

"Huh?"

"Well, you are married to him. As his wife, legally you probably could take it."

"I don't want his money."

"It's a lot, Rose. I looked him up before I called you. The man had millions."

"Still don't want it. Did she give you the lawyer's number?"

"No. She wanted yours, though. I hope that's okay. She said he'll call tomorrow. I'll talk to Steven when I get home and see if there's anything he thinks you need to do."

A couple of hours later, Steven called. He told her that all she'd have to do is sign some papers waiving her right to any inheritance. It should be pretty simple, and he'd be happy to look over everything before she signed it. As far as her record, she'd probably need to wait until she had a death certificate before she could get married again, just to be safe.

Arthur's lawyer called the next day. It was as simple as Steven had said, after she explained that she wasn't looking for anything from Arthur. He said that was good, because Arthur's children were willing to fight her in court over it. He'd send over some papers for her to sign and would make sure she had a certified copy of the death certificate.

The show in Atlanta went well, and the host, Jay, was much nicer off-air than Nancy in New York had been. He asked some questions about her latest husband, and Rose told him that, though she didn't know him well, she was very saddened because of the way the marriage ended. Jay had done his research and knew that Arthur was wealthy. She told him that she didn't want anything, and that the lawyers were handling all of that. His children seemed kind, and she had already promised not to try to take anything from his estate.

It took until October 12 to get the papers signed, get a death certificate, and have everything in order so that Rose could get married again. She got herself in a good routine during that time, though.

Rose had her web site up and was doing some marketing online. She had one new client and was almost finished with her work for Joey. Thanks to Crissy's help, she had filed the appropriate paperwork to have her own business name, had the new client sign the right contracts, and felt hopeful about the new business. Crissy also advised her to get at least half of the money upfront, which she did as a deposit. She was excited about her new venture and let Kenneth know that she was going into business for herself and was hoping she didn't need his job offer.

CHAPTER 40

On October 15, Rose married a man named Doug. He said he'd been following the blog for almost two years and finally got his chance to marry her. He wanted to ask a million questions about her marriages and especially about Arthur. She wouldn't talk much about him, telling him that it was all on the blog. She didn't keep many secrets.

There were even more reporters at her wedding to Doug, which helped her avoid most of his questions. It was easy to deflect him nicely when reporters were also asking questions. After the reporters started packing up, she tried to find him to apologize if she seemed rude, but Penelope told her he'd already left. Oh, well. There was nothing she could do about that now.

She booked some more shows, another one in Atlanta and one in Los Angeles. She was getting closer to reaching her goal, and people seemed to want to meet with her more and more. She only had two left. She thought maybe it would get easier towards the end, but everything seemed to be more hectic than ever. Penelope had the last two arranged and was having to constantly tell others that she was booked up, and Rose was getting more calls from reporters in addition to trying to start her freelance business. She was starting to feel a little overwhelmed, but knew it would be over soon, and they were starting to make a decent amount of money from her appearances and the ads on the blog. She and the girls finally decided to hire someone to answer questions and help them with scheduling and other assorted tasks. Jane quickly suggested Alice, a sweet girl who was a senior in college. She was majoring in journalism and interning at the paper where Jane worked. Jane thought she would be amazing for them, and she thought she'd be willing to work for a reasonable wage. The next day, Jane called and told Rose that Alice was excited about the opportunity and would love to meet with them.

The girls met Alice and Jane over coffee and went through everything she would need to do. Alice gave them some ideas on publicity, too, and Jane agreed with most of them. They found out after only a couple of days that Alice was as wonderful as Jane said. She booked three more talk shows for Rose, and when Leann went to check the blog, there was nothing for her to do except post what she'd written.

Rose didn't have to send Doug any papers to sign. On October 20, a couple of days before she would be sending him the standard divorce agreement, there was a knock on her door.

She answered it, and there was a young man standing there. "Hi. Are you Rose Wilson?"

"Yes," she answered.

"I'm serving you with divorce papers from Douglas Ambrose."

"I'm sorry?" she said. He didn't answer, but handed her a manila envelope and walked away.

She opened the envelope. It was divorce papers. She read through it and laughed. It said that Doug would get half of all her assets. She knew from talking to Steven that it was ridiculous; unless she had lied to him, it was almost impossible for him to take anything from her. There was nothing to take, anyway. She didn't even have a job at the moment, and her web development business was just getting started. There was a little money from the blog and show appearances, but she really didn't have much for him to try to take. This was just another road bump she'd have to get through.

When she called Steven, he confirmed what she already thought. She would need to get Jim involved again. Steven didn't want to handle some man wanting to take all of her nonexistent assets. Penelope said she would try to call Doug and see what was going on, but it was only a few minutes later that she called back.

"He's an ass," she said. "He thinks you inherited money from Arthur. I tried to tell him you didn't, but I guess they didn't cover that in the press well enough. He refused to listen. Said that if you can make money from a one-week marriage, so can he. He hung up on me."

Rose called Jim's office. He had a cancellation the next day, so she took the appointment.

"My best client," he said, extending his hand, as she walked through the door. He was waiting for her next to the receptionist's desk. "I haven't had anyone use me for as many divorces as you."

She shook his hand. "And you've only handled four of them. The rest were too easy for you."

"Or you just didn't want to pay my fees for a simple divorce, and I don't blame you." He led her into his office, closing the door behind them. "Joann tells me you're having problems with Husband Number 50 or whatever he is."

She laughed. "28. I've only got two left when this one is done. Assuming you can help me get it over with."

"What's this guy's problem? Doesn't want to divorce you like the last one I helped you with?"

"No. We have a different problem this time. He wants to talk about assets and everything. We had a verbal agreement about that, and it's in emails how things go, but of course he's trying it anyway." She pulled the divorce papers out of her purse and reached across the desk to give them to Jim. He started chuckling soon after he started reading.

Jim couldn't stop laughing. When he finally finished, he had a question. "So, he's asking for half of everything you have. What do you have?"

"Basically nothing. I even lost my job a couple of weeks ago." She explained about the situation with Arthur and what Doug thought, that she was taking an inheritance, even though she'd signed it away. "I really don't want to have to go to court, but do you think a judge would give him anything anyway?"

"Absolutely not. I don't know of any judge that would. You never even lived together, if what I remember from your little project is right. A marriage of less than a week doesn't usually entitle the spouse to anything. This is one where we could potentially work out an annulment since it seems that he

196

married you just to try to take money, but I don't think it's worth even that." He pushed a button on his phone. "Joann?"

"Yes, Jim?"

"I've got some papers I need you to copy for me. And find the number of the attorney listed on them. I'm going to need to make a call for Miss Rose."

Joann walked in a moment later and took the papers from Jim without a sound. While she was gone, he talked to Rose about the plan.

"No court if possible, right?"

"Right. I'm so close to finishing this project, and I don't want to draw it out any more than I absolutely have to. I wanted to be finished by Christmas, and it takes about a month for each marriage. Unless you can get this fixed up in the next few days, Christmas isn't going to happen."

"It's possible, but not likely. It depends on how serious he is. His attorney probably knows he can't get much, if anything. When Joann gets me the number, I'll call and see what I can figure out from this guy. If we can't work something out over the phone, I'll see what we need to do next. Probably mediation. It'll be just a regular divorce if his attorney can't talk him out of this nonsense."

It didn't take long for Joann to come back. She gave Rose her original paperwork and gave the copy to Jim, along with a paper that had the attorney's phone number. He started dialing before Joann got out of the room.

"Hi, I need to speak to Erica Mulder, please. This is the attorney for Rose Wilson, who Erica's client Doug is suing for divorce."

Erica must not have been very busy, because Jim was able to talk to her right away. Rose tried to listen in, but Jim didn't use the speaker, and most of it was simple, one-word answers. The only thing she knew for sure is that he explained to her what Rose already knew. The marriage was for record-breaking purposes only, and Rose did not get an inheritance from Arthur or any money from any of her now-28 husbands.

Jim looked at her when he got off the phone. "She didn't believe me. Said that they weren't dropping it. She wants all your financial records from the last two years. She also said that if you don't want to go through all the hassle, her client will take a settlement of $100,000."

Rose laughed, "As if I have anywhere near that much."

"Oh, I know. Just thought I'd tell you. I'm going to file an answer with the court. We've got thirty days, but I'll get it in early next week. I've got a hearing in that courthouse Tuesday, so I can just take the answer to the judge while I'm there. Maybe I can get him to make it quick, but I'm not going to guarantee anything. I'll go ahead and tell you to plan on this being a long, drawn-out process. It could end up being worse than that last one I took care of for you. The end result will be that he gets nothing, but it could come down to the court going through all your financials and everything. It's not likely, but possible."

She wrote a check for his retainer and left, praying that he could get it taken care of much quicker than that worst-case scenario.

CHAPTER 41

Rose spent the weekend hanging out with Leann and the kids. She decided to just stay there Saturday night, not because they were drinking too much, but she figured that way she wouldn't drink. She had been drinking most nights since Jessica fired her, and she didn't want to get back into the same routine she'd been in earlier that year. She knew she would only have maybe one drink if she stayed with Leann because the kids were there, so that's what she did.

"I'm glad you're staying here, and I know why. That drink in your hand is it for the night, right?"

Rose didn't think anyone knew about her recent drinking. "Yeah. How'd you know?"

"I know you better than you think. It's not really that I noticed you'd been drinking, but I know how you deal with problems sometimes and had a strong suspicion. You've had that job through almost 30 husbands. I'm sure getting fired is worse than any breakup."

"Pretty much. But I think it's okay. My freelancing is starting out pretty well, and you know how many talk show appearances Alice has me signed up for. What Jessica did may actually be for the best for me. I've got so much more freedom now. I didn't know that it was even possible."

Leann was happy for her. "Well, if you ever need it, I can schedule you for a few shifts at the store. I think I told you that before, but if not, I'm saying it now. I'm glad working for yourself is going well, though. And about the talk shows, I have a surprise for you."

"Oh?"

"That one in Huntsville? Penelope and I are coming with you!"

"Really? Isn't that one months away?"

"It's not until February. Alice and I already talked about it and arranged it with the station. Penelope said they're still getting a lot of calls about you at the agency, but they should definitely stop in the next few weeks. She'll ask for the vacation time then. She's sure it won't be a problem, and I've already arranged to make sure I have those days off, and Brent said he's good with the kids that week. Alice said the show figures you'll have the record broken by then. They want to be among the first on your schedule after you break it. It'll be fun. We can make it a long weekend. Maybe see the Space and Rocket Center there or something."

"Sounds perfect. A vacation would be amazing. You know it's been at least a couple of years since I took one, and even longer since we've done a girls' trip?"

"That's exactly why we decided to go. Plus, the talk show will be paying at least part of the expenses, so it'll cost us less. Perfect trip! It's not the beach or anything, but sooo much better than just sitting at home while you're doing all this traveling."

"Yay!" Rose shouted.

"Shh. The kids," Leann whispered, but then started giggling with Rose.

"Well, are you going to break the record by February, do you think?"

Rose filled her in on her conversation with Jim. She hadn't done that yet. She'd been too busy with finishing up a web site to really talk to either of the girls. "So, I have no idea. Jim's hopeful, but it really just depends on how much of an ass Doug is. I can't believe he thinks I took millions from Arthur."

"Don't you have a show appearance next week?"

"I do. It's another one in Atlanta. Same area, different station."

"Talk about Doug's stupidity. Call it something else, though. It really is stupid, but you don't want to call him anything like that on the air. But make sure to make it public, and make sure to call him out by name. It'll get you sympathy, and maybe he'll just drop it. I'm sure he'll start getting all kinds of calls from reporters after you do it."

"Oh, that's an awesome idea! I'll ask Jim about it when he calls me back.

The show's not until Thursday, so I've got plenty of time."

Jim called Tuesday afternoon and let her know that he was able to talk to the judge when she was finished with sessions for the day. She didn't promise anything, but after his brief explanation of the situation, agreed that it sounded pretty ridiculous. She had her clerk file his answer to Doug's papers and told Jim that she'd get to it as soon as possible.

Rose told him about Leann's suggestion, and he thought it was perfect. "Just make sure you stick to the facts. Don't add your opinion, and don't say anything that isn't absolutely true. Basically, you married him with the same agreement as all these other husbands, and he served you with papers asking for half of everything you have. Don't call him names. Don't speculate about what he was thinking. You don't want him suing for defamation of character or slander. The truth is fine, but if you go even a tiny bit off from the simple facts, he could at least try to sue. And absolutely do not talk about what we're doing on our end. Just that we've filed an answer."

"And if they ask how I feel about it?"

"Hurt, betrayed, maybe even frustrated. It's the truth. Just don't go into more detail than that. You want the media to do their own digging. If they publish an opinion about what he's doing, that's on them, but don't give them yours to use."

So that was settled. Rose also called Jane and let her in on the plan, making her promise not to publish anything about Doug until after she was on the show. Leann had already published a blog that just said that they were having problems with the divorce with Doug, but she didn't want to go into much detail yet anyway. She didn't want him to read it and find out that Rose even had a lawyer, much less what Jim was doing about it.

Thursday went perfectly. Rose arrived at the TV station at 6:00, thirty minutes earlier than they'd asked her to. The host, Richard, was happy to talk to her while he was going over his notes for the morning. She gave him the basics of the situation.

"This is perfect," he said. "And I get to break it this morning?"

"Yes. I wanted to see what my lawyer could do before I said much to anyone else about it. There's a reporter who has an article ready, but she's not publishing it until just after we talk this morning."

"You are amazing for letting me have this. It'll be great for ratings. And you said you don't want to go into a lot of detail, right?"

"Right."

He smiled mischievously. She decided right then that he was her favorite talk show host. "I'll take care of anything rude about the man. You could say something about how you're not judging him for it, but you want it to be over. He's not going to try to sue me for slander, and if he does, the station has good lawyers. But you'll look sweet and innocent, and you'll make it clear that you're not giving your opinion about him."

They couldn't talk much after that, because the show's producer came to take her to get ready. Richard was amazing on the show, though. She walked out when he announced her, and they waited until the audience died down.

"Rose, you're on Husband Number 28 now, right?"

"Yes."

"You're so close to breaking the record. I know you have it all on the blog, and some of my colleagues have covered it on shows and everything, but how many problems have you had along the way?"

Rose was pleased at how quickly he started bringing up the subject. "Only a few. I had one husband early on who didn't want to divorce me, and another who unfortunately died before we could sign the papers. There have been a couple who wanted to make the marriages more than we agreed, but overall, everything has gone pretty smoothly. My friends Penelope and Leann have been amazing at making sure everything works out the way it should."

"And are you currently married?"

"I am."

"What's his name?"

"Douglas Ambrose. He's from the Atlanta area."

"Do you think he's watching?"

"I have no idea. You know I don't really talk to them very much. It's a thing, keeps it professional."

"I understand that. And how do you think the divorce with Douglas will go?"

Rose looked down for a second before she answered. "I'm not sure, Richard. He filed his own agreement with the court before we signed the standard agreement I have. He's asking for more than we talked about before we got married."

Richard expressed the appropriate concern, and the audience gasped. "What do you mean? What's he asking for?"

"He wants half of everything I have."

The audience gasped again. Rose was sure that there was probably something telling them what reaction to have, but it was perfect. She was sure that Jim would be pleased.

Richard lightly touched her arm in sympathy. "After he agreed that there wouldn't be any kind of exchange or payments?"

"That's right," she said softly.

"And how long were you married when you were served with his papers?"

"Less than a week."

The audience gasped again. "What kind of crazy person would do that?" Richard asked. "It sounds like he's completely ignoring the agreement."

"I can't speak about his mental state. I have no idea. I just know that I have an attorney, and he's doing what he needs to do."

"But this is costing you extra money for the attorney, too, right?"

"Yes."

Richard still had his hand on her arm. He removed it. "Do you think this man will actually be able to take any of your money?"

"I really don't know. That's all up to the lawyers. I just want it over."

"Of course you do. So Douglas Ambrose, Husband Number 28, is just in it for whatever money he thinks he might be able to take. He sounds like a jerk. What do you think, audience?" He turned to the audience, and they all shouted. She heard things like "jerk," "asshole," and "gold digger." She made sure she didn't smile as she looked out at the audience, but she was happy about how it was going. She wanted to join them in shouting, but didn't.

Richard let them shout for a few seconds, but changed the subject when he turned back to Rose. He asked many of the normal questions then. He also asked what Rose's plans were after she broke the record, and she still hadn't thought much about it other than going back to her normal life. After they finished talking about Doug, she was a lot more carefree about the conversation. She didn't realize how much she was thinking about what to say until she didn't have to anymore. She was the only guest scheduled that morning, so they spent a lot of time talking. She didn't mind. She was starting to really enjoy her appearances on shows. She thought she might be sad for them to be over after she broke the record and everything died down, but she definitely didn't bring that up to Richard.

When she left, she called Jim. Surprisingly, he was available. She usually had to leave a message. "I had Joann clear my schedule this morning so I could watch the show. Normally, I wouldn't, but I had to make sure you didn't say anything awful," he joked.

"Well, how did I do?" she asked.

"Perfect. Absolutely perfect. I'll call you when I hear from either the judge or Doug's attorney. And if they try for slander, I've got the show taped. You didn't say anything wrong at all."

"Good," she said. "But Richard and the audience did."

"Oh, of course. That's the idea. He'll have reporters calling him soon. I looked up the show's ratings. It's pretty popular."

Rose called Jane a little later. "Oh, I've already called both him and his attorney," she said. "They're pissed. It sounded like I wasn't the first reporter to call either of them. You were amazing this morning."

"Did you get anything from them?"

"Oh, of course not. They're not going to talk about an open case. They both said something to the effect of 'no comment' and hung up on me. I think I heard Doug call you a bitch as he was hanging up, but I can't be completely sure."

Rose was satisfied. Even if Doug kept trying to get his version of the divorce papers, at least he was sufficiently annoyed at this point. Like Jim said, he could try to say she talked badly about him, but it was all recorded.

Jane's article was published first, before Rose even got home. It had the facts of the newest events in the record project and included the basics of what Doug was trying to do. She included that she had tried to reach both him and his attorney for comments.

CHAPTER 42

Rose had to field a few calls from reporters over the next two weeks, but at this point, it was just a normal part of her life. They all wanted to know how she felt about being so close to breaking the record. She chatted with each of them for a few minutes. Most of them were very nice.

She also got a couple of new clients for her business. They wanted web sites built, and she was happy to consult and then send them quotes. Things were going pretty well for a new business. It wasn't anywhere near enough to fully support her yet, but she would keep at it. She still had severance until the end of November, and it was just October. She was also saving money since she didn't have to drive to the office every day or go out for lunch. The money from appearances about her record was coming in, too, so she thought she would be okay financially until she got the web development going full speed, and she suspected that some of her new clients were actually coming from the appearances. She wasn't really spending money on marketing, but that was okay. She'd take the new clients however they came in.

On November 9, Jim finally called. He had heard from Doug's attorney. "He said he'll take a settlement of $20,000."

"No," she replied without hesitating.

"That's what I thought, but I had to ask. I'll call back in an hour or so."

It was only a few minutes later that he called again to tell her that the attorney said he would see them in court.

"Fine," Rose said. "But tell him to make it soon. I want to be divorced already."

On Friday, Jim called again. "I had lunch with the judge today. We've got a hearing scheduled before Thanksgiving. November 18. It'll be first on the docket. Bring me a copy of the waiver you signed when that Arthur guy passed away and a copy of your separation agreement at work. And any emails or whatever with your friend that have the terms of the marriage. Can you have them to me tomorrow?"

"Sure," she said. As soon as she got off the phone, she called Penelope and asked her to send the emails, and then started making copies and printing the emails. She drove to Jim's office and handed everything to Joann the next afternoon. Jim walked into the office just as she was leaving.

"Got the papers to Joann?"

"Yes. Didn't you say that Doug was asking for all kinds of financial records, though?"

"His lawyer asked me for them, but she didn't actually request them through the court. We're not giving them those unless we have to."

On November 18, Rose walked into a courthouse for a divorce hearing for the fourth time. Jim was waiting for her. She saw Doug and a woman she assumed was his lawyer sitting in the waiting area. She and Jim talked until they were called, and they walked into the courtroom and got settled.

The hearing was actually over pretty quickly. Doug's attorney, Erica, stated what he was requesting, basically echoing what was in the papers they'd filed. She stated that they had reason to believe that the marriage to Doug directly caused Rose to earn some huge amount of money over the six weeks they'd been married, and Doug believed he was entitled to half of Rose's assets, including an inheritance she received while they were married. There was more to her speech, but Rose couldn't remember all of it.

Jim countered with what he'd already said in the answer he filed. He added that he had a copy of the waiver Rose signed stating that she wouldn't claim any of her previous husband's estate. He also had proof that Rose had lost her full-time employment of many years due to her hobby of marriages. When he told the judge that he could also prove that Doug agreed that there would be no exchange of money or assets as a result of the marriage, Erica looked shocked. Jim didn't actually need to submit any of the evidence, because she asked for a brief recess. The judge agreed.

Rose and Jim sat quietly and waited. She saw Erica whisper to Doug for several minutes, and then she walked over to their table.

"Hi, Rose. It's nice to meet you. I've seen you in the news."

"It's nice to meet you, too," Rose replied. They shook hands.

Erica turned to Jim. "What proof do you have that they agreed to terms before the marriage?"

Jim pulled the emails out of his file, letting her glance at them, but he didn't hand them over. "When arranging the marriage, Doug exchanged emails with Penelope, Rose's manager. Doug specifically agrees to the terms in those emails. This was supposed to be one week, sign the papers, file them, and be done. No living together, no payments, nothing. Everything's in the email."

"And she didn't inherit anything from the previous husband?"

"Absolutely not," Jim said. "She follows her own terms. They're the same for every one of these marriages."

"Thank you," she said and walked back to her table. She and Doug talked until the judge called them back to order.

"Ms. Mulder? Are you ready?"

"I am, your honor," Erica said.

"Do you have anything new to bring to the court?"

"My client would like to change his request. He wants to revert to the original agreement with Ms. Wilson. He would like to see the divorce granted, with both spouses keeping all assets and monies that they currently have."

"Mr. Carter, is this acceptable?" the judge asked.

"It is, with one exception. In my response to Mr. Ambrose's original filing, I requested that he be required to pay all attorney's fees on the basis that his request for my client's assets is fraudulent."

This was new to Rose. She hadn't bothered to read Jim's answer. She thought he had sent it to her, but she trusted him.

Erica did give a brief argument against Doug paying Jim's fees, and Rose noticed that Doug looked a little frightened.

The judge didn't care. "Ms. Wilson's request is granted. Mr. Carter, please file a new divorce decree with my office for me to sign."

"I will have it to you Monday, your honor."

As they were leaving, Rose told Jim that she didn't really care about the attorney's fees. He wouldn't let her dismiss it. "You don't need to have to pay me just because this guy tried to milk you. You know I'm not cheap. The jerk deserves to have to pay. Leave it alone."

So she did. Jim was true to his word and copied her when he sent the new divorce agreement, which was really only different from the standard agreement she already had in that Doug would pay her attorney's fees.

The judge signed it on November 28. She was finally finished with Doug, and Jim refunded the retainer she'd paid. Given the circumstances, Jim got it through pretty quickly – only six weeks – and she would have been happy to let him keep the retainer for that alone. Still, she figured she could use the money since she wouldn't be getting any more severance checks after that week.

CHAPTER 43

As soon as Jim called to let her know the divorce was final, Rose texted Leann and Penelope. "I don't actually have papers in the mail yet, but it's done. Jim told me the clerk put them in the mail already, so I'll have them in the next couple of days."

They wanted to go out to dinner that night to celebrate. Rose immediately agreed. She needed to get out of the house for a little bit. Working from home was starting to get a little boring. Even though she was a little bit of a loner, she was used to being around people most of the day. Dinner was at their favorite Mexican restaurant. The girls were already there, along with Luke, Steven, and Kurt.

"Oh, my God. You guys got a real party together on short notice, didn't you?"

The girls were pleased. "It didn't take much. Just a couple of calls. These guys never say no to food," Leann said.

Luke stood up and gave her a hug, "Plus, I haven't seen you in weeks. I was starting to think you were avoiding me."

"I'd never avoid my favorite husband!" she replied.

"Wait," Kurt said as he stood. "He's your favorite? What about me?"

"Fine, fine. My *two* favorite husbands."

Kurt hugged her, too. "That's better." He looked questioningly at Leann, who nodded. He sat back down next to her and kept talking. Rose was taking the empty seat next to Luke. "And since we're on the topic of marriages, since we almost always are, thanks to Rose, Leann and I have an announcement."

Penelope squealed. "Really?" she shouted. "I thought we were just here to celebrate a divorce!"

"We can celebrate more than just my divorce. It's not like there haven't been a million of them. Really, Leann? You guys are getting married?"

Leann showed them her ring. It was a modest single diamond, a beautiful ring. "We're thinking June. Rose's marriages will be over, and I think we'll be ready for a real one by then. And, of course, I want both you girls to be bridesmaids."

Rose and Penelope agreed right away. When the girls were finished looking at the ring, Kurt spoke up again. "And I've already asked Luke to be best man. Steven, will you be a groomsman?"

"Of course!" he said.

"Good," Kurt replied. "Xander will be one, too. And now, I can counter Rose's earlier comment by saying that my two favorite *wives* are at the table, the ex-wife and my future wife. And I'm incredibly glad you two get along. It would be really awkward if you didn't."

The girls bored the guys with talk about the wedding for a while. They decided to get together the next weekend to start doing some real planning. Leann already had a call in to a couple of venues she was thinking about, and Kurt was going to go with her Sunday to look at them.

"So we have one more marriage to talk about before we can really have fun," Penelope said. "Rose, are we good to go ahead this weekend?"

"I don't know. It's cutting it kind of close to make sure I'm divorced by the end of the year, isn't it?"

Penelope shook her head. "There will be absolutely no problems with this one. He'll sign the papers as soon as you want him to. You know him from work. It's Terry."

"Terry, like my employee Terry?"

"Yep."

"I've talked to him, too," Leann added. "And he said that Jessica's fine with it. He talked to her before he even emailed Penelope about it. The only thing is that your whole team wants to be at the wedding. They said you never went to lunch with them like you said you would."

"Oh, no!" Rose exclaimed. "I totally didn't, did I? I got so caught up with starting the business and getting married and divorced that I just never got in touch with them. Sure, I'll marry Terry. Let's go ahead and plan for it whenever. I'm pretty sure we can get the divorce done by the end of the year if it's him."

They had an amazing time that night. Everyone had a drink to celebrate, and Rose decided she'd pay for the meal since she had the refund from Jim. It was a gift to Leann and Kurt, and they accepted graciously.

CHAPTER 44

Thankfully, Rose's wedding was easy to plan. Penelope called Terry and confirmed that Saturday morning would be fine with him, and Leann asked Alice to take care of letting reporters know. Even though they didn't think it would be necessary, Rose reserved one of the covered picnic areas at the park, just in case of rain.

The wedding to Terry went perfectly. He was great with the reporters and never told them where he worked, just that he was a web developer like Rose and that they knew each other because of the work they both did. There were new questions this time, since she was now tied with the world record. After the wedding and interviews, they waited for the reporters to leave. The girls had packed a picnic lunch, so they all ate lunch and caught up with Terry (Husband Number 29), Elsa, Bianca, and Will. Rose told them all the details about the divorce from Doug that they didn't already know. She was happy to see them and apologized several times for forgetting to get in touch with them about lunch.

"That's okay," Elsa said. "We figured you were busy. We've still been keeping up with the blog and your TV appearances and everything. It's been fun, even though we don't get to ask you about it every day."

"Good. I didn't want you to think I'd forgotten you."

Bianca didn't mind, either. "Today's fun, though," she said. "And Terry, how was it in front of those cameras? You looked great."

"It was actually kind of fun, but I wouldn't want to do it all the time like Rose is doing. It would be annoying after a bit."

Rose laughed. "It is, but I think it'll die down after the next marriage. I've got some show appearances scheduled for the next couple of months, but then I should be able to concentrate on my new business."

Bianca had news. "Jessica knew we were seeing you today. She wanted to let you know that things have died down a bit at the office, and she wants you to call her."

"I might," Rose said. "I don't know yet. I can't come back right now, though, if that's what she wants. I've got clients lined up, and I'm kind of booked with traveling for a bit."

"That's okay. Call her anyway. She kind of wanted to come today, but didn't think you'd want her here," Will said. "She was afraid you'd be upset with her over the whole firing thing."

"No, I'm not. Tell her that. And tell her I'll call when I can, but I can't promise when that will be."

After lunch, Rose and Penelope went to Leann's house. They started going through wedding magazines and thought they had everything almost figured out before the end of the day. Of course, there would probably be a lot that they'd figure out as they went, but Leann wanted a small, simple wedding. She had already been married once and didn't see any point in doing another big one. The kids were there, and they joined in the fun a little until Jeremy got bored with looking at "girly stuff" and went to play video games.

Late the next week, Rose decided that she would go ahead and call Jessica to see what she wanted. She was offering Rose her job back, but understood when Rose told her how much she had going on over the next few weeks. "Well, do you think you'll want to come back in a few months?" she asked.

"I don't know. It really depends on how this freelancing goes."

"Well, I need a manager. I'm thinking that if you don't come back, I'll promote Bianca. She's doing great as lead."

"Go ahead and promote her," Rose said. "I don't want you to wait for me when I don't know what I'll be doing."

"I'll do that. And if you decide you need some extra work, let me know. With Bianca managing, we could definitely use you as a contractor."

"I'll keep that in mind."

"I'll send over a couple of project summaries for you. Let me know if you want to do any of them. You can start contracting anytime you want."

Rose was happy when she got off the phone. Bianca would be great as manager, and she had some potential new work.

Terry signed the papers as soon as she sent them, and Rose got them filed quickly. On December 26, the divorce was final. It was a nice after-Christmas present. Rose let the girls know, Jane published another article, *World Record – One Wedding Left*, and Rose took a tiny break from being married before the last one.

CHAPTER 45

"The last husband's name is Gerard," Penelope said. "When do you want to marry him?"

It was New Year's Day, and Penelope had called way too early. Rose had gone out with her team the night before. She drank too much and needed a few more hours of sleep before she felt anywhere near human. "What time is it? Why are you calling right now?"

"It's 9:00. Time to get up and tell me when you want to get married."

"Well, not today. That's for sure."

"Your newest ex-husband got you drunk last night? Was it fun?"

"Not as much fun as you want to make it. Yes, I drank. No, Terry didn't try anything. Actually, I think he may be dating Elsa, but I can't be sure."

"Really? That's awesome."

"Yeah. It's just the way they stayed close and kept glancing at each other. They never did any of that when we were at the office, but it looks like something's changed between them. I'm happy if they're dating. They would get along really well."

"Well, are you ready to date? I think Gerard would be up for it," Penelope said.

"Hell, no," Rose said groggily. "I'm still not dating. But good for you. You haven't asked in a while. I'm proud of you."

"It's been how long? Are you sure? He's really cute!"

"It's been a while. I'm too hung over to calculate. And I'm sure. It's never happening. There's no point in dating. It would just turn out like every other time."

"So you're basically a nun now? Do you miss him?"

"Yes, but I don't want to talk about it. Can I go back to sleep now?"

Penelope laughed, but didn't press the issue. "You can go back to sleep as soon as you tell me when I can set up this wedding. It'll be big. There will be tons of reporters. Alice already emailed this morning asking if I have an update for her. She's not technically working this morning, but I think they're all driving her crazy."

"Ugh. Next weekend, I guess. Get it over with. I don't have any plans. Just tell me where to be and when, and I'll be there. *Now* can I go back to sleep?"

"Go ahead. I'll text you later. Sleep tight! Oh, and Ahhhhhhhh!" she screamed.

Rose pulled the phone away from her ear. When the scream was over, she put it back long enough to say, "That hurt my head, bitch." She hung up while Penelope was laughing and threw the phone onto the other side of the bed.

When she woke up a couple of hours later, Penelope had texted. The wedding was set for Saturday at 2:30. She was meeting Gerard Thursday night for coffee and questions. She didn't bother answering the text; Penelope knew she'd be there. Instead, she got coffee and ibuprofen. She thought it was a good day to be lazy and read a book. None of her clients expected anyone to work on New Year's Day.

The next day, however, was busy. She had two web sites to build that week and needed to get them finished by Thursday. She had started one of them the week before, so it was absolutely doable. She'd just need to work more than she'd been doing the last few weeks in order to do it. Not a problem, because she didn't think it would be any more than the time she used to spend working for Jessica.

Around the middle of the day, she got a call from Alice.

"Hey, Rose. I've got a question for you."

"Sure. Shoot," she said, picking up her coffee cup.

"I got a call today from some movie producer's assistant. They want to set up a meeting and talk about doing your story."

"My story?" Rose asked.

"Yeah. About your marriages. They want to make it into a movie."

"Is this for real?"

"It is," Alice said. "I did some checking on them, and even got Jane to do her own check to be absolutely sure. They're in Atlanta. They want to meet at their office later this week, if you can."

Rose looked at the web site she was in the middle of building. "I don't know about this week. It's looking like I'm pretty much booked. Can you see about next week?"

"Sure," Alice said. "I'll call them back."

"Great. Oh, and I know you took care of the Guinness record thing a while back, but did they respond? Will they be there Saturday?"

"They'll be there. I talked to Hal. He said he met you before?"

"Oh, good. He was nice. Is he coming again?"

"Yes. He said to remind you to bring all your certificates and divorce decrees, but just the ones he doesn't have yet. So marriages 24 through 29. We'll have the certificate for Number 30 for him Saturday."

"You are awesome, Alice. Thank you."

"No problem. I'll call you back after I talk to the studio people again."

She called back a few minutes later to tell Rose that she was scheduled for a lunch meeting Tuesday. They'd meet her at the office and have lunch catered. Alice had already checked with Penelope and Leann. They were invited, too.

Rose barely had time to think about anything other than work and marriage for the rest of the week. She finished the web sites Thursday morning and met Gerard for coffee at 6:00. He was a little arrogant, but she didn't think they would have any problems. After 10 minutes, she told him she'd see him Saturday and left.

She fell asleep later than she'd planned because one of the clients sent back notes for revisions. She'd be driving a lot the next day, so she wanted to take care of the changes quickly. She finished up while in her pajamas lying in bed. When she set her laptop down at midnight, she fell asleep quickly. The next morning, she left the house at 5:15 and arrived right on time at the tv studio.

The show went well. All of the questions were easy at this point, and there was nothing new to tell them. The only thing she really had to talk about was that the record was tied, and she was getting married again the next day to break it.

She was barely home at 10:00 when Alice called. "Messages are crazy right now. I just thought you should know. We're going to have like a million people at the park Saturday."

When Rose pulled into the park the next day, she thought that maybe Alice wasn't exaggerating. Thankfully, Jane and Alice were both already there, helping to direct people to where they should go. Marty was set up. He'd gotten there early enough to get his pick of spots.

Rose hugged Jane. "How many people are actually here?"

"Something like 30 reporters. It seems like a lot more, though, since they all have photographers or videographers and everything. I talked to one newspaper reporter from California. You're pretty popular right now."

"I can't wait for it to be over. Will today be a circus?"

"Probably," a man's voice said from behind her. Rose turned.

"Hal!" she said. "I'm happy to see you again."

"Me, too," he replied as he shook her hand. "I'm glad you've made it to 30. It's a pretty big deal. One of my coworkers tried to take this trip away from me, but I wouldn't let him."

"We'll see. I may run away screaming if any more reporters show up."

"I doubt it. There's more chance of your groom running away, but they always like the spotlight. He'll show."

Rose handed over the copies of all the paperwork, and Hal took it to his car. He snapped a couple of pictures and took his place at the front. As the representative from Guinness, he had priority over the reporters.

Leann, Luke, Kurt, Penelope, and Steven got there a couple of minutes before Gerard. They worked their way through the crowd, which Rose saw was still getting bigger. She was afraid there wouldn't be enough room in the covered area, but she figured some of the reporters could set up outside if needed.

Gerard walked closer to her as they made their way to the front. "Is it always like this?" he asked. He didn't seem as arrogant today. She thought it was the cameras.

"Not usually this bad. But since you're the last one, they're all out today. I hope you're okay with it."

"Not a problem," he said. By the time reporters started asking questions, his arrogance had returned. Rose didn't like it, but at least she didn't have to deal with more men after him.

Leann loudly asked all the reporters to quiet down, and she performed the ceremony. Rose and Gerard signed the certificate, which Leann picked up for safekeeping. Jane and Alice took care of directing everything during the interview. Marty had microphones set up already, and he and Jane asked the initial questions. They brought Hal into the interview, too. He reminded the reporters that the record still needed to be certified, and he would be working on that as soon as he got back to his office.

The interview took a lot longer, too. They didn't get to leave until after 5:00. Gerard walked with them to their cars and said he'd send the divorce papers the next week.

Penelope suggested dinner, but Rose was far too tired. She went home instead to relax, promising they'd celebrate everything being over very soon.

"Tomorrow!" Leann said. "We're celebrating tomorrow. My house. If it's not cold, we'll fire up the grill."

Rose read for a couple of hours that night. It was January 7, and she had just gotten married for the thirtieth time. It was an accomplishment, but at that moment, she was just glad it was over. Well, almost over. Gerard needed to actually divorce her. Hopefully, that wouldn't be a problem. And she still had some people to talk to about the whole thing. She was intrigued by the whole idea of someone doing a movie about her marriages. There was still some work, but at least she didn't have to get married again. She could spend most of her free time helping Leann plan her wedding now, one that would be a lot happier than any of hers.

She slept peacefully that night after she was able to push thoughts of Matt out of her mind.

CHAPTER 46

Rose decided to go to Leann's as soon as she got up the next morning. She could help Leann get ready for whatever she had planned, and it was almost noon anyway. They all knew that Rose slept late as often as she could.

It was a little chilly outside that day, but it wasn't bad. Rose was carrying her jacket and it felt like maybe the mid-40s. She knew they probably wouldn't grill, or spend much time outside, but they would still have fun inside.

When she got to Leann's, Penelope's car was already there. "Dammit," she said when she walked in. "I wanted to surprise you, Leann."

"Well, you did surprise me. I figured we'd have to call and wake you up in a couple of hours."

Penelope agreed. She was planning to call Rose soon, but they were happy to see her then. "We're just waiting for the guys to get here, really. They went hunting or fishing or something. I was thinking about a nap."

"You know I'll take a nap whenever, but I've only been up for about 30 minutes. What's for lunch?"

Leann shrugged. "Kids are at Brent's. I've got a roast in the crock pot for dinner tonight, but you're on your own for lunch. Make a sandwich or something."

Rose walked through the doorway to the kitchen. She could hear Leann laughing. There was sandwich stuff already out on the counter. It looked like the girls had already eaten and just left it out so the guys could make sandwiches when they returned. She made a sandwich and took it back to the living room. They talked while she ate, but after that, Leann found a movie for them to watch. None of them were very talkative for a while.

The guys came in while they were watching the movie, made their sandwiches, and cleaned up the kitchen. By the time they were finished, all three girls were asleep, so they left them alone. It had warmed up a little. When Rose woke up a couple of hours later, before either of the other girls, the guys were outside at the table. She joined them and talked until Leann woke up, then joined her in the kitchen.

They started a cake to go with dinner. Penelope added icing to it when she woke up.

By the time the cake was ready, it was almost time to eat. Leann put a loaf of French bread in the oven and made a salad to go with the roast, potatoes, and carrots. They talked and laughed over dinner.

Luke pushed his plate forward slightly when he was finished. "I was thinking. Maybe we should just get married again in case someone has a plan to break your record."

"Jane did some checking. It doesn't look like anyone's trying."

"They probably will, though. I'm not saying get married for keeps. Just one more marriage and divorce to make it a little harder for the next person. You've got the system down now. Might as well make sure no one else is going to take this from you anytime soon."

Rose smiled. "Okay. When Gerard's done, we'll do it."

They talked for a while about the meeting with the movie producer, wondering what they would be walking into the next day. Steven said he would take the day off, but had some important meetings that he couldn't reschedule. "Don't agree to anything, though. Whatever they say, just tell them you'll think about it and talk to me first."

"Yes, dear," Penelope said.

The next morning, Penelope picked Leann up first, and then Rose. They pulled up to the studio a few minutes early. Leann asked the receptionist for the woman Alice had told her, Adria Hanson. She walked out to the lobby after a couple of minutes and escorted them into a conference room. There were chicken sandwiches set out at each of the places. "Sit wherever you'd like," Adria said. "My partners will be here shortly."

Another woman, Dana, and a man, Ted, walked in a couple of minutes later. They introduced themselves and sat down. It was clear that Adria would do most of the talking.

"Please feel free to eat as we talk. We're very interested in your story, Rose. And, of course, your parts in it, Leann and Penelope. We know that a lot of the information is in the blog, but I can see from the ring on Leann's finger that there's more to gather."

She took a few minutes while they were eating to explain how she would like to get the story from them. She wanted to start with the blog, but also have interviews with each of them, getting as much of the story as possible. From there, the company's writers would take over.

"It took you how long to complete the record?" she asked.

Rose answered. "Something like two and a half years. And that was starting when I already had three marriages."

"Right. That's what I thought. So what I'm thinking is a movie to kick things off, and then a television series. We couldn't possibly cover 30 husbands in one movie, and there's starting to be a trend to do both movie and tv. We think your story is perfect for that, and I already have a streaming provider interested in the series."

Leann had a question. "So the movie wouldn't be in theaters, but on the streaming provider instead?"

"Oh, no!" Ted said. "We want to put the movie on the big screen. From all the media attention you've gotten, we're sure it'll do great. It's the perfect time, too. A lot of the studios are doing action movies right now, and they make good money, but it's time for a good romantic comedy."

Rose shook her head. "You understand that there isn't any romance in my story, right?"

Dana nodded. "We may want to add a little, just for interest. But we'd also like to know about relationships you've had while you were going through this. How men you've dated have felt about it. All that."

"What kind of say would we have in what you put in all this?" Leann asked.

Adria spoke again. "We can arrange it so you have final approval on certain aspects of the production. Maybe not specifics like the actual script, but events that happen and all that."

"Okay," Penelope said. "We'd definitely want as much approval as possible."

Adria nodded. They were all finished eating at this point, and she went to the door to call her assistant in. The girl cleared their leftovers and walked out without saying a word.

"We'll work it to make sure you have approval. We know the interviews and the whole process will take a lot of time, so we've prepared an offer for each of you." The assistant walked back in, handed Adria a folder, and walked back out. Adria pulled papers from the folder and placed one face down in front of each of the girls. "We'll need to revise the papers in front of you to add the approvals. For now, though, we'll let you look them over, talk about it, and let us know what you think." She, Ted, and Dana started walking out of the room.

"Wait," Rose called when she realized what they were doing. Adria turned around. "We're not deciding anything today. You don't have to leave."

"Well, I can assure you that it's a good offer. Understand that Rose's is a little more than the others since she'll need to spend far more time interviewing with our team, but you won't get the same from another production company. We have the funds to make this project a success, and we're sure you'll be happy helping us out. Do you want to take a minute anyway?"

"No, thanks," Leann said. "We'd actually prefer to talk it over at home, if that's okay with you."

Dana took over. "I'll give you my card. I'll be your contact and make sure Adria and Ted get any messages. I'll also email you an updated copy tomorrow with the approval information in it. Can you get back to us by the end of the week?'

The girls looked at each other. "Sure," Rose said. They still hadn't turned the papers over, but it didn't matter since they weren't planning to accept anything that day anyway. She stood. Leann and Penelope did, too. They'd been there less than 30 minutes, but felt it was time to go. They each picked up their paper and shook hands all around. Dana pulled a card out of her pocket and gave it to Rose. The girls thanked everyone and walked to the car, where they finally turned over the papers and looked at them.

"Good God," Leann said. "$75,000? Why didn't we go ahead and accept? Penelope?"

"Same," Penelope said.

"Rose?" Leann asked.

"150," she said. "Want to split it?"

"Nope," Leann said. "Like she said, you're going to have to spend more time with these people. And you're the one who married all the men. We just helped. What they've got on here sounds pretty good to me. Let's go home and let Steven look at it."

They did. After Dana sent the updated contract the next day, Steven went through it, too. He didn't see anything wrong with it. On Thursday, all the girls had signed it and sent copies back to Dana. They would get the first payment of half the money shortly after signing. Interviews would be scheduled starting in February. A second payment of one fourth of the total would come when they finished the initial interviews, and they were supposed to get the final payment when they approved the events plotted for the movie. The new contract had an additional payment of $2,000 per television episode, payable upon their approval of the plot points.

Rose was overjoyed at how things had worked out. She would be busy for the next few months at least, and while she'd have to pay a good chunk of her payment from the studio in taxes, it was enough to keep her going for a while, even if her business didn't build as quickly as she hoped.

The day after the girls signed the papers, Rose met Gerard for coffee and to sign divorce papers. She was almost afraid that, since other things in her life weren't going well, he wouldn't show, but he did. He signed quickly, not even getting a cup of coffee, and left. She took the papers to the courthouse to file them and was finally finished with getting married.

Almost. She had agreed with Luke that they would get married one more time. The divorce from Gerard was final on February 1, and the next evening, she and Luke met at Leann's house to go back to a quiet ceremony. Only the two of them, Leann, Penelope, Steven, and Kurt were there. They celebrated with a glass of champagne. Rose quickly got Leann and Kurt talking about their own wedding plans, which were well under way. There was a lovely garden not far away, and they had it booked for June 10. They already had a caterer, a band, and flower arrangements taken care of. The girls had appointments to find dresses, and they had over four months to finish planning. Judging from the way things were going so far, no one doubted that the rest of the planning would go well.

Rose wasn't as adamant about the divorce papers this time. There wasn't another wedding to plan, and she knew Luke would sign whenever. She had them ready and signed for her part within a couple of days, but it was almost two weeks before she happened to see Luke again, the night before the girls left for their trip to Huntsville. They would all be on the talk show this time and were ready to talk about Rose breaking the record, plus one, and how it felt to finally be finished.

Luke signed the papers while they were talking about the trip. He was going to drive the kids to Brent's so Leann could go to bed early. The next morning, Wednesday, Rose had Leann stop by the courthouse so she could file the divorce papers before they left town. She paid the final filing fee and walked out to the car feeling free. She had been free of relationships for a while, but now she was free of marriages and everything except her job. She had found out how amazing self-employment could be and was hoping it would stay that way. Most of all, she was happy to be getting a girls' trip in before Leann's *real* wedding.

Leann started the car when Rose got in. It was almost four hours to their hotel in Huntsville. Penelope pointed out that they could have flown, but after making their way to the airport and the flight itself, it would have taken almost as long. Besides, what was a road trip without the road?

Leann turned the music up, and they listened to it for a while, singing along often. After a while, Penelope, who was in the front passenger seat, turned it down. "Are you guys ready for this show?"

Rose answered first, "They're getting kind of boring for me, actually."

"Well, duh," Penelope said. "But it's over now. There may be different questions. Are you going to tell them about the movie and everything?"

"Nah. The studio will announce that when they want to. I think we should just keep it quiet for now. Jane did tell me something we should do the other day, though."

"What's that?" Leann asked.

"She said that the three of us should get together and write a book before the movie comes out. You know they're basing it on what we say, but it's not going to be completely real. Jane said she has a contact at some publishing company and thinks we can get it published if we write it."

"Why don't you just do it?" Penelope said.

"I could, but you guys have been with me through all of it. You need to help me with this, too. Besides, Leann's the best writer. She'd at least need to edit the crappy grammar we put into it."

They all laughed at that. Leann had a suggestion. "That's true. Why don't we start going through the blogs when we get home? We probably already have most of it written. Maybe just a few additions or deletions. But you're right. We didn't sign over any book rights to the company. Even if no one buys it, it's a new project. We probably need one. We'll be going crazy without your marriages to figure out."

"After your wedding," Rose said. "Maybe we can start going through blogs and maybe even start writing some, but we're going to concentrate on your wedding next. It's the most important one we've had in years."

They chatted for the rest of the drive, stopping once for gas and a restroom break. When they got to the hotel, they all wanted a nap before doing anything else. It was 4:00 in the afternoon, so they slept for a couple of hours. They weren't supposed to be in the studio until Friday morning, so they went to dinner and then to the hotel bar. They were up late and all woke up with hangovers.

CHAPTER 47

Leann got a call from Alice that morning and put it on speaker. "Hey, Alice. How's it going?"

"Everything's great here. Still finishing up some messages from men asking if Rose is still getting married."

Rose thought she was going to die laughing. "Tell them I'm done," she said. "There's no way I'm getting married again, ever."

"You're on speaker by the way," Leann told Alice.

"I kind of figured. And yes, Rose, I'm telling them very nicely that you hate marriage and won't be doing it again."

"Good."

"But I actually called for two reasons. First, Hal from Guinness called. The record's yours, and I made sure he included the marriage to Luke. All's good. Press release, in the book, everything, just like before. I also got a call from the tv studio you're going to tomorrow. They want to know if you mind doing the interview somewhere other than the studio."

Penelope and Rose shrugged. Leann answered. "We don't care. Where are they thinking?"

"They want to do it in the lobby of the courthouse. They would have asked sooner, but they had to get permission from the county or something to set everything. They just got it today. They said it would make a good location. Something about how many times you've been in a courthouse over the last couple of years."

"Works for me," Rose said.

Penelope added, "Just send us the address and whatever else. We'll be there. Still 9:00?"

"Yep. I'll text all three of you the address. It doesn't look like it's far from your hotel."

"Thanks!" they all said before hanging up.

The girls drove around a little bit that day. They went to the Space and Rocket Center, which was just a few miles away, and walked around there for hours. Then, they went shopping. By the time they got back to the hotel, they just wanted to order room service and stay in for the night. They'd be in Huntsville for a couple more days and wanted to see what else there was to do for the weekend.

The next morning, they got up at 6 and went downstairs to the hotel's restaurant for breakfast. The breakfast was pretty good, but none of them were very hungry. Rose didn't eat breakfast often, and the other girls were a little nervous about the talk show. "It's nothing," Rose told them. "You've been in interviews a thousand times already."

They knew it, but this was a little different. They weren't at home. The park they used was close to their houses, and they'd been to it often enough before Marty started coming to the weddings that it wasn't a big deal. They had time to slowly get used to more cameras. This was different. Rose didn't have a new husband there to deflect some of the conversation from them, and it was live. No one would be editing before the segment was aired.

They had nothing to worry about, however. The courthouse was beautiful. There were windows all along the front, so they could see the show's crew setting up before they even went in. They walked through the metal detectors and were immediately greeted by Sam, the show's producer.

"Hi, girls," he said. "We're almost set up. Do you want to meet Al before we start?" Al was the host, and he was the friendliest one Rose had met so far. She knew Alice had some more lined up for her over the next few weeks, but she found herself telling Al they'd come back anytime even before they went on air. He was thrilled.

The show itself was routine for Rose. She answered questions just as she usually did. Leann and Penelope were as natural as they always were when Marty filmed them. They did talk about being finished with everything, and Rose told Al that she had gotten married to Leann's brother again. That conversation took a few minutes. It was perfect, though. Luke was the beginning and end of the marriages for the record, and also her friend's brother. Al thought it was amusing. They ended the show not long after that, since they'd already been talking for almost an hour with a couple of breaks.

Al thanked them and walked away to help the crew start packing everything up. Rose, Leann, and Penelope stood just out the way, trying to decide what to do for the rest of the day. It was almost time to start thinking about lunch, so Penelope suggested they just drive around until they saw a restaurant that looked good. Rose agreed as she watched the traffic through the window.

She hadn't noticed before, but there was a man standing on the sidewalk. It looked like maybe he'd been watching the show, but there was no way of knowing how long he'd been there. He was wearing a black jacket, holding a briefcase, and was looking towards the studio's crew, not far away. He turned a little, apparently to get a better view of the crew working, and Rose saw his face. She gasped.

When Leann and Penelope turned to see what was bothering Rose, Leann stopped midsentence. They both looked at Rose, waiting to see what she would do.

It was Matt. Rose had no idea what he was doing in Huntsville, but he was here. At the courthouse. Right where she was. Was it fate? Were they both meant to be there?

She didn't know, but she knew what she wanted. She wanted to run out to him and hold him. She wanted to tell him that everything was okay, that she was there and if he wanted, they could be together again. That she hadn't forgotten him, and that, even though he dumped her with no explanation, she still loved him.

But she couldn't. She had to believe that he had seen her if he'd been watching the show. If he walked up after it was over, he was still looking inside now and probably would have seen her at some point. If he wanted her, he'd already be inside, telling her that. A tear escaped her eye and fell down her cheek. He didn't want her, and so she couldn't go to him, no matter how much she wanted to. She wanted to catch his eye and have his look prove her wrong, but she couldn't bear to wait for him to look her way. If he didn't recognize her, or if he saw her and walked away, it would break her heart all over again, and she thought that might kill her.

She had forgotten that Leann and Penelope were there. All she saw was Matt, watching the crew. He started to turn, and she couldn't bear to know that he could see her, so she turned away, tears coming more quickly now. She was looking at a hallway, and there was a sign for restrooms about halfway down it. She started walking that way, still wishing she could go to him and have everything be okay. Instead, she would give him time to leave and take time to compose herself, and then she and the girls could leave. The hallway was blurry through her watery eyes, but she kept walking, wishing that things could be different. Wishing that it had all been a nightmare and she was waking up now. Wishing he had never left her life, but knowing that he had. There was nothing she could do about that except walk away and keep trying to forget him. She may never forget, but she knew he didn't want her, so trying to forget was all she had left.

ABOUT THE AUTHOR

Amelia has been writing for most of her life. In addition to *The Sanctity of Marriage*, she has published *Heart and Blood*, a poetry book, and other works. She lives in northwest Georgia with her family and pets and loves creating artistically, especially through the written word.